## Books by John Braine

# The Pious Agent

# JOHN BRAINE
# *The Pious Agent*

NEW YORK   *Atheneum*   1976

For my friends Doreen and Philip Colehan

He who fights the dragon becomes the dragon.

FRIEDRICH NIETZSCHE

Let every breath of regret be far from the clarified seer,
Not from the hunter alone, who, when seasons mature,
Acts without failure or fuss . . .

Killing is only a form of the sorrow we wander in here . . .
The serener heart finds pure
All that can happen to us.

RAINER MARIA RILKE
*Sonnets to Orpheus*

Render therefore unto Caesar the things which are Caesar's;
And unto God the things which are God's.

MATTHEW 22: 21

# Note

Every year in the London area fifty unidentified corpses or pieces of corpses are found. Using this figure as a basis, and taking into account the corpses which are not found, the undetected murders in England alone cannot be less than five hundred.

Here is another fact: since the Krogers and Lonsdale in 1961, no Soviet agent has been brought to trial in this country. One explanation is that none has been caught. If this is unacceptable, then the paragraph above must again be considered.

# The Pious Agent

# ONE

## *1 December 1960*

---

### DIRECTOR OF COUNTER-ESPIONAGE DEPARTMENT TO CONTROLLER AND CO-ORDINATOR OF SECURITY PERSONNEL

It's taken me long enough to find you. Here was I, feeling absolutely chuffed, with a lot of pennies in my hot little hand. How? My tame politicians and tame Civil Servants and various manufacturers and contact men have set up a completely useless and gloriously expensive public project. I won't say what it is, but you'll know when you hear about it, because its cost, in a quiet, steady, remorseless way, is going to escalate.

This is incidental, a piece of useful information if used at the proper time in the proper way. I bestow it upon you – with no strings attached – to prove to you that I still regard you as a colleague and a friend. What's past is past. Everyone's agreed to forget Maclean and Burgess; after all, you weren't the sole person to be taken in. And don't blame me because now SIS* is being dismantled in such an underhand way. The decision was taken far above my head – and, as you damned well know, far above the Government's head.

What you've done is to use your Services connections to build yourself a cosy little kingdom. There'll be no spectacular balls-up there, because you'll be able to keep an eye on everyone, walk round the country in a day, so as to speak. But there won't be any spectacular successes either. Of course, you've still an official connection with M16, though it'd take the entire Queen's Bench a year to explain it. You know your way through the labyrinth all right. Don't forget that others do too; nor that there's more than one Minotaur.

Now we come to my shopping list. Time was when I'd just have taken it in to one of my chums at Whitehall and have stag-

---

* Secret Intelligence Service, later redesignated as M16, later redesignated as D16.

gered off in a matter of minutes, so as to speak, with my Union Jack carrier-bag crammed with goodies. But my chums don't seem to be there any more, or perhaps all the goodies have gone. So I've come to you after making a Cook's Tour of all the Ministries because you, unless you've changed a great deal, have a God-given instinct for discovering what I want. Which is killers. Nothing fancy. I don't want sadists, because they're always liable to blow up on you. I want intelligent patriots (not, if you'll forgive me for saying so, the dopey kind SIS was filled with) who know that dirty jobs have to be done quickly and efficiently. And who, furthermore, have no illusions about the kind of world they live in. Killers of the War generation are no problem to find – though I can always do with extra if you ever spot one lying around – but I need young ones.

We have to think of the future, you have to recruit the new generation, or else all of a sudden all your operatives are middle-aged. The problem is that there really isn't any Empire any more. So no-one's being killed in any appreciable numbers – at least, not being killed anywhere to which we can officially send our chaps.

Let's get down to it then. I want at least fifty of the article in question. Not immediately – it's quality not quantity that matters. No-one above thirty, give or take a year. I'm relying upon you to supply me with nothing but first-rate stuff. And no damaged goods either. I'm not running a clinic.

# TWO
## 5 December 1960

DIRECTOR OF COUNTER-ESPIONAGE
DEPARTMENT TO CONTROLLER AND
CO-ORDINATOR OF SECURITY PERSONNEL

Don't try it on, Nigel. I made it clear enough what I wanted. The list you've sent me just won't do: I don't even have to see the chaps. They're public-school muttonheads, decent chaps, gentlemen – which is the last thing I want.

I've tried to be nice; after all, we worked seven years together and shared quite a few monumental booze-ups. And I'm well aware that it's not easy at present to meet my requirements. But if you don't do what I ask, I'm going to drop you right in the shit, then push you down. There isn't, as I've pointed out, any SIS to speak of any more and MI5 is being reorganised. Everything, to quote O'Casey, is in a state of chassis. Those of your chums who've got themselves jobs in the new set-up are so relieved to be in the clear that their attitude towards you is going to be the classic *Fuck you Jack, I'm inboard*.

So I'm just going to mention two names: Igor Maklevitch and Mikhail Kotolynov. And two dates: 2 January 1944, and 4 December 1946. And a Swiss bank account number: ZX45203. There wasn't any harm done; you weren't even dealing with the enemy. Still, Laughing Boy Philby could, technically, use the same excuse. It's evident to me that you were simply indulging in a bit of good old-fashioned private enterprise with these two splendid chaps – both of whom, you'll be surprised to hear, are still alive and well. No thanks to you, but at any time under the Boss there was so much denunciation going on that the machinery got jammed. To cut a long story short, they'd love to meet you again.

Do what I ask you to and this never need be mentioned again. It's no trouble to you. In fact, just for once you're not doing anything even slightly underhand, but actually serving your country. And I have you by the balls, haven't I?

# THREE
## *10 December 1960*

CONTROLLER AND CO-ORDINATOR OF
SECURITY PERSONNEL TO DIRECTOR OF
COUNTER-ESPIONAGE DEPARTMENT

FLYNN, XAVIER ALOYSIUS, OFFICER CADET
BORN 12 APRIL 1939, LIVERPOOL
EYES: BLUE
HAIR: BLACK
COMPLEXION: FRESH
HEIGHT: 6 FEET
CHEST: 44 INCHES
WAIST: 36 INCHES
WEIGHT: 13 STONE
BUILD: HEAVY, MUSCULAR
FEATURES: REGULAR, BUT OF HIBERNIAN CAST
SCARS: KNIFE WOUND 11·3 IN. ABDOMEN
FATHER: JAMES PATRICK FLYNN:
       BORN 1914, LIVERPOOL
MOTHER: ROSE MADELINE (née HOOLEY):
       BORN 1914, LIVERPOOL
SIBLINGS: CLODAGH (BORN 1940), SEAMUS
       (BORN 1941), PATRICK (BORN 1945),
       ROSE (BORN 1947)
EDUCATION: ST KENNETH'S R.C. PRIMARY,
       LIVERPOOL, 1944–48
       ST BLAISE'S CATHOLIC PRIMARY
       SCHOOL, WEYBRIDGE, 1948–1950
       ST RAYMOND'S R. C. GRAMMAR
       SCHOOL, WEYBRIDGE, 1950–58
CALL-UP UNDER NATIONAL SERVICE ACT, 1958,
       SERVED FORTY-SECOND FUSILIERS, MALAYA,
       1959-60
OFFICER CADET 1960

COPIES ALL RELEVANT SERVICE RECORDS, SCHOOL
REPORTS, MEDICAL REPORTS, ATTACHED. ALSO
RECENT PHOTOGRAPH.

## SUMMARY BY CONTROLLER AND
## CO-ORDINATOR OF SECURITY PERSONNEL:

I had an hour's conversation with Flynn – I didn't of course let
him know what I was really after, but spun him a story about a
special personnel survey. Told him his name was picked out of a
hat. Then I bought the kid a drink afterwards, which he very
much appreciated. He's a nice kid, with old-fashioned ideas. I
think he's going to be a damned good officer. I've made pretty
thorough enquiries and everyone likes him. Not that he's a brown-
noser – I don't think he's scared of anybody. And there's a wild
streak there too, which he's only just learning how to control.

There's a lot of bumf attached, which all adds up to him being
normal and poking everything which moves. He's fit enough,
but not a nut about it, and he likes chess and reading and the
theatre. He's not an academic type despite his six Credits and
three Distinctions – I'd say a good all-rounder with a quick mind.
He enjoys any kind of game as far as I can see, but he isn't
obsessive about any one of them.

Altogether too normal?

There are two odd things about him. One is that he's a fervent
Catholic, the other that he likes children's books. The superior
stuff mostly, like E. M. Nesbit and C. S. Lewis's Narnia series.
Mind you, his being a Catholic doesn't seem to affect his poking
everything that moves – everything female, that is. He has it
off regularly with a colonel's wife in Camberley – he picked her
up in a café one morning – and he started his sex life at the age
of fourteen with a neighbour's wife. (There was a lot of trouble
about it, but his father managed to hush it up.) As far as I can
discover, though, he has good taste, and he doesn't seem
overmuch attracted to booze or gambling.

Chuck Eustace – remember him? – was out in Malaya cleaning
things up with the Special Branch when he ran across Flynn. He
had a few casual words with the boy. Then he gave him a little
practical test, which he explains in the attached report. He did
have some idea of using him, but then he had to go home. Any-

15

way, I'm using Chuck and some others as contact men; they'll have to be paid *in cash*, but we can sort this out later.

I'm sure that he's what you want. It's a shame, because he struck me as being a decent human being and you are going to spoil him. I'll put you in touch with him – we may as well continue to use the fiction of the survey – and in the meantime I won't forget your bloody shopping list.

# FOUR
## *10 December 1960*

MAJOR CHARLES EUSTACE TO DIRECTOR
OF COUNTER-ESPIONAGE DEPARTMENT

Nigel told me what you wanted, and I've found it: name, Xavier Flynn. To cut a long story short, I was somewhere in Malaya, clearing out old stock when I ran across him. I knew straightaway; he had the expression they all have – or rather that *we* all have. I was with the C.O. at the time – he was, for the time being, Flynn's C.O. – and I told him that I'd got what I was looking for.

He isn't in our line of business and asked me how I could tell. I said, 'Instinct. I always go by my instinct and that's why I'm still alive.'

Anyway, he pooh-poohed this and said *his* instincts told him that Xavier was a nice decent English boy, not one of our mob. 'OK,' I said. 'Put your money where your mouth is. I bet you a tenner that this same boy obeys an order to kill instantaneously. It'll be an order to kill, not to fight, and if there's more than five seconds' hesitation, you win.'

We went to the processing centre and I had this Chinese brought in whom we'd been keeping for three years. We'd extracted as much information from him as ever we were going to and he was rather dusty and frayed at the edges. Sometimes it's worth keeping a chap because you can do some kind of a deal, but I'd already tried that, and no-one wanted him. He'd been quite a figure in his day but now his day was over.

To cut a long story short, I had Flynn brought in, gave him this very nice Colt ·45 automatic – I've always liked a gun which *stops* people, if you see what I mean – and I told the Chinese to stand up. (He was looking all inscrutable, but when I told Flynn to take the gun he understood all right. Actually, he looked rather relieved. I think he was; he hadn't much future.) 'Kill him,' I said to Flynn, and he did just that. Well within the five seconds, and I collected my tenner from Flynn's C.O.

Flynn's C.O. was a bit disgusted, actually. I don't see why he should have been; the reason for the Chinese looking a bit frayed around the edges was that a new guard had recognised him as one of the chaps who'd rather messily killed his little brother.

'Don't you feel *anything*?' Flynn's C.O. asked him. Flynn said rather huffily that he'd heard what sort of things the terrorists did to women and children and so it didn't bother him. Then he gave us both a long and very cold look. I still had the ten one-pound notes in my hand. And he said – I remember his exact words – 'I obey all lawful orders without question, gentlemen, but I'm not a bloody horse for you to bet upon. Thank you for the ten pounds, which I now propose, with your permission, to get pissed blind upon.' And he took the money, saluted smartly, and marched out

We had to laugh at his impudence. He was quite right, of course. There are situations in which it doesn't matter a toss about rank; he knew that this was one of them. The funny thing is that I know if I'd offered him the ten quid he would have thrown it in my face. He was also telling one something else; he could do the job all right, but this was the first time and he was a human being, not a machine.

I liked that boy. I don't say this very often, but he's leader material. And there's not much of that around these days.

# FIVE

## 22 December 1960

---

DIRECTOR OF COUNTER-ESPIONAGE
DEPARTMENT TO CONTROLLER AND
CO-ORDINATOR OF SECURITY PERSONNEL

You'd better not forget my shopping list because, I repeat, I have you by the balls. However, I feel well disposed towards you now. Flynn is exactly what I want. I had a very interesting conversation with him and a suprisingly enjoyable lunch, and the temptation is to dispense with the jumping through official hoops and have him commissioned and in the field straightaway. (After a crash course at Bleak House first, naturally.) But he may as well be properly processed and make some useful connections. Needless to say, he's never going to be a fully-fledged member of the Establishment. But who wants that anyway? I want agents who can go anywhere, and an agreeable young grammar-school boy holding Her Majesty's commission is just the ticket.

When we had a brief word on the 'phone you asked me if I proposed to recruit exclusively from the Services. Not at all. What I want is rarely to be found in the Services. A soldier is only a killer incidentally. His function is first and foremost defence and when he goes to war he has to win battles. It doesn't really matter if he wins battles without killing anybody at all – though in fact he doesn't. He's a *fighter*, who kills if he has to.

Xavier is a killer. He will fight if he has to. (And at Bleak House he'll learn some tricks about fighting which they'll never teach at Sandhurst.) But fighting for the sake of fighting he considers childish. He approves of OPERATION PURGE – presented to him, it goes without saying, as one of a number of counter-espionage choices. Flynn said, without prompting, that since the Operation's Third Directorate permanently maintains its own Operation Purge all over the place, it would be suicidal for us not to do the same. He also brought some very complicated theological theories forward to support his case, which I won't

19

bother you with. But that boy almost had me persuaded that killing a Soviet agent and saving his soul are synonymous. You can almost imagine Gentle Jesus beaming His approval every time he pulls the trigger.

Mind you, all this was with his tongue just ever so slightly in his cheek. He's a bit of a card on the quiet. In our job you have to have a sense of humour to keep going. My pal Nat Weiberg, from whom I pinched the idea of Operation Purge originally, is a bit of a card too. He's pretty high up in the CIA now, and we've always kept up our connection, even after Bedell Smith got so stroppy about Laughing Boy. Which is yet another reason for Flynn being so suitable. His father is a working-class boy who made good – *his* father was a dock-labourer – and he got a scholarship to the grammar school and eventually became an accountant. Dad isn't rich – £9,000 a year, actually – and I'm afraid he's rather liberal, but he's definitely made it into the middle classes through his own efforts and he is by all accounts a genuine lace-curtain Mick, going to Mass daily, leading a clean and sober life, and all that.

Which is the sort of background I want for my boys and girls (if I can get any). I want people who'll basically be idealists, believing that they're serving the people even if, to quote the old saying, they're serving them like a bull serves a cow.

This is to amplify my instructions. You'll hear from me again. And when I speak, you've got to listen, haven't you?

# SIX

# 21 March 1964, Washington

---

## DIRECTOR GROUP 71 CENTRAL INTELLIGENCE AGENCY AND DIRECTOR OF COUNTER-ESPIONAGE DEPARTMENT.

*(The contribution of the latter has for some reason been edited out. This doesn't matter very much; the general effect is that of a monologue, the speaker being very much on his home ground. The other was, it's reasonable to suppose, cast in the rôle of listener and feedman right from the start.)*

You make yourself at home, Piers. Believe me, I mean that. If there's anything you want – and I do mean *anything* – just you ask. What's that? Jesus, you can have her right now if you like, she's a real Anglophile, that little girl . . . And she'll haul your ashes for you like they've never been hauled before . . . Or we'll install her in the bridal suite for you, all gift-packaged . . . No, I'm not joking. Whatever your tastes are, I won't be shocked. You're entitled, my friend, if ever man was . . . Just relax now and taste a mite of this Scotch. I know you can't get it in England now . . . And when you go, which I hope won't be for a while, you'll take a crate away with you. As I say, you're entitled. Nothing? Ah, crap! Last year I'd made my mind up – this was the end. I'd taken everything else – the Bay of Pigs, the Cuban crisis – and now he was going to top it all. Talking about a *détente*. A *détente*, when in 1945 we had them over a barrel. He was issuing a cordial invitation to Ivan to come and screw us deaf, dumb and blind, that's what. Not as bad as all that? Don't be so fucking English, Piers. You know damn well what you think. He was a crooked Mick politician who kept all his brains in the end of his prick. I give you my word, the only asset he had apart from his Pop's dollars, was his face. If only my poor buddy Joe McCarthy had had his face and he'd had Joe's, Joe would have been in his place, and then it'd be a different story. And, believe me, Joe, though not the world's brightest, was a genius compared with our Prince Charming. However, I got to thinking about all this

21

in April or so – I figured that what the hell, I couldn't be the only one. I wasn't, not by a long chalk. And very high-up – the real high-up, not the shop-window high-up – I was given to understand that, yes, they felt as bad as me about the situation, naming no names, and were prepared to admit that under certain circumstances stringent, if not drastic measures might be advisable in the best interests of the country. But I was on my own. If it blew up in my face, then they would wipe away a tear and send for a bowl of water and a clean towel and make a damned thorough job of the old hand-washing too. As for the details of the operation, it was not for them to put forward any suggestions, but to their minds right at the centre of the operation must be a professional, not an American and not, repeat not, anyone connected with any political party anywhere. Whoever was fall-guy, the button-man had to be dependable. You wonder why I didn't think of the Mafia? Piers, you've got to be joking. We're still in trouble because we had them co-operate with us in Sicily. Besides, Prince Charming was a Catholic. And – this'll amuse you – they'd refuse to do it. They'd say it was unpatriotic. Not that you can depend upon any hood. That's when I came to you, and you sent me Xavier ... Well, it's all history, and it went like a dream, except for one bad moment when Superslob was so hopped up that his gun was pointing anywhere but in the right direction, and I'd practically to hold his hand for him. Christ, he did sweat and he did stink ... Meanwhile Xavier was at my home drinking tea and his very special MI was a cube about the size of a hand, safely at the bottom of the heap in a junk yard. Xavier stayed with us for the week before the operation, which you didn't approve of, if I recall. I have to get to know a guy I'm depending upon. Depending upon – that's what they called meosis at high school. If Xavier had misjudged by one millimetre or one millisecond, if his nerve had cracked – I wouldn't be here and neither would have Betty Lou, and they wouldn't have spared the kids either. No, no, Piers, don't tell me. I know what they'd have thought. There isn't one of us would have got near a courtroom, that's for sure. I – and Betty Lou and the kids – exist only as long as it's necessary for me to exist. Which is quite a thought. We're Government property really, like guns and ammo, and who notices a gun or a slug more or less? But Xavier's

a prince, a real prince, a good Mick. Served Mass one Sunday –
I was told all the women had hot pants for him, and no doubt
these days some of the men . . . He was with us for a month; I
got to know him pretty well. You can talk to Xavier, really *talk*,
I mean, he's damned good company, always in there with the
wisecracks and the good old blarney; but that boy's got just
about everything, and he can be serious. Before I met Xavier I
was just – well, just a Sunday Catholic, making my Easter duty,
saying a quick Act of Contrition last thing at night . . . not really
thinking it through. But Xavier has it all worked out, he has the
real gift of Faith, he makes it all so damned *interesting* . . . Hell,
I'm not saying I'm a living saint now, but being a Catholic
really means something to me . . . Christ, we're finishing that
bottle. Once in a while with an old friend a man has a right to
get stoned, hasn't he? The kids loved Xavier and he loved the
kids. Oh, yes. Girl aged five, Lynne, and a boy aged six, Barry.
Xavier didn't put himself out to be agreeable to the kids, but he
was nice and gentle with them. He talked to them, he was interested in them. But when he told them to do something, boy,
that was it. They still talk about him. They didn't know he was
an agent, naturally. Though Betty Lou guessed. That's another
thing. He's a Grade A cocksman. I mean, I love her and I trust
her, but I wouldn't have left her alone with him . . . But I'll give
you an example of Xavier's technique. We went to this party one
Sunday evening, and Xavier gets his eye on a woman. 'Excuse
me,' he says, then I meet someone and have a drink and the time
passes – and Xavier sort of materialises into the room and then
the woman, and she has been shafted and she's glad of it and
proud of it – and the remarkable thing is that she's a very
eligible divorcée and just about every man in the room has
tried and got nowhere. I ask Xavier how he does it. 'I just
talk gently to them for a moment,' he tells me, 'then say, "*Let's go
upstairs and have a fuck.*" It never fails.' Well, not with him it
doesn't. I'd get a swift kick in the rocks . . . Don't let your glass
get too low. And don't worry about us security-wise. You just let
your tongue go free. Yeah, there's still some who hate my guts
for that operation. Baked Beans, we called it, but there's nothing
down in writing. A lot of people have sniffed around, but not for
long, if you see what I mean and I'm sure that you do . . . Oper-

ation Purge? Sure I remember. You need help, my friend, and I'll come running. Baked Beans did me a powerful lot of good and, not that it matters, it was very economical too. A hundred thousand covered it all, so you might say we almost owe your gang something, which makes a nice change. And do you know what was the bonus, the big fat juicy bonus? Not long after, I got a call from the White House. There the Man is, having a snack – a snack, for Christ's sake, there was enough there to keep a Chinese family going for a week – and he belches and wipes his mouth and scratches his crotch and puts on a deeply distressed expression. He didn't have that many expressions; he just tried not to look shifty. 'Nat,' he says, 'I know you're a man whose word I can rely on.' 'Mr President,' I say, 'you ask me a straight question and I'll give you a straight answer.' Which was fair enough; I don't tell lies, because you always get found out. Just the same, I was shitting bricks, because I knew damned well what was coming. 'Jesus, this is a question I'm scared to ask you,' he says. 'I'm scared just *thinking* about it. But there's no-one else to ask it but me, and no-one to answer it but you, Nat. I've heard a terrible thing. The most terrible thing I've ever heard. I've got to ask you: *did a CIA agent shoot JFK?*' And then came the moment to be treasured: I looked him straight in the eye and I said: 'I give you my sacred word, Mr President, a CIA agent did *not* shoot JFK.' 'OK,' he says, and he mops his brow and scratches his crotch – I never did see such a man for scratching his crotch – he wasn't what you might call an elegant Southern gentleman . . . 'OK, Nat, that's it, that's enough.' There's a big thick file on his desk marked MOST SECRET; he scribbles CLOSED, *LBJ*, across it, and tosses it into a drawer. 'The shits,' he mutters to himself, 'the rotten lousy lying shits . . . Thank you, Nat. From the bottom of my heart, and don't think that I haven't got a warm and loving heart – and there'll always be room in it for you . . .' So that wrapped it all up in silk ribbon with a nice fancy bow; like I say, I'd told the truth . . . What's that? Fuck Operation Baked Beans, you feel good right now? Well we're in our prime . . . Listen, I'll call her, she has a friend too. Believe me, they'd rather do it than eat . . . But you take good care of that boy Xavier. He'll go far. Very far. Why, Piers, what an expression! (*Laughter and a fit of coughing.*)

# SEVEN

## 21 May 1974: 18.00—23.00 Hours

'The First Joyful Mystery,' Xavier Flynn said, his finger on the beechwood rosary which he had brought back, along with a purple knife scar across his left forearm, from his last trip to Poland. 'The Angel Gabriel tells Mary she is to be the mother of Jesus,' he said, very quietly. 'Hail Mary, full of grace, blessed among women . . . ' The figure on the crucifix was stylised with elongated limbs and an impossibly narrow face, almost, in fact, trendy, but somehow, Xavier mused, the man who had carved it – the tiny irregularities were proof that a machine hadn't been near it – had expressed a genuine human agony. He had seen that expression too often not to be able to identify it. He knew too that to hold such thoughts in his mind for too long would be dangerous, break into the tranquillity which was now gently enveloping him, saying the familiar words along with his sister Clodagh and her four children, part of the circle of bowed heads – Clodagh and the five-year-old twins, Jenny and Bernadette, hair black like Xavier's, and Maurice and James with red hair like their father Rory's. Maurice and James at first sight seemed to be twins, but Maurice was six and James seven and not only taller than Maurice but more heavily built.

This was what it was all about, Xavier thought – the large untidy room with worn red carpet of the kind once called Turkey, with a mustard and sage lozenge pattern, and on the mantel-piece a cheap alarm clock, four dusty invitation cards and a sheaf of letters, a small vase covered with silver paper by the twins, with six pieces of palm drooping from it, a cheap crucifix about a foot high which was supposed to shine in the dark, but never had done so, and a bundle of old letters and dusty forms. The big sofa with the faded fawn loose cover he remembered from his parent's home. It had cost thirty pounds in 1946, a great extravagance, but it was still as good as new, and was where Clodagh had her afternoon nap in preference to the brand new sofa in the sitting-room. The dark-green velvet curtains

25

with most of the pile gone, like the fur of a sick cat, the streaky pale-green walls, and the two old plum-red high-backed chairs with sagging springs, part of a long discarded suite also from his parents' home, should have been sordid and depressing, but in fact it was the one room where he felt completely at home.

The day had been bright but there had been coldness behind it. And now it was drizzling; it seemed soft, not spiteful as sometimes it could be. But it was odd weather for May; he was glad of the gas-fire and the bulbous old radiator bubbling away too hot to touch; the old saying was right, and he shouldn't have changed into lightweight clothes at the beginning of the month. The second Joyful Mystery: Mary goes to visit her cousin Elizabeth . . . There was a smell of meat cooking from the kitchen next-door; it was shin beef for a stew tomorrow. It took a lot of cooking, but if it were cooked properly he preferred it to fillet steak. It took him back, and back was where he always wanted to go, and where he always did go when he stayed with Clodagh.

The 'phone rang; he stood up in one movement and went next-door into the narrow room, half taken up with two cupboards running its whole length, one from the floor with a green formica shelf on top, the other above it to the ceiling, which they still called the butler's pantry.

'Harfield 748,' he said. 'Xavier Flynn.'

'I have a little job for you.'

It was Aslan, as he knew it would be and hoped it wouldn't be. Though there wasn't such another voice – high-pitched and penetrating, always on the verge of a sneer, each word pronounced with a contemptuous precision as if teaching elocution to a not very bright class – he gave his operating name and the identification number for the day and the hour and the place. 'Drinian Five Six Three. Identify.'

'Aslan, you fool. Trumpkin is coming –'

'Identify,' Xavier grinned. There was an open packet of Silk Cut King Size on the cupboard top; he had a split-second debate with himself – it would be his fifth today – then took one out and lit it with his Cricket lighter.

'Aslan. Five Six Nine. You *are* a clever boy, aren't you?'

'A cautious boy. That's why I'm still in good health and permanent employment.'

'I dislike that sort of talk. We are discussing a perfectly ordinary business transaction. What concerns us now is that the date of the Wilkinson contract has been brought forward. You will sign it tonight.'

'I rather like that word, sir. *Sign*. It's beautifully concise.'

'*Sign* is what I said, Xavier. To inscribe in one's own hand. It is a most specific word describing a specific action. It should hardly be necessary for me to point out that this contract is extremely important to our export trade. An opportunity presents itself to conclude an agreement more quickly than we had hoped.'

'I take it that the usual person will be along to dot the i's and cross the t's?'

There was a dry chuckle. 'The Disposer? He too has had his week-end broken into. He's a most meticulous worker, but he does hate a change in his plans . . . He won't be in a good mood.'

'You're breaking my heart. At what address do I sign the contract?'

'Trumpkin will give you all the details. There is one small one to attend to now; put on a suit and collar and tie. Wilkinson is a very serious and conscientious man and will expect it of you. Trumpkin will inform you about whatever else may be necessary.'

'Why do I need Trumpkin?'

'We all need others, Xavier.' There was another dry chuckle. 'Wilkinson has acquired a colleague. A young lady.'

'She has to sign too? It might complicate things.'

'Inevitably. But blame Wilkinson, not me. I'm terribly sorry about it.'

'Why are you sorry about it? Isn't she in the export business?'

'Unless I've been gravely misinformed, she isn't. I doubt if she's even remotely interested . . .'

'Then we'll have to put off signing the contract.'

'That just isn't possible. It must be signed *now*. You can't make an omelette without breaking eggs, Xavier.'

'I've heard enough about that bloody omelette, thank you. I don't like it. It means trouble.'

'Not if you deal with the matter with your usual expertise, my dear chap. And now I've a great deal of paperwork to catch up with. Trumpkin will be along at seven; report to the Woking number immediately the contract is signed. I'll see you Monday. Goodbye.' He hung up.

Xavier put the 'phone down and walked back into the room. They had reached the Third Joyful Decade. He took out his rosary and joined in, by an effort of will closing his mind to the telephone conversation.

At the end of the decade he rose – for a second finding his limbs reluctant to obey him. 'That was the boss, Clodagh,' he said. 'Something's come up. I have to go out.'

'Wouldn't you think the devil'd leave you alone on a Friday night?' she said. 'Will you be late?'

He shook his head. 'Tom Drage is calling for me.'

The children started to giggle and chatter. It was their innocence that overcame you, he thought, the clearness of their eyes, the movement and gestures which were not graceful and which weren't clumsy either – coltish, not surprisingly, would be the word for it.

Clodagh rose, not with great ease; at thirty-four, after four children and four miscarriages, her figure was already beginning to thicken; her skin was as flawless as ever, scarcely lined, but the black hair wasn't as well groomed as it once had been and she didn't bother overmuch about laddered tights or down-at-heel shoes. Xavier often wondered whether his brother-in-law Rory's more frequent absences were due entirely to the pressure of business.

'Go and have your baths now, the lot of you,' Clodagh said. 'Then you can come down in your dressing-gowns and watch TV. And for God's sake, tidy your rooms before your father comes home . . .'

Xavier slumped down in the armchair. The telephone conversation was on his mind again. The boys rushed out of the room, slamming the door behind them; the girls came and sat on his knees, warm and surprisingly heavy. He squeezed their waists; they were extraordinarily comfortable to have near one, but they weren't going to solve his problems.

'What are you thinking about?' Jenny asked. He knew it was Jenny because of the tiny mole on her cheek.

'Business,' he said. 'Earning a living. You wouldn't understand, pet. It's what grown-ups have to do.'

28

'What's your business, Uncle Xavier?' Bernadette asked. Even without the mole, you could tell her apart from her sister; she always had a slightly worried expression; when she grew up she'd probably worry about the state of the world, like her father – the silly sod.

'I negotiate for the Department of Trade and Industry,' he said.

'What's negotiate?'

'I arrange for different people to meet, really. And in the end what happens is that things are sold abroad. Which is good for the country. Which is good for all of us.'

They nodded their heads and slipped off his knees, running out of the room and leaving the door wide open.

'Were you born in a field?' Clodagh screamed after them, but they were already out of earshot. 'Jesus, Mary and Joseph, they have me worn out,' she said. 'Close the door, Xavier, there's a draught like a stepmother's breath.'

She leaned back lighting a cigarette, her knees going apart as she relaxed, an old woman's habit which never failed to annoy him. 'I'm sure you'd like a cup of tea,' he said to Clodagh, whose eyes were already half closed. She sighed and levered herself out of her chair. 'You're worried about something,' she said.

'I don't think it's going to be as easy as the boss thinks.'

'I'll send up a quick prayer to St Francis Xavier whilst the kettle's boiling,' she said as she went into the kitchen. The cream Arran Isles jumper he'd bought her in Dublin after his job there last year was grubby, the black skirt uneven at the hem; this would have repelled him in another woman, but with her it added to his love. It was restful to be with a woman who was still bed-worthy and not have the faintest flicker of desire, restful even to be irritated by her leg-show.

The tea was almost exactly the colour of mahogany: the initial effect wasn't so far off that of alcohol. 'My God,' he said, 'when I makes tea –'

'I know,' she said. 'When I makes tea I makes tea, and when I makes water I makes water –'

'Then God send, says I, mam, that you don't make them both in the same pot,' they said in unison. It was an old joke; Joyce had been a secret pleasure which they had shared since his adolescence.

'You shouldn't look so worried, though,' she said. 'You get it from Mother. She's always been a great worrier . . .'

'The contract'll be signed,' he said. 'Someone new has been brought into it, that's all.'

'They're always doing things like that to Rory,' she said. 'He never knows where he stands two moments together . . .'

'Where is he now, did you say?'

'Birmingham. Some design problem with a kitchen equipment firm.'

'Sooner him than me.'

But Rory would never have the sort of problem which he had now; not the least of which was the growing suspicion that Aslan was hamming up the rôle of Grey Eminence a bit too much, becoming a bit too fond of treating human beings as expendable. Horace Wilkinson, born Klementi Pletnev in Leningrad in 1949, had served his time in the Third Directorate of the KGB; he was a killer and had come to kill. He wouldn't be used for anything else; which made it puzzling that he should be where he was. The girl was another matter. It shouldn't have been impossible to prevent her coming and then there would have been no harm done at all. He didn't even know the girl's name. He had fucked girls without knowing their names but he'd never killed one without knowing her name, and for no other reason than that someone was too lazy to get her out of the way.

Walking up the stairs to his room he felt for no good reason physically weary. The largeness of the house usually elated him: there was room to move, room to breathe, room to be private. Tonight it depressed him: there was something official, something oppressive about the high ceilings and deep skirting boards and the broad staircase; it reminded him too much of Whitehall. He went into the guest-room and lay down on the double bed for a moment. He could hear the children's voices from the two bathrooms along the corridor; tonight that didn't make him happy either. He got up impatiently and took off his sweater and washed his face with cold water at the washbasin in the corner. He took out of the wardrobe – a big old Victorian mahogany piece which always reminded him of the wardrobe in *The Lion, the Witch and the Wardrobe* – and changed into the navy-blue lightweight suit and blue shirt and tie and black shoes which he had arrived in. He lay on the bed again and lit a cigarette; then he heard the front doorbell. It was just as answering the 'phone had been; he wasn't eager about going into Aslan's world after he had thought he was going to escape from it for two days.

Tom was looking healthy and bright-eyed in an aubergine suit with waistcoat and flared trousers with turn-ups, a pink checked shirt and pink tie, trendy but not outrageously so, his fair hair full at the back rather than long. Xavier went to the kitchen door. 'I'm going now,' he said to Clodagh. 'I don't think I'll be long.' He kissed her cheek. 'Don't worry,' she said. 'I've got St Francis Xavier on the job.'

Tom had brought the old Zodiac shooting-brake – the long bonnet kind. It had a 300-horsepower Mustang V8 under its bonnet and various complex operations had been effected on its brakes and steering, but he felt that it was beginning to be a little too well known, and that Tom was growing too used to it.

'Sorry about this,' Tom said. 'I know you treasure your family week-ends.'

'You're responsible for all this rush then?'

'I'm bloody glad to get it over with quick; but it wasn't me.'

'This girl – what do you know about her?'

They were on Thames Street now, passing by St Maur's; it was an odd road, never quite sure of its character. He wondered if Portmore Park on the right had ever been a park; but through the half-open window was the smell of trees and grass. This was as much of the country as he wanted, with the river not far away. It was a narrow road with nothing of any note along it but St Maur's Convent with the green expanse of its playing fields on the left. You couldn't see much of them but they were there. And the houses were mostly the older type, real houses, not concrete boxes, all well kept. It was a quiet road but life ran through it; it was in the mainstream.

'I'm talking to you,' Tom said. 'Stop dreaming beautiful dreams. The girl: her name's Shirley Mason. Twenty-two. A receptionist. Here,' he handed Xavier a mimeographed sheet with a large Press photo attached. The photo showed a smiling blonde, all breasts and eyes and white teeth, a man in a dinner-jacket next to her, his hand on her shoulder. He had fair hair, worn short, a little tousled, and an open, boyish face.

'That's Pletnev,' Tom said.

'Clean-cut type, isn't he? They've stopped sending sinister Slavs with gold teeth . . . I've seen a picture of him before. Christ, Tom, this is ridiculous. According to this report, she's merely off for a dirty week-end with him.'

'Brighton actually,' Tom said. 'These chaps seldom lose an opportunity to sample the capitalist fleshpots.'

'I wonder that he didn't go straight there from London. After, presumably, collecting the girl.'

'He has to make a 'phone call to his cousin in the Midlands.'

'The cousin will actually be one of our lot?'

'Something like that ' Tom sounded preoccupied.

It had stopped raining now; suddenly the sun was dazzling. Tom put on his sunglasses as he did at every opportunity.

'Aren't we trendy?' Xavier said.

'Fuck you,' said Tom.

'I don't like this,' Xavier said, glancing again at the mimeographed sheet 'Is there something you haven't told me about this girl?'

'It's all been checked.'

'Respectable working-class background, left Salford at twenty to better herself, took a secretarial course, ended up in London with what seems like a reasonably good job. Hasn't any politics. Not a natural blonde – how did they find that out?' He grinned.

'Our agents don't spare themselves in the pursuit of information,' Tom said. He glanced at his watch and stopped the car just past the British Aircraft factory on the right. 'We're a bit in advance. Look, Xavier, what's eating you?'

'I'm not in favour of killing the girl. And please don't tell me about that bloody omelette again. At least we should wait until we can get Pletnev on his own.'

'Which probably won't be until much later in Brighton. So there'll be no Disposer to tidy things up.'

'We've tidied up ourselves before now.'

'Yes, and it's time-consuming and complicated and we've been damned lucky to bring it off. You can't count on being lucky.' Something in his voice made Xavier look at him more closely: there were beads of sweat on his forehead and lines suddenly round his mouth as if actually cut, lines too deep for a man of twenty-seven.

'There's something wrong at Morgate's, isn't there?' Xavier asked.

Tom put his hand to his mouth as if to wipe the lines away, and turned the ignition key. 'Of course there is. That's why I'm there. But it isn't as simple as I'd expected. I know there's something wrong, but I can't put my finger on it. And I've got a hunch that it's something to do with Operation X.'

'Operation X?' Xavier laughed. 'That's a myth to begin with. But what's your evidence?'

'I haven't got any. But I'm going to Guildford tonight. Meeting a chap there who might be able to tell me something.' He paused. 'His name's Dykenhead. Export Department. Can you remember that?'

'If you want me to. But Operation X means the KGB. How would they come into it?'

'Through FIST, of course.'

'But how exactly?'

'I can *smell* it!' Tom's voice rose to a shout. Then he was silent for a moment. 'Oh hell, I don't know . . . May all be a waste of time.' He sent the big shooting-brake into the roundabout for West Blyfleet at 20 mph more than the standard model could have taken it; it cut into the path of a white Audi 100 GL and straightened out without a lurch, its oversize tyres squealing only slightly. The driver of the Audi, a young man with a white face and a black beard, shook his fist at them.

'You stupid bugger,' Xavier said. 'That sod in the Audi is going to remember us. Be your bloody age.'

'You needn't take it out on me because you're turning squeamish all of a sudden,' Tom said sulkily. 'Frankly, it's a relief to me to know where my orders are coming from . . . It's a nice, straightforward job.'

'It was going to be,' Xavier said. 'But I'm not happy about the girl being brought into it . . . Hell, I wouldn't mind if she were – well, political. Longing for the Revolution and all that . . . But she's just a decent normal girl looking forward to a rousing fuck at Brighton.'

'I once saw a decent normal girl carried out of a shop after a bombing,' Tom said. 'She hadn't any lower half to her face. What difference does it make in the end?' He turned to the right and parked the car on the intake by Bishop's Supermarket. He looked at his watch again then picked up the 'phone under the dashboard. 'Trumpkin Ten Three Two Five,' he said. 'Yes. Over.' He turned to Xavier. 'They're here,' he said. He opened the glove compartment and handed Xavier a small notebook with NOTES embossed on it in white, a police warrant card, and a small plan with half a sheet of typescript attached.

'When?' Xavier's throat felt dry, as it always did at these moments. It was late opening night and there were still customers in the supermarket; he wondered for a moment what it would be like to be one of the customers, living in a kind, gentle, civilised world where death, when it was thought of at all, was thought of only as the consequence of accident or illness or old age.

'Five minutes,' Tom said. 'The story is that we've found his stolen car, but there're a few things puzzling us. Details attached to the plan and repeated on the first page of the notebook, by the way.'

Xavier put the notebook carefully in his inside pocket then glanced at the plan. He didn't try to memorise it; the reality was always different, and if he hadn't learned when very much younger mentally to photograph his surroundings in a split second, he wouldn't be alive now.

'You've seen the notebook before?' Tom asked.

Xavier nodded. 'The operating position is the normal reading position. The safety catch is off when I open it.'

They got out of the car. It was dull again but, he noted with amusement, Tom still had his sunglasses on. 'For Christ's sake, Tom,' he said with sudden irritation, 'take those bloody sunglasses off. Are you trying to look like a Mafia hit man? And why the hell have you got all that Carnaby Street gear on anyway?'

'Because younger cops dress like that,' Tom said. 'Otherwise they'd look conspicuous. And short hair would look conspicuous.' His tone became spiteful. '*You*'re not under the illusion that you look anything other than what you are, are you?'

'And what's that?'

'A Mick thug. When you're a bit older and you've put a bit of weight on you'll look like a crooked Mick politician.'

34

'As long as we look and behave like coppers now, that's more to the point,' Xavier said. 'Don't get worked up about nothing.' He took in his surroundings with one quick glance; it was easy enough to get away quickly if they had to. But there was no necessity to consider it; this should be a smooth straightforward operation. From the moment they had got out of bed that morning Pletnev and Mason – it was better to think of her as Mason – were dead. They would disappear; it would be as if they had never existed. If there were no bodies, there were no problems: a bonus was that the KGB could never be completely certain that Pletnev hadn't defected. The process was described as Hooverising; in the first two years of Operation Purge they'd arranged various accidental deaths, but it had grown too complicated.

There seemed to be as many men as women around the supermarket; he noticed with amusement that the men were all dressed casually. Suits were still the rule in most middle-class jobs; in order to ceremonially announce the beginning of the week-end they must have changed immediately on coming home. They should really have been stockpiling baked beans and fruit juice and condensed milk and putting in some intensive target practice. But instead they'd be piling up their grocery carts with bundles of spaghetti and Schwartz's herbs and a dozen different kinds of cheese and pâté and pickles and relishes, engaging in long debates about unpretentious little wines, acting out the Supercook Sunday supplement Good Housekeeping Weekend charade for all the world as if they weren't living on a knife-edge.

'Don't waste any time,' Tom said, as they turned to the right by the featureless bulk of the supermarket block.

'Don't worry,' Xavier said as they crossed Lavender Road. 'Here, down this rather nice little alley. Frisby Court, and very nice it is . . . A very pleasant little pseudo-Georgian square. But that awful supermarket block overshadows it . . .'

'You talk too bloody much,' Tom said.

The entrance hall was at the side of the square nearest the main road; there was an enquiry desk there but no-one was sitting at it. The walls and ceiling were plain cream and the floor a mottled black and white. Xavier glanced at the list of tenants and then pointed at the empty desk.

'He's at the police station,' Tom said, as they entered the lift. 'The matter will be straightened out, with profound apologies, as soon as the Disposer has tidied up.'

They walked briskly along the beige-carpeted cream-walled corridor at the third floor, not bothering to tread softly. They were policemen asking for information from the owner of a stolen car; they assumed that naturally he would wish to see them in order that he might have his car returned. After all, a Jaguar XJK was worth having back; if Pletnev didn't want to see them, it was as good as blowing his cover there and then.

Xavier felt the weight of the Smith and Wesson 9 mm automatic against his right hip. It was a special hand-engraved model with an alloy frame, his initials in gold on the walnut butt. It had been given him by Nat Weiberg at the Pentagon as the climax of a small and select celebration dinner. It wasn't the sort of thing which a police officer would carry, but if Pletnev did see it, events would have reached the stage where all that was relevant was who killed who and not who was who. He wasn't very keen on the notebook: it was too clever by half.

He rang the bell under the circular louvred opening on the the door of Flat 11. 'Who is that please?' a man's voice asked.

'Mr Wilkinson? This is a police officer, sir. It's in connection with your missing Jaguar.'

The door was opened by the man in the photo. He looked younger in the flesh; his bright-blue jacket with large yellow checks accentuated the width of his shoulders and the depth of his chest. It was also of a very full cut with room for large weapons, let alone the nasty little weapons in which the Third Directorate specialised. His blue slacks were of a good worsted and his black casuals weren't cheap: the KGB was learning the value of details – details which, when of this kind, would make assignments in the West even more popular.

The carpet was beige as in the corridor, light enough to show every mark. Though there shouldn't be any. He cleared his throat. 'We've got the Jaguar back, sir, but there's a problem.' The sod had moved away. The girl on the sofa, in a short grey denim dress which showed a great deal of leg, was sipping a drink. Pletnev was fiddling with a shirt in the black leather grip which stood open on the imitation-marble-topped coffee-table

36

by the sofa. It was a depressing room – large and light enough, but bland and neutral, with no trace of human beings having lived there.

Pletnev straightened himself up. 'I'm wondering why, officer, I should have different people dealing with the matter.'

Xavier took out his warrant card, coming closer to Pletnev so that he could see it. Tom followed suit.

'It's soon cleared up, sir,' he said. 'It's a question of some unusually active villains making good – or rather bad – use of your Jaguar. I'll explain . . .'

He took out the notebook and opened it, saw Pletnev's face harden, felt a sharp pain across his shins as the coffee-table hit them; even as he flung himself sideways, Pletnev's foot knocked the notebook from his hand. Pletnev was nearly at the door when Xavier rabbit-punched him; he grunted and fell with extra-ordinary suddenness, as if a wire holding him up had been cut. Automatically Xavier drew his foot back; you were never safe in assuming a professional to be dead.

'No,' Tom said, moving over to Pletnev and taking hold of his wrist. 'Don't gild the lily. He's dead all right.'

The girl's drink had dropped from her hand. 'Oh my God!' she said. 'I must be dreaming. You've killed him. What are you just standing there for? Why don't you do something?' She rose and went to the body. 'Aren't you going to help me?' She was weeping now and shaking violently. 'What sort of policemen are you?'

She really was attractive, Xavier thought, looking at her half-revealed breasts as she bent over Pletnev. It had been a long way from Salford: she had no trace of a Lancashire accent, the dress was Dior, and the gold bracelet was a Patek Philippe. He took hold of her shoulder, Tom's eyes on him. Now Tom was looking at his watch.

'Leave Mr Wilkinson where he is for a moment, miss. Just sit down and answer a few questions, please.'

She sat on the sofa, pulling her skirt down and fastening the top button of her dress. He said nothing, waiting for his instincts to send instructions. He would obey them, wherever they led him; he'd made it plain from that first occasion in Malaya that he was a man and not an instrument. The notebook had dropped

37

on the table: he picked it up, opened it again, heard her draw in her breath sharply, saw her fling herself sideways and, knowing that this would happen, knowing with a sharp pain under his breast-bone what he had to do, pressed the lettering on the notebook. There was a tiny hiss and a dart – red, a little longer than a bluebottle – hit her cheek. It fell off; her hand touched her cheek then stiffened convulsively; her face was suddenly dragged grotesquely out of shape as if in a fairground mirror; she grunted and dribbled and then slumped forward.

Tom took the notebook from Xavier and pointed it at Pletnev's wrist. Xavier pulled a face.

'They'll expect us to have used two,' Tom said. 'It doesn't make any difference to him now anyway.' He took out a pair of rubber gloves and a large heavy plastic envelope from his inside breast-pocket, picked one dart up from beside Pletnev and the other from the sofa beside the girl and put them with the notebook in the envelope. He carefully put away the envelope. His hands were shaking a little.

Xavier, his eyes closed and his head bowed, was making the Sign of the Cross. Tom picked up the 'phone. 'Four Three Six,' he said. 'You can come up now.'

'Was it the Disposer himself?' Xavier asked, lighting a cigarette.

Tom nodded. 'He'll be even more disagreeable than usual, you'll see.'

'D'you know, Tom, I find myself disliking him more and more each time I meet him.'

'I don't suppose he cares as long as you don't rabbit-punch him. Are you quite sure you've finished your prayers? I'm used to it, but I don't think that the Disposer will appreciate it.'

'I'll pray for them again before I go to bed.'

'You think they'll go to Heaven?' There was an edge on Tom's voice.

Xavier smiled. 'You always ask me that . . . I don't see why not, if they were doing their duty according to their lights.'

'Considering the number of people you've killed, it's going to be quite a party when you receive your eternal reward and you all meet again. You don't think that the atmosphere will be a little strained? Don't you honestly?' He was shaking and his face had gone pale. 'Jesus, you're wonderful. Straight out of the Middle Ages.'

'There is nothing but love in Heaven. At least, so I've been told.'

'You don't practise it here much on earth, do you, Xavier? I have of course said this to you before.'

'No doubt, Tom. And I have said this to you before: I prevent people from committing the grave sin of harming my country. That's *practical* love.'

Tom burst into hysterical laughter. 'You papists are absolutely incredible. Practical love! What do you do when you hate people? No, don't answer me, Xavier. I've heard it all before. I never believe it, so I ask you again and get the same answers. Practical love!' He was nearly screaming. 'You're like an automatic machine . . . And we have the same conversation again and again. And the worst of it is that right now there's something wrong –'

The doorbell rang. Tom answered it to let in a tall thin man in a rumpled navy-blue serge suit and a stiff white collar and nondescript blue tie. His dark brown shoes were unshined. He shook hands with Tom but merely nodded at Xavier. Then he knelt by Pletnev's body and pulled back an eyelid. He stood up, wiped his hands on a large white handkerchief and walked over to the girl. 'No need to check on what's happened to her,' he said. 'Why not with him?'

'A slight technical hitch,' Xavier said. 'They're being Hoover-ised anyway, so it doesn't really matter, Inspector.'

'You're wrong there. The job has to be carried out strictly in accordance with your instructions.' The Disposer's thin lips went through the motions of spitting. 'Once upon a time, Major, I was young, I had ideals. I was a creature of the light, a protector of the innocent . . . Quite poetic I was then. Imagine, me *protecting* people . . .'

'That's what I'm doing,' Xavier said. 'In a sense.'

'In my sense, you're driving a coach and horses through the law and I'm covering up for you.'

'You're obeying orders,' Xavier said patiently. 'We've been into this before.' The hatred in the Disposer's thin bony face disturbed him a little.

'One of these days some lawyer's going to make mincemeat of that excuse.'

Xavier shrugged his shoulders. 'Argue with my boss,' he said.

The Disposer waved at Pletnev. 'Another secret agent? Another fiendish Red spy?'

'I don't know about fiendish. A Soviet agent certainly.'

'And the girl?' Her skirt had ridden up round her waist, revealing pale-blue Bikini pants; the Disposer pulled the skirt down to cover her, his face averted.

Xavier smiled in the direction of Tom. 'Quite harmless. She was going off for a dirty week-end with this chap here. Who passed himself off as a respectable businessman. She didn't know he was a Russian. But you wouldn't be best pleased if you had her on your hands now, having hysterics and complaining to her MP and the papers and these Civil Liberties bastards . . .'

'No, I wouldn't be pleased. But I have a daughter her age . . .'

'All this is pretty futile, Inspector,' Tom said. 'We don't pick and choose our jobs, any more than you do yours.'

The Disposer pulled out a small cheroot from his inside pocket and lit it with great care. The festive smell of the cheroot masked the other smell which was now becoming apparent to Xavier, as it always did: it was acrid and animal and sad, it was the smell of violent death – you never mentioned it to anyone but everyone in their line of business recognised it.

The Disposer gave Xavier a buff form divided into twenty compartments of various sizes. 'Code name here,' he said to Xavier. 'And you,' he said to Tom. 'In block letters please. And both your identification numbers here and here.'

'There now,' said Xavier. 'Everything's correct, Inspector.' He pointed. '*Method of termination. Method of disposal.* I'd never really noticed these before. Amusing in a way . . .'

'I don't think it's amusing.' The Disposer picked up the 'phone and dialled. 'You can come up now,' he said.

Suddenly Xavier wanted to be out of the room. 'We've finished now, Inspector,' he said, going towards the door. 'I expect we'll see you again.'

'I'm afraid so.' The Disposer's mouth puckered up again as if he were actually going to spit; surprisingly, Xavier felt sorry for him, seeing him as a decent man who'd through no fault of his own been led into an alien world.

'I wonder why he dislikes me so much?' he said to Tom as they walked along Madeira Road by the post office.

'You always try to shock him for one thing. You don't think that that bloody form is amusing. And you needn't have told him about the girl.'

'It wasn't true, anyway.'

'What a clever chap you are.'

'I knew when she was frightened of the notebook.'

'She'd seen Pletnev's reactions, hadn't she?'

They got into the car; Tom turned to the right, back along the way they'd come, passing an ambulance on the way. Within ten minutes Pletnev and the girl would be out of the flat and everything tidied up; it would be as if nothing had ever happened, except that perhaps for a while the smell of violent death might hang about the place. But that would only be identifiable to those whose business was to deal with it.

'She'd seen Pletnev's reactions, surely?' Tom repeated impatiently.

'Only someone in the business would have known *what* he was reacting to. Shirley the receptionist from Salford just wouldn't have taken in such a detail.'

'Good thinking, Xavier.'

'Where is Shirley?'

'In the mortuary: a refrigerated drawer somewhere in South London. Her face is bashed about rather, but it's her all right.'

'You're a rotten sod, aren't you? Why didn't you tell me?'

'I was expressly ordered not to. Aslan's sense of humour, I shouldn't wonder. Likes the idea of you grappling with your conscience.'

'You do too, don't you?'

'It's just another job for me. I've only the Government as my employer. You've got God in on the act too.'

'I can't understand why they went to all that trouble to set up a cover,' Xavier said.

'Probably just an experiment. You find a girl in London living away from home, you get an agent to match, you get rid of the girl, and you've got a damned good cover. Clever, really.'

'It gave me a nasty moment.'

'Hard luck. Don't worry, Xavier, you've been put to the test and not found wanting.'

'Aslan's job isn't to test me. It's to get the work done.'

'Sorry your feelings have been hurt. I'm far more worried by what's going on at Morgate's.'

They were travelling fast along Brooklands Road now; a bit too fast, as if Tom were intent on proving that the Zodiac was no ordinary Zodiac.

'Slow down,' Xavier said. 'It's a straightforward case of industrial sabotage, isn't it?'

'It's FIST, to begin with, if you consider that straightforward.'

'Force, insurrection, sabotage, terrorism. That's straightforward enough. Just like a boy's adventure story.'

The work was finished and he was going to his sister's home for a quiet evening and, best of all, an hour in bed reading *Five Children and It*; he looked at the streets of semi-detached houses on the left with love and tenderness. He had done his duty; the people who lived in the semi-detached houses could live their quiet, safe, essentially cosy lives a while longer, violence merely a diversion on film and TV, something which they read about in the newspapers.

'Christ, I wish it were! I don't know what Aslan's playing at. *I do not know*.' He spat out the words. 'I'm supposed to take orders from amateurs. I don't like it, I smell trouble. I don't see why we're mixed up at all, except that Aslan's related to old Morgate.'

'I had heard.'

Xavier laughed. 'Probably got some shares in the business.'

'My job isn't to protect his bloody investments.'

'He knows what he's doing,' Xavier said, settling back more comfortably.

'I wish I did. I'm at the end of my tether.'

He looked at Tom in surprise: always before he'd been very much the smooth casual technician, too much addicted perhaps to going by the book, to sticking to his orders in every particular. The most important rule in the Department was that the less each agent knew what the other was doing, the better: you helped only when asked, and you were virtually never asked.

'I'll come along with you to Guildford if you like.'

'It might scare Dykenhead off.'

'I could just hang around. I'd be there if you wanted me.'

'It wouldn't solve the problem. It isn't just FIST, you see. It's something else that's going on. I can't prove it, either. I can't prove anything.'

Xavier nodded. 'I know the feeling.' He didn't like Tom all that much, but he could put himself into his shoes at this very moment.

'I'll bloody well get to the bottom of it if it kills me,' Tom said, sending the Zodiac squealing into the Hanger Hill roundabout.

'Just as you like,' Xavier said. 'But you know where I am if you need an extra pair of hands.' But he was aware as he spoke that the offer could have been phrased better, that he could have insisted upon going along with Tom. He rationalised immediately: this was Tom's assignment, he was an experienced operative despite his youth. He had to learn to cope alone, as he, Xavier, had had to many times in rougher places than Guildford. As they turned right into Thames Street, Xavier had already got rid of his slight but irritating sense of guilt and was looking forward to the evening ahead.

'There's something you can do for me,' Tom said. His voice had not its usual bantering tone. 'I've been shacked up with Sally Rowmarsh for a few months now.'

'I'm well aware of it. You haven't been the same chap since you met her.'

'I'm sure Aslan has told you. She's a bit of a Lefty, but not too bad . . . Anyway, I'd rather you saw her. If anyone must see her.'

'God, Tom, it's not going to come to that.'

'If it doesn't, what difference does it make? You see, Xavier, though you're a Mick thug, you're occasionally almost indistinguishable from a human being.'

'Beware of your tendency to flatter,' Xavier said sourly. 'I'll do as you ask – but I'm sure it's unnecessary. Jesus, it's unlucky to talk like that.'

'So you say. So you say.' Tom's voice was without expression.

At eleven that night on his knees in the spare room he asked St Thomas the Apostle to intercede for Tom's safety. It might not do any good; it certainly could do no harm. He didn't like Tom very much but he loved him as he was bound to as a Christian, just as he had loved Pletnev and the girl who had called herself Shirley Mason. Tom was shallow and a bit of an arsehole-creeper but he still had to love him. He wondered whether to pray for the Disposer, but decided against it; he seemed to have a long list of people to pray for that night and he didn't want the pint mug of strong tea on his bedside table to grow cold.

The room was an odd mixture of austerity and comfort, with a new and expensive divan bed with Dunlopillo mattress, thick fitted beige Axminster carpet, but a dressing-table and bedside table of unpainted whitewood which didn't match the large old mahogany wardrobe, plain white walls with only a large crucifix as decoration, and cheap ready-made curtains in royal blue which didn't quite meet. There was something impersonal and vaguely monastic about it: it was one of the few places in which he felt completely happy.

He said his final prayer – *O God let me know how best to serve You and my country* – made the sign of the Cross and got into bed. The tea – made in the pot with five teabags – was exactly the right temperature. It was five years since he had read *Five Children and It;* long enough ago for it to be almost like reading it for the first time. The pleasure wasn't only in the escape from probability, but in the background – an ordered, formal, safe society which in addition was robustly certain that its few imperfections would very soon be remedied.

He only knew that he was completely happy. It had taken him some time to learn it; but in a job like his you only kept your sanity if you learned how to escape and not to be ashamed of escaping. His way of escape was into innocence: he'd seen all too often what happened to those who used drugs and alcohol. Clodagh's home was escape too: Clodagh was no fool but she lived an intensely personal private life. The outside world didn't enter this house.

But despite himself he was tired. The job today had been a drain upon his emotions. In action a second was a long time. It had to be a hundred times longer than for ordinary people if you were to have any chance of dying of old age. And there had been at least ten seconds after the killing of Pletnev when he wasn't certain who the girl was.

He lit a Silk Cut King Size and, when he'd finished it, closed the book and put it down. He didn't mark the page: he would remember it. He pulled the cord that switched off the ceiling light, folded his hands over his chest as if ready for burial, and let himself drift off to sleep. For a minute or so he heard noises from outside – a passing train, a car, an owl, the squeak of some small animal swooped upon – and then he was asleep and warm and secure, his face as composed as a stone crusader's.

# EIGHT

# *3 June 1974: 10.00–17.00 Hours*

Turning into Victoria Street a silver Miura cut in across Xavier's Mini to take the left-hand lane, its deep burble scarcely changing in note as it accelerated. Xavier resisted the temptation to put his foot down and do the same thing to the Miura; he could see the gaps which would enable him to do it and, after that, just for the hell of it, to do it again. He enjoyed the Mini more than any car he'd ever had. He'd begun with a Clubman Estate, had Rogers of the CED Transport Section put in a 1275 cc GT engine, then had it, in Rogers's phrase, breathed upon. As he'd discovered when he got the bill, breathed upon was an understatement. A single double-choke Weber carburettor, a high-lift camshaft, a close-ratio gearbox, an extractor exhaust system, high compression valves, a Cooper crankshaft and various other additions which he didn't fully understand added up to nearly as much money as would have bought him another Mini; but he'd got an engine which produced a genuine 85 bhp and 105 mph. He'd had Dunlop Denovo tyres fitted; big fat racing tyres would have been more in keeping with the engine, but they'd be no safer than any other tyre if he had a blow-out. There were reclining seats in Connolly leather, electric windows, an electric sunroof, and fifteen coats of midnight-blue paint, each one sanded before the next was applied. There was a roll bar and an 11-gallon fuel tank with special foam filling; the foam was only five per cent solid and if punctured would take a long time to run dry. The windscreen was Triplex 10–20 laminated and the headlamps swivelled with the steering. No-one in CED had a car quite like it, and very few outside it. It wasn't conspicuous except in its performance and it didn't have any hidden missile launchers or an ejection seat or even a secret compartment. He'd had it over a year now and it had never given him the least trouble, though the tender loving care of Rogers was no doubt what accounted for that.

The air through the open sunroof had just enough edge to blow away the last traces of sleep; the sun was bringing out the girls'

46

summer dresses and, with any luck, would make them shed their tights. That was a minor but certain pleasure: revelations of feminine underwear instead of what always seemed to him an asexual garment, a kind of chastity belt, reminiscent of medieval page-boys, and who the hell could be turned on by them?

He passed Strutton Ground on the left, took the next turning and came up Strutton Ground towards Victoria Street. He turned at the narrow alley-way between the Grafton's pub and the iron-mongers at the top of the street. He pressed a small button on the dashboard: the big double doors at the end of the alley opened silently, disappearing into the wall. He drove forward and the doors clanged shut behind him. He was in an empty room some fifty feet square. The floor was concrete with six-inch ramps at intervals of five feet, the walls were plain white. The room was lit by fluorescent strips; their harsh green-blue glare abolished all sense of night or day, just as the bareness of the room abolished all hope of cover. Xavier drove slowly towards the left-hand side of the blank wall, the Mini's suspension working hard; when his bumpers were a foot away from the wall, it slid upwards and above it a notice lit up in red: ALL VEHICLES STOP AT CONTROL POINT.

He drove along the corridor for a hundred yards, still driving slowly, though now there were no ramps on the floor, and stopped at a steel lattice gate. To his right was a steel door and an opening beside it at waist level. The large man in the black trousers, white shirt and peaked cap sitting at the opening stretched out a gloved hand. The hand was of steel as was the arm; his face on the left side was purple and puckered almost up to the crown.

Xavier handed the man a small red plastic card; he pressed it into a slot under a large control panel in front of him, and a green light shone. All the time the man kept the TV screen in front of him in view. The alley curved in a deep crescent; the picture kept changing to take in the whole of the alley. The man handed Xavier back the card and inclined his head in a kind of salute. If the light had shown red he would have been authorised to shoot without asking further questions: the Smith and Wesson ·38 Special in the holster at his waist was loaded with Special Hi-Speed with a striking energy of 460 foot pounds, and a muzzle velocity of 1175 feet per second, which added up to a hole the size of a man's fist if you were hit, and – a feature which always perturbed him slightly – there were no manual safeties.

'Right, Major,' the guard said, and smiled, the teeth incongruously white in the ruined face. Having been changed from a handsome young soldier into what he was by an IRA bomb in Belfast, he regarded Xavier as one of his favourites; he knew what his job was and had heard, through devious sources, that only recently it had taken him to Ulster with the result that a thriving little bomb factory and arms store near the Border had blown up along with ten Provisionals. Whenever the guard's wounds hurt, he thought of the ten Provisionals dying and felt a little better.

'Thank you, Sergeant,' Xavier said, and drove forwards towards a large steel door which slid into the wall one second before the Mini's bumpers touched it. He drove slowly down the spiral concrete passage, noticing with a kind of hatred the slowly revolving lenses of the closed-circuit TV set at ten-foot intervals in the walls above him. For some reason those slowly revolving lenses always caused him to undergo something which he might almost have, if he'd been that sort of man, called fear.

At three hundred feet down, the ramp led into the car park, a concrete chamber of some two hundred feet square. It was almost full; but he parked the Mini next to Aslan's Rolls, noting on the other side a silver BMW 2002 which he hadn't seen there before. There were overhead TV lenses here too; he got out of the Mini, leaving the keys in the ignition. If he had not, then the light in the steel door towards which he now went would have been red instead of green and a buzzer would have sounded. He spoke into the grille in the centre of the door: 'Drinian. Three Six Seven Four.' In the control room on the other side two graphs and two photos were instantaneously compared; the green light flashed twice and the door slid into the wall.

He walked down the white-painted corridor, his footsteps echoing, towards the opening in the wall, where a guard sat, his eyes on the TV monitor. 'Good morning, Major,' he said, taking the card from Xavier. The light flashed green. Xavier counted: one, two, then green again; the light was dead, the corporal's hand was on his gun; then three, four, and the third green. 'The third green was late. Look into it, will you?' He grinned. 'Would you really shoot me if the light flashed red?'

48

'Of course, Major,' the man said. 'Blow your 'ead clean orf, this could.' The gun was out of the holster before he'd finished speaking, the finger on the trigger. If the trigger were pressed, there would be a slight resistance: once overcome, it was only necessary to continue pressure. The thin mouth smiled but the eyes did not. It wasn't a bad face, but the eyes stared a bit too much. Xavier rummaged through his memory: Corporal Cox, ex-Military Police, forty, widower, one child, complexion sallow, features regular. Corporal Cox had better be investigated.

'I believe you, Corporal,' Xavier said. Besides his duties in the field he had since the Deputy's death to exercise general administrative oversight over HQ; the job of the guards could be a dull one, and they had to be constantly reminded that in the last analysis it was a man with a gun who did the real guarding, not the super-sophisticated security devices. He made a mental note to discuss the matter with Aslan, and to check that Corporal Cox had reported the light's malfunctioning.

Another guard appeared from a door on the left, glanced at Xavier's card, and clipped an identity disc on his lapel. Xavier went through the turnstile on the right, stopped at the door lettered DIRECTOR and spoke into the grille. Behind the white plaster the walls now were steel, thick enough to withstand any non-nuclear explosive device which could credibly be brought into the place. 'Drinian. Three Six Seven Four,' Xavier said, yawning. The green light flashed twice and the door slid open. Xavier left the dank chilly steel and concrete world for a cosy untidy middle-class world, the world of Bristow's office strip in the *Evening Standard*; the white distempered room was identical with fifty others at HQ, but the shopping bags on the floor, the square of battered dark-blue carpet, the large battered Victorian desk, the bamboo coat-rack festooned with women's coats and scarves, and no less than five hats, the smell – sweeter than Virginian, less heavy than Havana – of Turkish cigarettes, made it into the sort of office which is an extension of home. Bunty Knowles, plump, fifty, rosy-cheeked, was making tea from a silver teapot. Xavier had never visited Aslan's office when she wasn't making tea.

'Drinian dear,' she said. 'I knew you were coming, you see. His Nibs is expecting you.' She stood up; she might be fifty but with her pink skin and fair hair she looked ten years younger, and her

49

figure, though undoubtedly full, was a long way from obesity. Xavier wondered, not for the first time, whether there was anything going on between her and Aslan; it made no difference to the efficiency of the Department if there were, but the information might help him one day. Bunty took out three cups and saucers and a milk jug from the dark-green steel cabinet behind her, making it somehow look like a brightly-painted kitchen unit.

Xavier smiled at her and spoke into the grille at the door. 'Drinian. Three Six Seven Four.' The green light shone. The principle was that even if somehow an unauthorised person got as far as Bunty he'd not be any nearer Aslan. If Bunty's office was blown up, he'd scarcely hear it. And of course CED never did any deals.

Aslan's office was carpeted in dark red, opulently thick Axminster. The walls were the same glaring white as the ante-room but very little of them was actually visible. Taking up one wall was a map of the British Isles with red and blue and green pins scattered about it; on another was a Mercator projection of the world, and on the two others were huge blow-ups of six news photos. There was a simpering Stalin apparently scrutinising his finger nails with his fingers extended straight out like a woman, there was Churchill with his mouth slack and dribbling, his eyes wide open in an idiot stare, there was Roosevelt leaning forward to whisper behind his hand to a young WAAC, his face expressing, by a trick of the light, ravening lechery, there was Eisenhower facing a group of German officers, his right hand extended in what was apparently a Nazi salute, there was John F. Kennedy at the dinner table, a tilted glass raised in his hand, obviously roaring drunk, there was Hitler with his hands clasped in prayer, his eyes directed upwards and, because of some mishap in the developing room, with what appeared to be a halo. Aslan changed the display from time to time, but these on display now were his especial favourites. Xavier didn't really like Aslan – though he wasn't the sort of person to whom words such as *like* or *dislike* really applied – but those photos were one of the reasons why, however reluctantly, he respected him.

Aslan didn't look up as Xavier entered. His feet were on his desk and he was reading *Playboy*.

'Sit down, my dear Xavier,' he said, still not looking up. 'Tea
50

is coming. And Bunty has brought some delicious home-made macaroons.' He put down *Playboy* and took his feet off the desk. 'Believe me, Xavier, I wish I'd discovered this before. I led a very sheltered youth . . .' He waved at the magazine. 'You wouldn't believe it, but I've never seen this before . . . It's marvellous it really is . . . Once you've bought the magazine, that's it. These young ladies are yours. You don't have to talk to them, they'll submit uncomplainingly to the most outrageous demands, and they don't answer back.'

'I often wonder what the most outrageous demands really are,' Xavier said. 'Not that I'd really know. I'm a meat and potatoes man, myself.'

'Yes,' Aslan said, 'it's all in your file. These days it'll mark you for advancement. I have a divided mind about it myself. In my experience really good agents often have some little kink. It makes them more human. And thus able to understand other humans.'

'It didn't do Alfred Redl much good, did it?'

'That was a long time ago. Times have changed.'

Xavier found himself growing irritated. He had heard it all before. It always had the same purpose, which was to make one feel that Aslan was a thoroughly decent chap, before whom one could let down one's guard, talk as a personal friend.

'Is that why I haven't heard anything about the Deputy's job?' he asked.

An expression of pain passed across Aslan's large pink face. There was never any trace of beard on that taut healthy smoothness nor, considering his fifty-five years, very much trace of age or passion. It was a face which, surmounted as it was with thick glistening white hair, belonged to a cathedral close or academic cloister. *Larger than life* was the verdict when meeting him for the first time; and the head was indeed larger then life, half again as large as Xavier's, and his body was in proportion. At six foot six and sixteen stone, everything that Aslan wore had to be specially made. It was extraordinary that in his youth he should have done so well in the field, because inconspicuous he was not.

'My dear Xavier,' he said, deepening his mellow voice perceptibly, 'Charles is scarcely cold in his grave.'

'God rest his soul, but he might as well have been in his grave for all the good he did these last six months.'

'I know, I know. And you've been doing most of his work. Without thought of reward, being the splendid chap that you are . . . And now you want some solid recognition of your services. But it's out of my hands. We aren't quite like other Government departments, you know. The Minister of Defence is only nominally in control of CED. And only nominally in control of D15 and D16. With which we have a rather complicated relationship. And beyond all that and beyond me and far, far above me, are two dozen extremely distinguished public servants. They comprise the Security Council. They belong to more than one Ministry. They meet when the fancy takes them. They behave as the fancy takes them. I have recommended you in glowing terms. It won't make a scintilla of difference. Most of them hate my guts . . . Of course, there does exist, vaguely, a sort of Court of Appeal . . . which is the Committee, which I shall not attempt to explain. But I'm sure that Bunty will.'

'It was explained to me a long time ago.'

'Frankly, I think it's a waste of public money. But it is there. Not that it would be of much help in this instance. It merely answers questions. I have been told that the answers are not invariably what one wants to hear.'

Bunty brought in the tea-tray; plain tin Government issue but covered with a white lace cloth. The tea-pot, hot-water jug, milk jug and sugar basin were silver, the tea-cups and tea-plates white Spode with a pink and gilt floral pattern. The tea-spoons were silver, of the same period as the tea-pot, heavy and ornate, most likely mid-Victorian. The tea was weak and tasted of lemon; Xavier didn't enjoy it very much, but found it rather less unpalatable than the smoky kind which was Aslan's favourite.

Aslan lit an oval Turkish cigarette and opened the red folder. In his dark-grey suit, white shirt and blue silk tie, he looked, Xavier thought, almost too much the English gentleman to be true. He'd switched off, one of his most annoying tricks; he was now absorbed in the red folder.

'What all that boils down to is that nothing is going to happen about my application,' Xavier said.

Aslan looked up as if awakened from sleep. 'Application? What application?' He looked away from Xavier; for a moment the pale-blue eyes were shifty, the pink smooth face cruel. 'Oh yes.

It's kindest to be truthful. The Chairman has told me in confidence that the matter is to be left in abeyance. Old Nigel, his successor will no doubt have already nominated someone. It'll no doubt be someone I dislike and mistrust. Nigel dislikes and mistrusts *me*, I'm sorry to say. He's been in the wilderness a long time and is all bitter and twisted. But let us turn to more pleasant things.' He blew a smoke ring. 'Your handling of the Pletnev case has given me great joy. A nice smooth job. The KGB thought quite a lot of him.'

'What did they think about Shirley Mason?'

'Elena Agranov. Her father was in the KGB too. Her grandfather was in the NKVD. In the Cheka under Dzerzhinsky to begin with. Then the OGPU. He wasn't a nice man.'

'Never mind her grandfather. You could have told me she was an agent.'

'I'm not entirely my own master. As I've already indicated . . . The truth is that recently I was sent a memo. Nominally from the Chairman of the Security Council. Of the Destroy when Read kind. It concerned you. Its gist was that you're the kind of man who has to find orders acceptable before you'll carry them out.' He sighed. 'I say nominally from the Chairman because he's too nice a chap ever to make such an insinuation. He's all for a quiet life. Nigel is the one responsible. And Nigel is a real stirrer.'

'I'll say he is. When did I ever disobey an order?'

'No-one says you have ever disobeyed an order, dear boy.' Aslan grimaced. He was now, Xavier recognised, about to adopt his favourite persona, that of the journalist he'd once briefly been – all pals together, two decent hard-working chaps helpless in the hands of the bureaucrats. 'I admit it. Whatever your feelings, you do what you're told. And whatever shit or set of shits wrote the memo, they admitted it. But, they said, you'd been lucky. Their estimate of your character was that one of these days you were likely to disobey an order. They've made a study of you in depth, you see.'

'So I had to be tested, is that it?'

Aslan laughed. 'The boy's quick. The principle is that you must obey all orders without question, Dalek-style. You can't possibly know how those orders fit into the pattern or indeed what the pattern is . . .'

53

'What pattern did it fit into when you sent Tom with me? Were you afraid I wouldn't kill Miss Agranov?'

'No use trying to deny it, is it?'

'Christ, I've a good mind to go back to the Army.'

'You can't. Even if you could, you wouldn't enjoy it. With the lot we have in power now, you have to sign a form in triplicate before you can fire a shot.'

'At least I'd know whom the orders were coming from.'

'From a politician, my dear chap. From a politician who believes in anything, absolutely anything, except reality. Which is who kills who.'

Xavier's tea tasted bitter. He lit a cigarette. Aslan always made him want to smoke too much. 'You needn't tell me that,' he said coldly. 'We didn't do very well with Yuskevitch, though, did we?'

Aslan winced. Like all his facial expressions, it was as if assumed for the purposes of a melodrama to be played before an exceptionally stupid audience: the full mouth grimaced as if in pain, the huge white hand flew up to the eyes. 'Don't remind me,' he said. 'How was I to know that D15 would suddenly come to life?'

'I have heard that someone activated them.'

'Probably my pal Nigel. Not that we'll ever know . . . My God, how relieved Yuskevitch must have been . . . To find himself in the hands of English gentlemen, not thugs like us . . . But that's three years ago, and D15 has now relapsed into its usual torpor . . . And Yuskevitch is safe and cosy in jail.'

'The Russians might suggest an exchange. It's rather surprising that they haven't before now.'

'Probably internal politics. Yuskevitch's face may not fit somewhere. He's one of the old school, but he's short of friends inside the KGB. I have heard, with horror and amazement, rumours of him and Nigel trying to cook up something just after the war. Mind, I didn't say that . . . Anyway, we've nothing to exchange. Still, they're quite capable of hauling in one of our nationals on a trumped-up charge. I would hate that to happen. I've never got over the Brooke deal . . . Brooke for the Krogers – it just didn't make sense.'

'Yuskevitch is a damned sight more important than the Krogers, too.'

Aslan sighed. 'I know. And they got damn-all out of him . . .

54

But it's history now. Possibly our Security Chairman to be may be still interested, though. But that isn't what I wanted to see you about.' He opened the red folder. 'I'm worried about Morgate's.'

'Tom thinks that there's something odd going on there –'

'Odd?' Aslan's dark heavy eyebrows shot up. He took out a sheet of white foolscap and handed it over to Xavier. 'FIST in red at the top, a stencilled fist underneath it. Dated First January 1974. Woolworth's paper. Remington's typewriter. No finger-prints. The message is admirably succinct. *We will destroy you blow by blow and bring the revolution nearer.*' He brought out four more sheets of white foolscap. 'Third February 1974, tenth March 1974, fourth April 1974. The messages are even more to the point: *Blow Number One, Blow Number Two, Blow Number Three, Blow Number Four.* They were received the day after a fire in Number One Stores, a fire in Number Two Stores, an explosion destroying a load of electrical fittings, and a fire in the main offices. Isn't that enough to be going on with?'

'Tom seemed pretty sure that there was something else going on.'

'What made him sure?'

'He said something about seeing a chap called Dykenhead. In the Export Department. Dykenhead may have something to tell him.'

'The stupid bugger!' Aslan's face flushed: Xavier, fascinated, realised that he'd never seen it that colour before. The effect was as if rouge had suddenly and unskilfully been applied. 'That settles it. You'd better go there and sort Master Tom out.' He rubbed his face fiercely as if it actually were rouged and he was getting rid of the rouge. 'He's as thick as two planks. I told him what he had to do and he hasn't done it.' His colour had returned to normal. 'He's had his orders, and instead of carrying them out, he's gone on a wild-goose chase, playing detectives . . .'

'He rather thought that he was getting orders from the wrong people.'

'He wasn't. Morgate's is employing a private detective agency. They claim to have an operative under cover in FIST too. I've gone into all this in the report.' He tapped the folder. 'Naturally you'll clear everything with me.'

'It's all rather irregular.'

55

'Irregular! Xavier, you are only *technically* a Civil Servant. For Christ's sake don't talk like one. Just about every bloody thing we do is irregular, didn't you know that?'

'Why bring amateurs into it?'

'They're not amateurs. They're very hard men indeed, and they're on the scale of Pinkerton's. And paid by Sir Geoffrey, incidentally. We can't do the job ourselves, because we're too thin on the ground at present. And we can't very well ask D15. Because they're still essentially the same sort of decent, humane, thoroughly nice chaps. We want FIST to be destroyed. They won't do it.'

'Is it absolutely certain that it's FIST?'

'Please don't use the third person, Xavier. You mean am I certain? Yes, I am certain. You were sent a fifty-page report in December. What did you do with it? No, don't tell me . . .'

'I'm fully conversant with the report,' Xavier said stiffly.

Aslan grinned. 'Translation: you've read it. Tell me about FIST, then. Briefly, I hardly need add.'

'About a hundred members. Trotskyite, to over-simplify. Virtually all bourgeois. Tightly organised: they use their own variation of the good old cell system. No connection with any other Left Wing organisation. Or any trade union. It's been in existence about six years. Their visiting card was left after a couple of explosions last year. An armament factory in Birmingham, I can't remember the name. Nothing serious, nobody hurt. There was the red clenched fist and the name spelt out. Our estimate of the situation is that they've spent the last six years building up a really tight organisation and accumulating funds. They're now ready to begin in real earnest.'

'The Birmingham explosions were a dummy run. They're very clever. They're a model revolutionary organisation.' There was a note of admiration in his voice. 'No involvements with any other Left Wing organisation and self-financing. Which means no-one else's finger in the pie and no danger of anyone talking too much.'

'Are you absolutely certain that they're receiving no help from the KGB?'

'It isn't impossible, but it wouldn't be in character. Complicates matters enormously and takes control of operations out of their hands.'

'Tom thinks that the KGB is involved. Also – mind you, this is just what he said – that there's some sort of link with Operation X.'

Aslan stared at him, seemingly genuinely surprised. 'Did he have any solid information?'

'He thought that he might pick up something from this Dykenhead chap.'

'He won't,' Aslan said simply. 'There's no Operation X. I've been hearing about it for years. It's devilish cunning and is doing the country no end of damage – and then you ask how the damage is done, and no-one can tell you.'

'Tom had a hunch.'

'And a great waste of time it will be. Frankly, I think that Operation X is just that. An Agitprop invention to make us waste our time. Let's concentrate upon FIST and its specific, concrete acts of sabotage.' He paused, took out a gold Parker rollball pen from his pocket and fiddled with it. 'A Christmas present,' he said. 'From my youngest daughter. Twenty-five quid at Christmas. They're forty-five now . . .'

He opened the folder and scribbled in the margin. 'In fact, I'd like you to look into the situation very soon. Bunty will arrange the details.'

'Tom won't like it.'

'Then he can bloody well lump it.'

'Let's get this straight. Do you want me to take over from Tom?' Just as the air at HQ didn't have the taste of real air, always gave the sensation that sooner or later it would become tangibly solid and choking, so sooner or later with Aslan words would lose their meaning, he would be left uncertain of what he was to do. He acknowledged the truth of it then, rather shocked, pushed the thought to the back of his mind.

'Not quite. But with your experience you should be able to push things in the right direction.'

'I'm not sure we are in the right direction. Isn't this a job for Special Branch?'

Aslan snorted. His snort was very loud, almost as if he were trying genuinely to imitate a horse. 'Special Branch? Well, they might conceivably catch them. Then they'd take them to Scotland Yard and give them tea and cakes. Then there'd be a trial. And after about six months of their Communist pigs of lawyers

57

blackguarding the police, they'd all be put on probation and given five quid each from the court poorbox for a taxi home. I just want you to' – the white hand reached up as if to pluck the euphemism from the air – 'escort them to the terminus.'

Xavier frowned. 'If that's what you really want. But we've confined ourselves to Russians up till now. And a few IRA.'

Aslan laughed. 'You may have a Mick name, but by God you're British, you really are. It's OK with foreigners, but not our own nationals – that's positively immoral, isn't it?'

'It's a question of where it may lead to. And where you stop.'

'Where you stop with the enemies of your country? That isn't for you to say.'

'Does Tom know about me coming to – give him a hand?'

'He hasn't bothered to inform us of his whereabouts for the last twenty-four hours, so how can he know?'

'I'd better find him before I go any further.'

'He'll be busy playing detective.' Aslan closed the folder. 'Don't look so worried. It just might not be necessary to be too – boisterous – with these chaps. When we've confirmed their identities, there are other possibilities . . . Before I forget, there's this girl Tom's shacked up with – she's a journalist. I don't like it.'

Xavier grinned. 'Do you want me to be *boisterous* with her?'

'Don't be frivolous, Xavier. I want you to find out more about her, that's all . . .'

He took out a large yellow silk handkerchief knotted in five places. 'Now what the hell are all these bloody knots for? I know. Morgate's having an At Home tonight. I want you to go. He'll look out for you.'

'Will Sally Rowmarsh be there?'

'In her professional capacity.' Aslan looked at him sharply. 'I didn't tell you her name.'

'Tom did. He seems to be rather fond of her.'

'Most unhealthy and unwholesome. Action must be taken.'

'I wouldn't be in favour of our usual sort of action, sir,' Xavier was careful to keep emotion out of his voice.

'I'm not suggesting it. She's been cleared anyway. I want to know a bit more about her. Bunty has all the material.' He fiddled with the gold pen again. 'Just get to know her. She might even tell you where Tom is . . .'

He took out a gold key-ring with his initials, PRD, engraved on the large medallion which hung from it, unlocked the drawer to his right, and pulled out a thick green folder. 'I'll see you tomorrow,' he said, and opened the folder. He smiled. It was an accomplished professional smile, going as far as the eyes, but the wrinkles which appeared at the corners were as if suddenly incised. 'Use your sudden request technique, Xavier,' he said. 'I've heard that it never fails.'

In the ante-room Bunty, her face animated, was talking to a man of Xavier's age. His hair was smooth and butter-coloured, full but not too full at the nape, and he wore a lavender lightweight suit with flared bottoms and turn-ups. The spotted lemon shirt and matching tie were of heavy silk.

'Hugh Droylsden,' Bunty said. 'Xavier Flynn.' The two men nodded at each other, their faces expressionless. 'Hugh's father and mine were in the Army together, isn't that a coincidence? Daddy was only talking about him the other night . . .'

'My code name is Ninian, I see,' Droylsden said. 'Does it have any particular significance?' His face was evenly brown and as smooth in its contours as if it also had been brushed. It would have been much the same, Xavier thought, ten years ago and would be much the same until ten years from now when suddenly, almost overnight, it would become old and wrinkled. It was an upper middle-class face, as his own was a navvy's or a bookie's face.

'No-one was using it, that's all,' Xavier said. 'Actually, our administration is rather informal. Aslan's the Director, and Caspian's the Deputy, but the Deputy's dead. Otherwise it's like the Army – Sir for the Colonel, and Christian names for the rest, since we're supposed to be a band of brothers . . . The code names are for official identification in reports and so on . . .'

'It was much the same in D15,' Droylsden said. 'Who acts as Deputy?' His accent gave him away. It was faultless: too faultless, as if learned like a foreign language. It had been assumed, as his expression had been assumed. If his father had been in the Army with Bunty's father he'd either have been a NCO or what they used to call a temporary gentleman. It was an advantage to know these things: whatever Aslan might say about Philby once and for all sickening the Service of the Old School Tie lot, Xavier had no illusions about who stood the better chance when it came to the really important jobs. That accent might mean that Droylsden wasn't serious competition: it wasn't one hundred per cent genuine, which often antagonised the sort of people who still, after all, ran the country. He himself might just get by; if he'd defined his accent it would have been as Seventies Classless.

'Anyone who happens to be around. Chiefly me.'

'Haven't they found a Deputy yet?' Droylsden's tone was, Xavier decided, a shade too casual.

'Not yet. I don't think that they know that the Deputy's dead yet . . .'

The green light shone over Aslan's door and Bunty tapped Droylsden on the shoulder; he moved away from her and round to face the door in one instantaneous movement, his eyes narrowing. Xavier recognised with no surprise why he had been transferred to CED.

Bunty held out a white folder to him. 'This will put you in the picture Morgate-wise,' she said. 'Typed in my own fair hand. Your invitation's clipped to the folder.'

'Tom won't be pleased,' he said.

'Ours not to reason why.' Bunty rarely talked for very long without using a cliché; sometimes she'd use nothing else. 'His Nibs is very keen on this matter being cleared up. Geoffrey Morgate is one of his favourite persons.'

'What about the cover?'

'You're to see Josef K at the DTI. Three o'clock.'

'We've met before. He doesn't like me.'

'Nobody does like us, ducks. We don't like each other all that much, do we?'

The round jolly fresh-complexioned face with the small mouth hardened for a moment, reminding him of someone. 'I don't have any choice about liking you, Bunty,' he said. 'You know where all the bodies are hidden. Twenty years is a long time.'

She grimaced, and he saw the resemblance, even in the fair eyebrows: her face was rounder and softer, but it was unmistakably like Henry VIII's. Hers was, he'd been told once, a very old family.

'It's been a long journey,' she said. 'A long journey over a hard road. Aslan has got by until now, because he could manage the Security Council. It's going to be different in the near future.'

60

'Because the new Chairman doesn't like him?'

'You can say that. Aslan can say that. I can't. Least said, soonest mended.' She put a sheet of paper in her typewriter and lit a cigarette, her eyes screwed up against the smoke. 'I've got work to do, ducky.'

'I'll leave you to it. By the way, can you give me a photo of Sally Rowmarsh? Aslan wants me to see what sort of a person she is . . .'

'Unsuitable for Tom. *You* might cope.' She went over to the green filing-cabinet by her desk and handed him a large shiny photograph of a dark-haired girl in her middle twenties. 'Looks discontented,' she said.

'Well, there's a cure for that . . .'

Bunty frowned and returned to her desk.

'I'll see you,' Xavier said, and strolled out of the office, outwardly undisturbed, since nothing had happened to be disturbed about, but inwardly wondering why somewhere in the recesses of his mind was a shape which was indefinably out of alignment. There had been a sound, like spurred boots clattering over marble, which he hadn't expected to hear in the vicinity of dear old Bunty.

In his own office, half the size of Aslan's, with a map of England on one wall, a map of the world on another, a small beech desk, swivelling chair, a small bookcase, plain black studio couch, coconut matting on the floor, and a dark-green filing cabinet, he looked through the folder Bunty had given him. Like all the reports by Aslan – or Bunty – it was very easy to read. A picture built up of an old family coming over to England with the Conqueror, increasing in power and wealth and then, from the reign of Mary onwards, consistently backing the wrong side, at its lowest ebb in the early 1900s, then climbing back again because of the interest of the youngest son, Everard, in motor-bikes. Now Morgate Inc. was that rarest of organisations, a large family firm which hadn't gone public, with ninety per cent of the shares in the hands of the family. One by one the firms supplying it had all been bought out; they continued to sell tyres, electrical accessories, and so on, to other firms but the Morgate 1200 would never cease production for lack of essential components. *The organisation of Morgate's is almost childishly simple and it has no personnel or public*

61

*relations department. Their statistics department was scrapped long before Henry Ford scrapped his. It is true that to get ahead at Morgate's you must be connected with the Morgates through blood or marriage, but no passengers are carried and the firm is obsessively cost-conscious. The price of the 1200 is well below that of its chief foreign rivals, the BMW and the Harley-Davidson . . .*

Xavier read on to the end, photographing the words on his mind. If every copy of the report were now lost he would be able to rewrite it word for word and figure for figure from memory. He threw the report down in the letter basket on the desk and walked up and down the room restlessly. It was a model of what such a report should be, it gave him virtually all the information he needed, but it didn't explain more than cursorily why Morgate's should have survived and prospered when almost every other British motor-cycle manufacturer had gone out of production. Why had they gone out of production when the market was booming at home and abroad?

He lay down on the studio couch with his hands crossed, perfectly still. The answer was that it wasn't his business. Helping Tom to nail the boys and possibly the girls from FIST was his business. Details of the sabotage were summarised in an appendix; under the heading SUSPECTS was a brief note SEE TRUMPKIN. He presumed that Tom would fill it out. But what were Tom and he supposed to do about it when they'd filled it out? The answer was obvious: he did what it was his job to do. But killing KGB men – or women – was a different matter from killing Marxist loonies. Once start doing that and you were well on the way to an Ulster-type situation. Once FIST started killing, of course, then there was no option. But they hadn't started yet. But what did Aslan have in mind? Why did he indicate action, then say that it just mightn't be necessary? And, above all, why were they concerning themselves with the matter at all? Because Sir Geoffrey was a cousin and one of Aslan's favourite persons? And why were they poaching on Special Branch's preserves? He felt a dull twinge just below his heart. It was the familiar sign that he was worried; his body was telling him to watch out.

He swung himself off the studio couch in one movement, went over to the filing cabinet and took out a bottle of Bison vodka and a small glass. He filled the glass, sniffed the aromatic smell – a

62

country smell totally unlike the bland faintly medicinal smell of the English makes – and sipped. You weren't supposed to, you had to knock it straight back, but it was his palate and his stomach. The red light above the door went on and a woman's voice said 'Polly. Three Four Seven One.'

'Come in.' He pressed a button under the desk and the door slid back. A small dark-haired woman in her early thirties came in, an almost visible smell of Yardley's Khalimar preceding her. She was wearing a starched white blouse, and a checked blue skirt which did nothing to minimise her broad hips. She was carrying a black briefcase. He kissed her on her cheek and gave her bottom a light pinch; it felt firm and resilient.

She showed no reaction to the pinch, but nodded towards the bottle. 'Yes, I will have a shot of the good old Bison.' She sat on the studio couch. 'It settles the stomach,' she said, as she always did. 'Not a drink but a medicine.' She downed the drink in one gulp, took out a packet of Kent from the briefcase, and lit two.

'OK, what have you got for me?' Xavier asked, taking the cigarette.

She handed him a metal roll-ball pen, thicker in the barrel than usual. 'To operate it as a pen, twist the top round once, anti-clockwise, then press once,' she said. 'To operate as a weapon, just press it three times.'

Xavier pressed the top; three inches of needle-pointed metal, the thickness of a bicycle spoke, protruded.

'Now once again,' she said, and the metal lengthened by three inches. 'Now once again,' and the metal lengthened by another three inches. 'To get it back press the top once and you have a roll-ball pen.'

'Won't there be a danger of it snapping?'

'It's made from the same stuff as moon rockets. It would hold your weight without bending.' She held out her glass. 'Knives are ridiculous really. Awkward to carry and not easy to get rid of. And messy in their effects. And sometimes they hit the bone, and what's the good of that?'

Xavier sipped his vodka: the pain was already going. 'No good at all, my darling,' he said. 'It may mean the other chap killing you instead of you killing him. Does the KGB have it?'

'Of course. But ours is better.'

63

Xavier retracted the pen. 'It's all right as long as it works.'

'It can't go wrong.'

'So you say. The more ingenious the bloody thing is, the more possibility there is of it leaving you with egg all over your face.'

'Aslan wants you all to have one.'

'He won't have to depend on it, will he?'

'It won't do any harm to keep it in your pocket.'

'As long as nothing goes wrong with the spring. I'd hate to be skewered.'

'It won't go wrong for you. How many Russians have you killed, Xavier?'

'Fifty,' he said. 'And various other odds and sods.'

'Fifty,' she said. 'May God spare you to kill fifty more. Put the pen in your pocket. I pray for you every night.'

'Be seeing you,' Xavier said as she went out. He put the pen in his pocket.

She turned. 'Be seeing you.'

Polly's real name was Wanda. Her father, an ex-Army officer, had come to England in 1932 and had anglicised his name, not because he was ashamed of it, but because it was, more than most Polish names, a sustained explosion of consonants to the British ear. He had rejoined the Polish Army in 1939 and had been shot at the Katyn Forest, his hands tied behind his back. Wanda, who was born in England, had joined the ATS on leaving Cambridge with a science degree; strings had been pulled, and for four years now she had been in charge of Armaments and Interrogation. She had been married briefly, but her dedication had not mixed with marriage. Aslan had not yet allowed her into the field; possibly Xavier thought, looking at the intensity of her expression now, because she was a bit too dedicated, because she was too personally involved. And perhaps because she was too useful on the weapons and interrogation side, particularly interrogation. It put the toughest KGB man off balance when examined by a young and attractive woman; it seemed subtly to devalue his manhood. And Wanda was inspired at finding ways to make them crack; which was quite unfairly why he'd never fancied her. He had no scruples about interrogation himself, having no illusions about what would happen to him if ever he fell into the hands of the KGB or, for that matter, the IRA. But it wasn't his cup of tea;

64

it did odd things to the personality. Killing was a nice clean job, and you could continue with it as long as your reflexes let you, happy and wholesome and well adjusted. He thought of the Katyn Forest and the mass grave of the Polish officers. They would have done better not to have surrendered; they would have died just the same, but quicker, and perhaps with the happiness of killing some of the enemy first.

He finished the vodka, hesitated, then put the bottle and two glasses back in the filing cabinet. He turned to the Morgate report again, taking it more slowly this time, but still not finding the clue which he was looking for.

That afternoon at the Department of Trade and Industry he brought the matter up again.

'I can't see how Morgate's has survived when so many others have gone under,' he said to Josef K. The code name was Aslan's little literary joke; it was used in this instance to underline the fact that its holder was involved in a secret operation. But in practice you only used code names in official reports. Josef K, however, he never thought of, or addressed, except as Josef K.

'Quite simple,' Josef K said briskly. 'Solid financial basis. No administrative frills. First-class product. No dependence upon outside suppliers. No labour trouble. And it's the parent company of a large, prosperous, and reasonably diversified group. Quite simple to understand, even for you.'

The thin lips spat out the words as if he would rather be spitting out abuse. Xavier had long since become used to the hatred which his job evoked, but this afternoon he wasn't in the mood to bear it meekly.

'Perhaps I understand all that better than you do,' he said. 'It still isn't an answer. You have to give me all the answers I need.'

Josef K scowled. It was an expression which didn't go very well with the small pale neat-featured face. 'It will have to do. We're here to arrange your – cover.' He spat the word out. 'Though the DTI is your permanent cover, of course. God knows what people must think of our department if they judge it by you . . .'

'It probably helps recruitment,' Xavier said. 'The public visualises Civil Servants as being timid, dim and devious . . . Why don't you just get on with giving me a plausible excuse to go to Morgate's?'

Josef K stared at Xavier's grey check Huntsman suit, blue flowered shirt and Bally crocodile shoes. 'You should pay more attention to detail. Burton's and Marks and Spencer's are where we Civil Servants buy our clothes, Major Flynn.'

'I shall change into something more suitable.'

'I hope that you do. You are, of course, already on the establishment here, Major Flynn. You are a Senior Export Negotiator, a new and fundamentally meaningless title. You even have an office, the same size as this, with a ten-foot square of red carpet, an executive-type desk, an armchair for visitors, a small table for flowers, and you're allowed three pictures. I've chosen reproductions of Constable for my office, but you no doubt would prefer battle scenes. Or nudes if the Ministry of Environment has any in stock.'

'I know all that. What am I going to Morgate's for?'

'You know that better than me, *Major*. It will have something to do with violence, I'm sure.'

'Not necessarily, but you know damned well what I mean. What am I there for as in my capacity as Senior Negotiator?'

'They're having difficulties with their American agents. They feel that it's time for a change. They also feel that it's time to rethink their whole export policy. They don't want to neglect the home market too much; if they do the foreigners will leap in. There is the possibility of a new outlet in the USA, and here you can help. But if they change their agent, there's a certain amount of risk involved. They want some sort of guarantee from the Government. Because the DTI wants them to divert their product from the home market to the export market. They'll have to disappoint a lot of customers, give up sure sales for sales which are, for various reasons, not quite so sure.' He handed Xavier a green folder two inches thick marked CONFIDENTIAL. 'You'll find it all in here. If there's anything you don't understand get in touch with me.' The neat features contracted, the short grey hair appeared to bristle. 'I'd normally say *By all means get in touch with me*, or *I'd be delighted*, or *Don't be frightened to get in touch with me*, but I can't say that to you.'

Xavier yawned. 'No reason why you should.' He tapped the file which Josef K had given him. 'I've already been given a load of bumf . . .'

'It's probably repetitious,' Josef K said. 'But it's better to have too much information than too little . . .'

'I take your point . . . Anything else you have to tell me?'

'Your salary – four thousand eight hundred gross – will continue to be paid, less deductions, into a bank. Which bank doesn't matter, because you're not ever going to be given it. It wouldn't matter very much to a person like you anyway – you don't pay tax, do you?'

'And we don't work nine to five or lead a nice easy safe life either.' He glanced round the room; for at least ten more years Josef K would spend forty hours a week here. He would empty the IN basket to fill the OUT basket, only to have it fill again the next day. He would change the Constable reproductions in another year or so. He would take out the roses in the vase on the small table as soon as they began to wilt. The flowers would vary with the season; and that was all that would vary about the room. Josef K had good reason to hate him.

Josef K's face assumed a neutral expression. 'Sign this, please.'

Xavier took out the pen that Wanda had given him that morning and manipulated it as he had been instructed. He signed his name on the buff form, rather surprised that it worked as a pen. He rose. 'Just one little thing, Josef.'

Josef K raised his eyebrows.

'You've signed the Official Secrets Act.' He twiddled the pen. 'You don't talk about my visit.'

'Of course not, Major.' This time there was no sneer behind the word Major.

'It's extremely important that you realise that.'

'Yes, Major, of course I do.' Josef K's voice was suddenly hoarse.

Xavier put the pen back in his pocket and walked out of the room; as he opened the door he saw that Josef K was staring at him open-mouthed, his forehead beginning to sweat.

Back in his office he 'phoned Aslan.

'I'm sorry, ducks,' Bunty said. 'He's been summoned to a conference with the Powers that Be. Won't be back today. Anything I can do?'

'You could put me in touch with Tom Drage.'

'Try Morgate's. The number's in amongst the bumf I gave

you. Is that all, my wild colonial boy? Because I have to work like the clappers now, I really have.'

'That's all,' Xavier said. He looked up the number, frowning to himself: agents in CED were supposed to work on their own and use their initiative at all times, but this was carrying it a bit too far. 'Flynn of the Department of Trade and Industry here,' he said. 'Could I have a word with Mr Drage?'

'I'm afraid he isn't here, Mr Flynn. I should try his home number.' The voice seemed pleased that Tom shouldn't be there; or was it his imagination? As he dialled Tom's home number he knew already that Tom wouldn't be there, or if he were there, wouldn't be capable of answering. Though his suit was light-weight and the heating was off for the summer he began to feel hot and sweaty. After he'd rung Tom's home number for five minutes he slammed the 'phone down and spoke to Bunty again.

'There's something odd going on.' He still could hear Tom's voice when he'd last seen him: it had had a final tone in it, a signing-off tone, a tone of acceptance. He'd never particularly liked Tom, but they were on the same side; even if no-one else were concerned, he'd got to be.

'Tom's just 'phoned,' Bunty said. 'So don't go into a flat spin again.'

'Why the hell didn't you put him through to me?'

'He hadn't got much time. He'll see you tomorrow at Morgate's.'

'Why not at the party tonight?'

'He's chasing various people round London.'

'Where exactly is round London?'

'Soho, when he 'phoned.' She giggled. 'The naughty Square Mile. What a marvellous way to earn a living.'

'Did he say that he was 'phoning back?'

'He'll keep in touch.'

'Tell him to keep in touch with me too. I'm going home now.'

As he hung up and put Aslan's folder into his brief-case along with Josef K's he realised disquietingly and unmistakably that suddenly he didn't like Bunty. And as he walked down the corridors of HQ, performing the requisite actions with his identity card under the eyes of the guards with their fingers itching on the triggers of their ·38s, he realised that it would be wisest not to show that dislike.

# NINE

## *3 June 1974: 17.20–18.05 Hours*

Xavier's flat was off Kensington High Street between Phillimore Place and Phillimore Gardens; he kept the Mini at the CED Transport Section off the Kensington High Street end of Earl's Court Road. He was fond of the district because, against all odds, it had kept its individuality: it was still essentially British middle-class, quiet and respectable. Even in Earl's Court Road you had the illusion that the tall terraced houses were still each inhabited by one British middle-class family, that the heterogeneous hordes, mainly young, who filled Earl's Court Road were private non-paying family guests.

He turned the Mini left off Kensington High Street and left again at Hiram Alley. The alley stood between two high buildings with blank dusty windows and curved sharply to end in a red-brick two-storey building with a steel door twenty feet across. There was a roughly-painted notice in red – PRIVATE. LEWIS INC. CENTRAL STORAGE. It was strangely quiet in the alley, as if one had gone into a different world; and in a sense, Xavier reflected as he drove the Mini straight at the door, one had done just that. As at HQ in Strutton Ground, the moment anyone entered Hiram Alley they were under surveillance at gun-point.

The door swung up when the Mini was three feet away, but the electronic eye which actuated it only operated when Xavier pushed the small button left of the steering-wheel the requisite number of times. Inside there was a concrete floor forty feet square and plain brick walls up to the ceiling. On the right there was an opening of twenty feet. He drove slowly up to the opening (Aslan's instructions were to fire at all cars moving faster than 5 mph) and stopped beside the glass-sided booth let into the wall. He put his identity card into the steel-rimmed slot at the side of the booth; the man in the navy-blue suit inspected it, put it in a slot in the control panel above him. A Colt ·38 rested close to his right hand. The strange thing, Xavier thought, was that this was always a bad moment; the light here for some reason took three

69

seconds to come on, and he always half expected the light to turn red and the guard to start firing, as he would be within his rights to do. The light turned green, the card emerged from the slot next to the one in which he'd put it, the guard made a kind of salute, and Xavier drove into the car park fifty yards further on, into a world approaching the normal.

The car park – an expanse of concrete with plain brick walls – held two hundred cars. There was every variety of vehicle there – taxis, hearses, vans, lorries, Land-Rovers, caravans, ambulances and even a small fire-engine. When a particular type of vehicle was needed, there wasn't always time to hire one. He looked around the car park, noting every vehicle; when he'd joined the Service he'd been told by Aslan that information was power and all information was worth having. And one piece of information which was worth having was the fact that the Ford which Tom had used on Friday was back in its usual place but Tom's own car, a white MGB, wasn't there. So Tom must have returned to London since Friday, whether he was there now or not. But why had he not 'phoned HQ until this afternoon?

He stepped through the small door at the side of the large steel doors at the far end of the car park, and into the noise and mess and smell of petrol and oil and metal of the Service Department. He couldn't see a MGB there. He told himself that it didn't mean anything; but deep down, not in his brain but in the pit of his stomach, he knew that something was wrong.

Rogers was drinking tea in his untidy little office. He was a small square man in overalls which he always managed to keep dazzling white. He was always somehow at attention, even when sitting, all his movements stiff and abrupt. 'The Mini needs servicing, Major,' he said.

'How long?' He offered Rogers a cigarette. Rogers took it abruptly, pulled out a gold Dunhill lighter, snapped it alight for Xavier, snapped it alight for his own cigarette, returned it to the pocket of his overall, and glanced at a notebook in front of him.

'Pick it up tomorrow at this time. Don't let it go so long past servicing again, Major. Doesn't matter so much with an ordinary Mini, but when you've got all these mods they really do need attention. Otherwise it'll go right out of tune, see what I mean?'

'OK. I'll pick it up tomorrow.' He turned to go, then turned back. 'By the way, you haven't seen Captain Drage, have you?'

Rogers's face, square, brick-red, deeply lined, was non-committal. 'Not that I recall, Major.'

'His car's gone. The white MGB.'

'I didn't check it in.'

There was the sudden bellow of an engine running full throttle in the workshop; for no reason a line of poetry came into his mind – *Heart of the heartless world* – and he remembered the contorted face of the girl whom he still thought of as Shirley Mason. It wasn't supposed to be good form in CED to be over-inquisitive about the comings and goings of other agents, even if they were your friends, and Tom had never been exactly a friend. Information could also be something of which you could have too much, and this kind of information it wasn't Rogers's job to give. But he persisted.

'Surely you have some record?'

The lines on Rogers's face deepened. He opened his notebook abruptly. 'Saturday morning.' He closed the notebook, keeping his hand on it. The engine in the workshop cut out; for a few seconds there was absolute silence.

'Thanks.' It didn't, of course, mean anything. Bunty hadn't said that Tom had come to London today, but that he was there today. Xavier had a feeling of absolute desolation. The line of poetry wouldn't leave his head. *Heart of the heartless world*; the poet had died in the Spanish Civil War fighting with the Republicans, as futile a death as it was possible to imagine. 'I'll see you tomorrow,' he said, and left the office. Rogers didn't answer; Xavier had the feeling that his query hadn't been welcomed.

Outside in Earl's Court Road he began to feel more cheerful. He was with the private people once again, surrounded by innocents, the sheep who'd never know that he was, if not one of their shepherds, one of their guard dogs. They had nothing on their minds but their next meal, their next drink, their next joint, their next fuck, their chance of promotion or a new car or new house or new electric cooker or colour TV – with nothing on their minds that wasn't private and personal, an individual fantasy which was part of the collective fantasy of living in a country where nothing was ever going to change. It was that terrible innocence which made him from time to time actually love his fellow-men. Or perhaps it was the sunlight and the cool breeze and the proximity of Holland Park and Kensington Gardens, the smell of grass and trees always faintly discernible above the smell of petrol and diesel oil, so that you felt able .to breathe – whatever the cause, he always felt happy and well disposed towards his fellow-men in this part of London. And Kensington High Street was still a high street, a main thoroughfare but not merely a motorway; it had a sense of space about it, one didn't feel hemmed in, its dimensions were still human. It was a promenade, you could stroll along it as he was strolling now, looking at the shop windows and the passers-by, the pressure off for a while. People lived here and in the streets running off it, there was always a current of life to warm it, it wouldn't die at half past five. Recently it had become rougher and tougher, just as Notting Hill Gate had become gentler and more civilised, but violence wasn't a real problem yet. The cold wind from the East would blow away the pink woolly blanket of illusion soon enough; in the meantime it comforted him that so many were warm and cosy.

There was time for a shower and a drink before the party and he had better change into something more suitable for a Civil Servant. He liked the Huntsman suit but at three hundred guineas it was too expensive for a Senior Negotiator to have come by honestly. He crossed the road at the zebra and quickened his pace.

The flat was on the first floor of an Edwardian terrace house which was much larger inside than its narrow frontage suggested. The front door opened into the entrance hall, with the door to the ground-floor flat on the left and the door to his own flat one flight up. He unlocked the front door, pushed it open a few inches slowly and steadily, then suddenly pushed it fully open with great force.

The entrance hall was empty. In the letter-box were two buff envelopes, obviously bills, which he put in his pocket unopened. The parquet floor was unpolished; he frowned. There were three other tenants and the entrance hall floor was done by each in rotation. In his case it should have been done today by Jeremy, his usual agency cleaner. Jeremy was an actor who maintained himself in this way between his professional engagements. He was due to clean the flat this afternoon, because Xavier had 'phoned the agency to check on it. Xavier glanced at the small mahogany table with the large glass ashtray on it which stood against the wall; there was a film of dust upon it and two cigarette ends which had been there this morning. It was the observation of details like that which had enabled him to survive so long. The day that he didn't 'phone the agency, that he just opened the hall door in the ordinary way, that he didn't look round the hall, even at the plain cream distempered walls, would be his last day. He walked slowly up the stairs, taking out the pen Wanda had given him.

The heavy oak door had a Banham lock; he turned the key slowly, then opened the door as he had opened the hall door, with sudden force. He heard a gasp, then flung himself inside the flat, his finger depressing the top of the pen, his right arm extended; within the first hundredth of a second he knew that the man behind the door wasn't Jeremy, within the next hundredth that he had a knife, within the next hundredth that he must strike at the heart; he drove the weapon upwards and under the ribcage and felt the point skewer not flesh but cloth, the other having side-stepped with professional quickness, his knife still in his right hand. It would take him three hundredths of a second to recover; Xavier had a shade over two hundredths of a second to hit him in the throat with a sharp left, and then all the time in the world, nearly a full second, to follow it with a right to the solar plexus, dropping the pen, since it wouldn't be necessary to kill him now.

Xavier kicked aside the knife, unlocked the small davenport in the corner opposite the TV, brought out a Baby Browning, and ran out of the door into the passage at the other end of the room. The bathroom door stood next to the bedroom door, the kitchen opposite it; he flung each door open in turn, the Browning at the ready. The Browning looked like a toy, measuring only four inches and weighing a fraction over ten ounces, but its cartridges would penetrate a seven-eighths pine board at fifteen feet, and if the man on the floor had brought anyone with him, he would be much nearer than fifteen feet. There was no-one in the bathroom or the kitchen; but supine on the bedroom floor was a body with a large red stain on its pink shirt, an upright model Hoover next to it. There was nothing to be done for him. Xavier scowled; to try to kill a professional like himself was all in the day's work; he bore no grudge. But to kill poor harmless Jeremy was murder. He stalked back into the sitting-room to where the man was still fighting for breath, put down the knives on the davenport, and aimed the Browning between his eyes. 'What did you kill him for?'

Panic came into the man's eyes, and he vomited a little yellow bile. Then he fought for breath again, tearing his collar open, the noise of his agonised wheezing filling the room.

'You're really very lucky,' Xavier said. 'I must have missed your Adam's apple – you ought to be dead by rights, like that poor chap in there.' He went over to the 'phone, his eyes still on the man on the floor, remembered his code number for the day with an effort and heard Droylsden's voice answering him; over the 'phone was now distinguishable a very faint Lancashire intonation.

'It's urgent. I've just dealt with an intruder.'

'I'd be obliged if you'd define *dealt with*, old man.'

'I've put him out of action. He'll live.'

'Is he a simple old-fashioned burglar, do you think?'

'I doubt it. He tried to kill me. I have a notion he came just for that reason.'

Droylsden chuckled. 'It's a hard life. I'll be over straight-away.'

'There's a dead body here too.'

'Was he another intruder?'

'No, poor sod. He was my cleaner. You could say that he got his hair caught in the machinery . . . Excuse me.' The man on the floor, still fighting for breath, was crawling towards the daven-port; Xavier put the 'phone down and kicked out as the man attempted to lift himself up. The man moaned, fell back, then started wheezing again. 'He's still in there trying. Look, there'll be a problem about the cleaner's body.'

'The Disposer will look after it. At least, so I assume.'

'Do we have to have that bastard along?'

'According to my instructions, yes. Otherwise there can be trouble with the authorities. He oils the wheels.'

'It's just that he gets on my nerves.'

'You'll have to put up with it – hang on . . .' Xavier kept the 'phone to his ear, his eyes on the man on the floor. Droylsden

74

spoke again. 'Drinian, Aslan says you must not kill the intruder. Repeat must not.' Droylsden hung up.

The man on the floor was broad and stocky, with short brown hair and a complexion which was now a mottled pink but which was returning to its normal pallor. The striped suit was a reasonable quality of worsted, probably in the forty pounds area, the blue nylon shirt looked like Marks and Spencer's. The finger-nails were short and clean. Holding the Browning at his head, Xavier went through his pockets rapidly. There was nothing there but one grubby handkerchief and one brand new one, a red and green Tempo pen, a Parker Skyline, a Schaeffer fountain pen, twenty Rothman's King Size, a Ronson lighter, a wallet, a set of car keys and a mixed bunch of keys. He threw them down on the davenport.

'I wonder why you didn't bring a gun,' Xavier said, more to himself than to the man. 'And I wonder who sent you.'

The man gulped for air, propped himself up on his elbow, and said in a hoarse voice; 'No-one sent me.'

'You just don't like me, is that it?' He flung over the cigarettes and the lighter to land beside the man. 'You may as well sit down.' He waved towards the chair at the head of the mahogany table in the centre of the room. 'Take the small ashtray from the top of the bookcase behind you.'

The man pulled himself to his feet painfully. He picked up the cigarettes and the lighter and the ashtray and put them on the table but left them there.

'I want the toilet.'

'We can't always have what we want in this life. Self-denial is good for the soul.'

'I tell you I urgently want the toilet.'

'You can do it in your pants for all I care.' Xavier was sure that the man didn't in fact need to relieve himself; professionals attend to such details before an operation. But if he did make a mess of himself, the physical discomfort could help to break him down.

'This is barbarous. If you're standing behind me with a gun when I use the toilet, how can I attempt to escape?'

'I'm not bothered about your trying to escape. I just want you to be uncomfortable.'

'Then why offer me the cigarettes?' The man looked very

75

young suddenly; Xavier realised that he couldn't be much older than twenty-six.

'The principle is to be inconsistent.' He lit a cigarette. 'If you'd asked for a cigarette I wouldn't have given you one, but I would have let you go to the toilet. And so it goes.'

'You're a sadist. Typical of your kind.'

'You'd do the same to me if you had the gun. Why did you kill poor Jeremy?'

'The cleaner? I was going to tie him up but he tried to resist.'

'You're lying. He'd served his purpose once he'd let you into the flat.'

The man shrugged. 'If you know that, why ask?'

'It passes the time. And it helps me to find out who you really are, and who sent you.' He pulled out the driving licence from its compartment in the wallet. 'I'm damned sure your real name isn't John Rothgar.'

'You'd be wrong. My parents live in Hastings. You can ask them.'

'If they exist, we shall ask them after we've arrested them.'

'You can't do that!' To Xavier's amusement, there was a genuine note of horror in his voice.

'We can do anything we want. As you're about to find out.'

'Within the law. Even pigs like you are answerable to the Courts.'

Xavier laughed. 'I honestly think that you're trying to be funny. Who sent you?'

Rothgar was silent. Xavier sighed, went over to the small inlaid walnut table on which the drinks stood and poured himself a Bison vodka, his eyes never leaving Rothgar. 'Honestly, if you tell me that, you'll save yourself a lot of trouble.'

'You'll kill me anyway.' This time there was no emotion in the voice.

'Not necessarily.' Despite his lack of height, Xavier thought with amusement, he was quite good looking, with regular features and intelligent blue eyes; poor Jeremy's emotions must indeed have been conflicting before the knife went home.

Suddenly he felt a blind choking anger; he went over to Rothgar and hit him on the nose, sending him toppling backwards. Standing over him, the Browning in his hand, he kicked

76

him hard in the ribs: Rothgar gasped, then moaned. He made no attempt to protect himself.

'That's for Jeremy,' Xavier said. 'Get up. Sit down again.' Rothgar rose stiffly, holding his side. Wincing, he sat down and put his hand to his nose. It came away bloodied. 'You might give me a handkerchief.'

'I wouldn't give you a cup of cold water if you were dying.'

Rothgar wiped his nose with his hands. The blood was running fast now. He sniffed and wiped his nose on his sleeve. It was a curiously pathetic gesture. Xavier went over to the table and put a handkerchief beside him. 'Smoke if you want.'

Rothgar wiped his nose and mouth and lit a cigarette. He put his hand to his side again. 'I think you've broken a rib.'

'That's too bad. I think you'll be lucky if that's the worst that happens to you.'

'I know I've run out of time now, but so have you.' Rothgar wiped his nose again; the handkerchief was already more red than white. 'You'll be dead soon.'

Xavier lit a cigarette. 'Don't worry about me. Tell me who sent you. It really will save you a lot of trouble.'

'I'll tell you nothing.' Rothgar shifted himself uneasily. 'Christ, I really do need a pee.'

'You're not going to get one. Though you might if you told me who sent you.'

Rothgar shook his head. Xavier shrugged his shoulders; let Interrogation sort him out. They sat in silence, their eyes never leaving each other. Rothgar kept wiping his nose until the handkerchief was soaked through; Xavier handed him the other one.

'Thank you,' Rothgar said incongruously.

Xavier stared at him, feeling for a moment strangely guilty. They sat in silence as in a dentist's waiting-room. And that, Xavier reflected, was the sort of room it had become now that violence had entered into it; the pearl-grey on white Sanderson wallpaper with the silk texture, the two buttoned leather armchairs, the big mahogany bookcase, the lovingly-polished mahogany table, the set of four Victorian dining chairs, the fitted Axminster carpet, were as if chosen by somebody else – the room never would be his retreat again.

The doorbell rang; he let in the Disposer and Droylsden. The

77

Disposer had the same suit and tie that he had been wearing on Friday but his shirt was brand new, with long collar points and broad black and blue stripes. It seemed to accentuate his general unkemptness.

'You must be getting past it, Flynn,' he said. 'He's still breathing. Knocked about a bit, though.'

'Quite recently too,' Droylsden said. 'You're supposed to leave that sort of thing to Interrogation, old chap.'

'Fuck you,' Xavier said. He turned towards the Disposer. 'There's a body in the bedroom. Second on the right along the passage.'

'And it was him who did it?' The Disposer gestured towards Rothgar.

'Couldn't have been anyone else.'

The Disposer left the room, whistling tunelessly to himself.

'Got anything out of him?' Droylsden asked Xavier.

'Nothing to speak of. No doubt you'll do better.'

An expression of panic came over Rothgar's face and he leapt up and lunged towards Droylsden. Droylsden hit him hard in the belly and he bent double, gasping and retching.

'Sit down and don't be silly,' Droylsden said. Rothgar went slowly to the chair and sat down. His head went down on the table; he seemed to be crying.

'I wonder if he's connected with Morgate's?' Droylsden said thoughtfully.

'Try asking him.'

The man who called himself John Rothgar raised his head. It seemed to be a great effort. 'I'm not saying any more until I see my lawyer.' His voice was shaky.

Xavier burst out laughing. 'My dear John – I might as well call you John – you've left the world of lawyers. You're in the Gulag Archipelago now.'

'You're a real intellectual, aren't you?' Droylsden said coldly. He took a small box out of his black briefcase, an ampoule and a hypodermic out of the box, and filled the hypodermic. 'This will put you to sleep,' he said to Rothgar, whose face had now assumed an expression of total withdrawal. 'It's quite harmless. If you resist, painful things will happen to you and you'll be put to sleep just the same.'

'I haven't much option, have I?' Rothgar took off his jacket and rolled up his shirt sleeve. As Droylsden pressed the plunger down Xavier found himself, to his surprise, feeling slightly sick. All that had happened since he'd come into the flat seemed to have happened within a human world, within a house off Kensington High Street in West London. It was violent and nasty, but he could take it. But the gleaming hypodermic, the colourless liquid going into the bloodstream, the concentration and composure on the face of Droylsden as he pressed down the plunger had suddenly and genuinely taken them all into the non-human world, the Gulag Archipelago.

# TEN

## *3 June 1974: 19.00–20.45 Hours*

The gold doors swung open and the white-robed, white-bearded figure of Time glided out, swinging his golden scythe. The clock struck seven; the tone was deep and mellow with an element of urgency about it which for a moment silenced the sound of a hundred voices in Sir Geoffrey Morgate's drawing-room. Time glided back and the gold doors shut and the voices started again. The girl in the silver lamé trouser-suit who had come up beside Xavier said, 'It's real gold leaf on the doors. And the clock face. The rest is Carrara marble.'

'I've seen something like it at Harrods.' The girl was very slim, almost emaciated; her face was evenly tanned and her hair, worn short, bleached almost white by the sun.

'This was made to order for my great-grandfather over a hundred years ago. Nowadays we don't buy anything that we can't put down on expenses.'

'That's rough.' He couldn't keep his eyes off her face: too long – almost hatchet-shaped – to be conventionally pretty, but too vivid, too full of expression, too intelligent not to be disturbing. You wouldn't ever be able to disregard her.

'It *is* rough,' she said. 'We should be able to keep our cash and spend it on mad and spectacular and useless things. Like the clock.'

'I rather fancy you,' he said.

'Shouldn't you ask me my name first?'

'I know it. It's Vanessa Morgate. I'm Xavier Flynn.'

'I know. I was told to look out for you. Do you really fancy me, or is it just to have something to say?' She put her hand on his sleeve. It was a very thin, long-fingered hand, with a large solitaire diamond ring and a thick wedding-ring on the third finger. She had a heavy gold bracelet which accentuated the thinness of her wrist. The hand was trembling slightly.

'To tell you the truth, I'd like to fuck you,' he said.

She smiled. Her teeth were a shade on the large side, but white and regular. 'I'd like it too, but not now.'

'Why not? There must be lots of places here.'

'Mrs Alvaston is bearing down upon us. I think that my father wants to see you.' She squeezed his hand. 'I'll see you later.'

Mrs Alvaston, tall and stiffly-corseted and nearing fifty, but with long legs which were strong yet graceful, the legs of a Cochran chorus girl, and auburn hair which gleamed softly, reminded him of Bunty, except that she had about her a sexuality which Bunty lacked. He knew that she had been Sir Geoffrey Morgate's secretary and mistress for twenty years. He knew also that she was a widow with no children, that she came from a county family, and that it was virtually impossible to get access to Sir Geoffrey except through her.

'Mr Flynn?' she asked. 'Of the Department of Trade and Industry? I'm Stella Alvaston, Sir Geoffrey's secretary.' She had a pleasantly clear, brisk voice; looking at her more closely, Xavier could see what her attraction must once have been. He smiled and held out his hand.

'How do you do, Mrs Alvaston. Very good of Sir Geoffrey to invite me. We Civil Servants lead very constricted lives.'

She lifted her eyebrows by a fraction and Xavier was aware that she was fully cognisant of what his function at Morgate's was to be.

'Quite so, Mr Flynn. Sir Geoffrey would be very grateful if you could spare him a few moments.'

'By all means.'

He followed her out of the room, along the corridor which had surprisingly shabby red carpeting and plain cream walls, and into a large room lined with books. A white-haired man in his early sixties was sitting in a large leather armchair reading the *Telegraph*. He put the paper down and advanced upon Xavier.

'Flynn? Delighted to meet you, my dear chap.' He put his hand on Mrs Alvaston's shoulder. 'You go off and drink some champagne, Stella dear. I shan't bother you again.'

Xavier was surprised to see Mrs Alvaston's face soften as Sir Geoffrey touched her, then wondered why he should be surprised. In the information he'd been given, it had been stated that there was almost certainly still a physical relationship between them and certainly a lasting *tendresse*. Perhaps what surprised him was the lack of discretion. He decided to make it clear that his cover was to be preserved.

'I have the idea that Mrs Alvaston knows what my real function is,' he said.

'Naturally,' Sir Geoffrey said. 'Won't tell anyone else, though. Do sit down, Flynn. I've got some rather good whisky here. Talisker. Over a hundred proof . . . Marvellous stuff . . .'

He was almost as tall as Aslan, but his face – thin, lively, with a large nose which only just escaped being grotesque – wasn't so smooth, and he had a jerky, clipped way of speaking.

'I'm sure she won't, Sir Geoffrey,' Xavier said. The armchair sagged uncomfortably, but the whisky which Sir Geoffrey poured for him was smooth and strong and peaty. Sir Geoffrey waved towards the open box of Romeo y Julieta on the small walnut table between them; Xavier shook his head and took out his Silk Cut King Size.

'Ours is very much a family business, Mr Flynn,' Sir Geoffrey said. 'I'm just *primus inter pares* if you see what I mean.'

'The *pares* being?'

'Mrs Alvaston, my son Brian, Roy Cothill, who's Acting Head of our Security Department, and my daughter Vanessa.'

'There mustn't be any more. Not if you really want your problem to be solved.'

'Of course, of course. Bloody well *is* a problem too. You'll have every facility, I assure you. Go where you like, ask whatever question you like. If something's not done soon, we're going to be in Queer Street. You know about our bike, don't you?'

'It's 1200 cc, water-cooled, shaft drive, much improved since its design in 1938, but basically unchanged. You go on from there, Sir Geoffrey.'

'It's never been cheap. It's not all that much cheaper than the foreign competition now. People don't buy the Morgate 1200 because it's cheap. They buy it because it's a damned good motor-bike. We don't have a new model every year, but we keep abreast of modern design, and we do have a brand new model in the pipeline – alloy wheels, automatic gearbox and all that . . . We don't have a public relations department but if any of our customers has any complaint or any suggestion they write to us and they get a signed answer – a proper letter not a form – by return of post and then a senior executive will look into it. And I *mean* look into it . . . And we deliver on time. Because if you don't there are other manufacturers that will.'

'You're not delivering on time now?'

'We've a thousand orders overdue. Never happened before.'

'We'll have to see that it doesn't happen again.' He wondered when Sir Geoffrey was going to get to the point; despite the quite exceptional strength and smoothness of the whisky, he found that the room depressed him. There was a musty smell from the shelves of leather-bound books, none of which, as far as he could see, were of a nature likely ever to have been read.

'I'd like some action,' Sir Geoffrey said. He smiled. He had the same large white regular teeth as his daughter but they made his face suddenly and strikingly savage. 'Piers tells me that you're a chap who likes to be where the action is.'

Xavier was silent for a moment; he hadn't for a long time thought of Aslan as possessing a Christian name, certainly not as someone who would have friends outside of CED. 'Let's get it straight, Sir Geoffrey,' he said. 'What exactly do you mean by action?'

'I don't mean just sacking them. Probably have a strike on our hands then. Or handing them over to the police. What happens then? A suspended sentence and lots of sympathy from the Leftists. And they become heroes. And they're still free to go on wrecking the country.'

'What do you mean then, Sir Geoffrey?'

Sir Geoffrey's voice became a whisper. 'Kill them. All right, don't look so pained. *Execute* them. Believe me, I'll help you. Godammit, I'll *pay* you. And sleep easy afterwards.'

The old boy certainly was turned on, Xavier thought with amusement. The idea of killing took some civilians like that: it seemed so beautifully simple.

'So far we're just investigating, Sir Geoffrey,' he said. 'I'm helping Tom Drage. So we've already got one of our men on the job. Under cover, of course. When we're sure who's responsible for the damage –'

'Sabotage. Deliberate sabotage. Politically-inspired sabotage.'

'– Sabotage, we'll take action instantly.'

'We've got seven names. That's why we brought Cothill in last December. Pensioned off the chap who was head of Security then.'

'Even if you've got the names, we have to check and double-check. And before taking action we have to clear it higher up.'

'Red tape,' Sir Geoffrey said. 'Nothing but red tape.'

'I'm sorry, but we must follow certain procedures. Or else we're in trouble.' Xavier lit another cigarette; that was two over his allowance already. He looked at the books again, then noticed that in amongst the leather-bound ones were some newer ones. *Das Kapital*, Lenin's *What is to be Done?*, Deutscher's *Stalin*, Conquest's *The Great Terror*, Kitson's *Low Intensity Warfare*, then an assortment of novels – the complete James Bond series, the complete Matt Helm series, *The Day of the Jackal*, *The Odessa File* and, rather out of keeping with the rest, Betjeman's *Collected Poems*. Sir Geoffrey saw what he was looking at.

'I do read, Flynn. Though most of my books are at my place in Sussex. Don't really care for London.' He rose and took the whisky over to Xavier. 'A spot more?'

Xavier nodded. 'Too good to refuse.'

'I'll send you a bottle if you like it. Got to show how much we appreciate chaps like you.' He half filled Xavier's glass. 'We don't know the half of what's going on, eh? The Reds are winning all the way. Not under the bed, *in* it and on the job . . . Say a word about it, point out the truth, and even Conservatives start yammering about McCarthy. What the hell's a dead American politician got to do with it? The Reds in the car industry have lost us the North American market, they've lost us shipbuilding, and now there's only us and one other in the motor-cycle industry. And God knows what's happening at Meriden, because I don't . . . These were words, Xavier thought, which evidently Sir Geoffrey had used often before; they might well be true, but they got him no further.

'You think that FIST's aim is to close you down?' he asked.

'Too damned true it is.' Sir Geoffrey banged his fist on his knee.

'But FIST, as far as it's anything coherent, is Trotskyite. I don't say that there's no connection with the CP, but we haven't traced one.'

'You won't, my boy. The Reds are too clever for that. There's no need for any connection, no need at all.'

'Tom Drage thinks that there's something else amiss at your factory.'

'Nonsense. Why should there be? We've never had any trouble

84

until FIST moved in. We treat our workers decently – always have done – and they make a product they can be proud of. I'd be the first to know if there were anything wrong apart from this damned sabotage. Christ, it's all that they can do, they can't get at us through stirring up labour trouble.'

It was all too pat, too quick, too reasonable; he didn't particularly like Tom, Tom had never struck him as being anything more than competent, but he was sure that when he said something was wrong, something indeed was wrong. His guilt at not going along with Tom on Friday night came back to him in a stab of sharp physical pain in his stomach. He sipped his whisky and it was gone. But this job wouldn't be straightforward and it wouldn't do to take too much notice of Sir Geoffrey. Or, he realised with surprise, of Aslan. He suppressed the thought fiercely, and drained his whisky.

'I'll be in touch with you very soon, Sir Geoffrey. Don't worry, we'll sort everything out.'

'Don't be so mealy-mouthed. Kill the buggers, and if you make a few mistakes – well, as the bishop said at the time of the Albigensian heresy, God will know His own.'

Xavier laughed. 'All right, Sir Geoffrey. If we have to, we'll make the factory floors run with blood.'

Sir Geoffrey smiled his wolfish smile, and as Xavier left the room, glad to be out of its chill and musty smell, he thought, and was not wholly amused at the thought, that the old devil was actually taking his words seriously.

Back in the drawing-room the party had perceptibly livened up, the noise increased. He noticed the sheer physical size of both men and women: this was emphatically an upper middle-class, if not upper-class gathering. He was six foot, and in one quick glance he could see half a dozen men who were taller than himself. About half the men were wearing dinner-jackets: these people were great ones for ritualising their lives. He didn't give a damn one way or the other, but it was depressing to realise that nothing had changed very much since this house had been built some time in the 1830s. These people had been in charge then and they were in charge now. He took a glass of champagne from a passing waiter and sipped it without any enjoyment. He felt a hand on his shoulder and turned round quickly to see Vanessa smiling at him.

85

'Don't look so gloomy. Daddy has that effect on people, I know. Why were you *glaring* so?'

'Thinking how decadent you all were.'

'That sounds rather fun. They're rather a dull lot here tonight, actually. Lots of politicians. Have you ever thought of going in for politics?'

'You must be joking.'

'No, I'm not.' She slapped his hand with surprising force. 'Why don't you look at me?'

'I can't help but look at you.'

She laughed. 'I'm not really pretty but you'll remember me once you've seen me, won't you?'

'As the saying goes, when they made you they broke the mould.'

She slapped his hand again. 'Your eyes have gone away from me again. I don't think that you look at people at all.'

He smiled. 'I'll look at you then. Can I give you dinner?'

'And then fuck me?' She was breathing quickly.

'If that's what you really want.'

'You don't give a damn do you?' She moved closer to him; her hip encountered the Baby Browning in his pocket. 'What's that?'

'You're far too curious. It's only a cigarette-lighter.'

Her hand touched his pocket. 'It feels like a gun Show me it?'

'It's supposed to feel like a gun. Great joke. But it doesn't work.'

It worked very well, in fact, and one of its tiny bullets between the eyes killed a man just as effectually as one from a ·45. The pocket of his suit had been specially reinforced to take its weight. Shoulder holsters were very rarely used in the Department; by the time you'd got the gun out you could be dead.

'I think it *is* a gun. What odd equipment for an export negotiator. Do you keep it to persuade customers with?' Her smile was like her father's but sensual rather than menacing.

'The Emperor's last argument? You're not very security-conscious, are you?'

'You don't understand. We're a family business.' Her face turned suddenly cold. 'We know when to keep our mouths shut.'

'I hope you do. My experience is that people like you don't.'

'I don't very much like your tone.'

'It doesn't matter whether you like it. Just don't talk about my job, do you understand?'

Her expression changed to amusement. 'All right, love. I'll be a good girl. I'll do as I'm told . . . You don't approve of me very much, do you?'

'Not really.' He looked around the room. 'Nor of anyone here, come to think of it.'

'You're not a Lefty, are you?'

'No.' He decided that he was becoming too serious. Agents were not supposed to have opinions which would make them conspicuous in any way. 'It's just the way I feel. I've had a hard day at the office.' He squeezed her hand. 'I still fancy you.'

'Even if I'm decadent?'

'I'm rather decadent myself.'

'Not you. You are rather frightening. But I don't object to that –' She turned away from him. 'There's someone I must see.' Her hand went to his shoulder lightly and he was conscious of her excitement. 'Later,' she said, and half ran towards a tall thin man with shoulder-length platinum hair and a blue denim suit, Saint Laurent from its cut.

Xavier put down his empty glass and looked round the room for Sally Rowmarsh. He half hoped that she wouldn't be there. If he went to bed with Vanessa it was simply a private pleasure: it had nothing to do with his job. But if he went to bed with Sally Rowmarsh he'd become a kind of whore, which wasn't what he'd joined the Service for. And then as he walked over to Sally Rowmarsh he realised that he would do what he had been ordered to do. If she were available tonight he'd sleep with her tonight. He'd obey his orders, and be grateful that they were orders that it would be a pleasure to obey.

Sally Rowmarsh had just detached herself from a fat middle-aged man whom Xavier recognised as Ronald Byrock, a moderately well-known Labour MP.

'Sally Rowmarsh?' he asked. 'I'm Xavier Flynn, a colleague of Tom Drage's.'

'He's spoken of you.' Her tone implied that Tom hadn't spoken of him with any degree of warmth. Xavier grinned.

'He won't have said anything good.' She was pretty, with good features and shining black hair, but she had a definitely discontented look; there were faint lines at the corners of her mouth which would, if she weren't careful, drag it down, and her forehead in the near future would lose its smoothness.

'He says you're a very thinly veneered Fascist. And a papist of a very nasty and hypocritical kind.'

'I'm worse than that. Believe me, he doesn't know the half of it.'

'Very good. Of course, he said you were a cunning sod too. Are you trying to pick me up?'

'I wouldn't mind, now that I see how pretty you are. But all I want is to know where he is.'

Her dark brown eyes opened wide. He was aware of being scrutinised.

'I can't think why. You aren't friends, are you?'

'I didn't say we were. Something urgent's come up, that's all.'

'Something urgent? At the Department of Trade and Industry? A likely story. But I can't help you. Haven't seen the sod since Friday morning.'

'That's awkward. We're in a mess without him, believe it or not. Hasn't he 'phoned?'

'Tom doesn't bother about things like that. He's not what you'd call the thoughtful type.' She shrugged. 'Still, I'm not married to him.'

The gesture lifted her breasts under her white blouse; they were full and unequivocally youthful. Despite himself, he looked at her sympathetically and lowered his voice an octave.

'He's too young,' he said. 'Older men are better. They understand what little things like a 'phone call mean to a woman . . .'

Her smile was genuine and the hard look in her eyes softened. 'You'd be kind to me, is that it? A real father figure?'

'I could start by giving you dinner.'

'Sorry,' she said. 'I have to get back to the office.'

The sudden approach was now out of the question; it would in any case have meant ditching Vanessa. 'Another time, then?'

'I'll give you my 'phone number.'

He knew it by heart; he knew a great many 'phone numbers by heart. But he wrote it down in his diary, reflecting as he did so that it was as equivalent to her saying that she couldn't go to bed with him now, but would at some other time.

He looked in the direction of Ronald Byrock. 'Strange to see him here.'

'He's a director of Jonquil Electrical Supplies. He and Sir Geoffrey are great buddies. Didn't you know?' She frowned. 'When you look at people you seem to size them up in a peculiar way . . . You're rather like Tom.'

He grimaced. 'I can't say that I'm entirely flattered.'

'Oh, you're attractive enough. I suppose *he* is. Sexually, anyway –' she gave him a sidelong glance to see if she'd shocked him – 'but what I mean is simply that you're not a Civil Servant.'

'I am, I assure you. I haven't ever had any other employer except the Government.'

'I think you're cold, like Tom.'

'That's with being a Civil Servant.'

'But what are you cold *about*?'

'You'll have to know me better.' So much for my cover, he thought. I might just as well be in the Classified Directory – Flynn, X.A.: Secret Agent and Fornicator. Murders by Arrangement . . .

'Mad, bad and dangerous to know . . . You're not mad, but as for the rest . . .'

'Like Tom, I have a very prosaic job, and you ought to be writing fiction.'

Sir Geoffrey came into the room; Xavier noticed that the material of his evening suit was so old that it actually had a greenish tinge. Ronald Byrock half ran towards him, his round pink face smiling. His evening suit was mohair with the gloss of newness still on it, his silk shirt was frilled, and his tie and breast-pocket handkerchief were scarlet.

'I suppose I must try to extract some quotes from the old monster,' she said. 'And his scrubber of a daughter.'

'That's rather hard.'

'She's got through two husbands and God knows how many lovers.'

'No-one's perfect.'

'You can say that again . . . See you.'

'See you,' he said. He suddenly felt tired and rather lonely. The large room with its faintly shabby white and gold wallpaper and its dusty chandeliers was too much a public room. What he had seen of the house didn't add up to a home.

There was no reason for him to be bothered by such thoughts:

he had done what he came for. He'd met Sir Geoffrey, and he'd begun a relationship with Sally Rowmarsh. In short, in the near future he was going to sleep with her. He'd virtually been ordered to do so by his superior officer, which, he reflected, was rather a moral conundrum. Since he would be obeying lawful orders in sleeping with her, could it really be counted as a sin?

But he hadn't been told to sleep with Vanessa. That was purely – or impurely – for his private pleasure. And yet it would help him in his job, it would open the locked doors which one always encountered in jobs of this kind. It was part of his job. Everything he did seemed to be part of his job. And for the first time that job had physically followed him into his home, and because of the job an innocent man had died. He had prayed for his soul and would pray for his soul again, but he was dead now, his great and true friend Ricky the unperformed composer with whom he'd lived for five years would be lonely tonight, his beloved Mummy (*She's completely fucked me up as a man, ducky, but I adore her*) in Bath would never hear from him again. And if Ricky enquired, the police would tell him that he'd been seen that very evening, giving the place and the time. And he'd be seen again the next day, and wherever it was, it would be far away from London. His body would never be found.

Where would it be now, and what was being done to it? That was a question he'd never asked himself. What was certain was that, that morning at ten, Jeremy had tripped along, humming cheerfully, into Xavier's flat, carrying his large Union Jack carrier containing his flowered pinafore and slippers and head-scarf and rubber gloves, a living and breathing though by his own admission imperfect human being, and now he didn't exist. The worst of it, Xavier thought, feeling something very close to fear, was that it could happen to anyone.

He sipped his champagne; it was too dry, of course, typical of the stuff the French exported. The best, in which you could taste the sweetness of the grape, they kept for themselves. As soon as he'd formulated the thought, he recognised it for what it was: an attempt not to think about what Tom had said to Sally Rowmarsh. He didn't mind being called a thinly veneered Fascist and a papist of a very nasty and hypocritical kind; these days to be summarised in such terms was rather a compliment. It wasn't expected from agents that they should always be loudly proclaiming their willingness to die for Queen and Country; the tone set by Aslan was one of cheerful cynicism, and what the political indoctrination of the Department boiled down to was that you defended the bad against the infinitely worse. Agents weren't supposed as private people to become involved in politics, and they had to keep their noses absolutely clean, but they still didn't have to exclude Lefties as friends or mistresses or even wives. There was a world outside the Department and they had to live in it and they had to learn something about it. Granted all that, from those words of Tom, spoken to that particular person, Xavier could deduce a way of thinking which was dangerous – dangerous to Tom, dangerous to the Department, dangerous to the country. And where did John Rothgar, if that was his name, get his address?

Suddenly Droylsden was beside him. He hadn't seen him enter the room; it was as if he'd literally materialised himself like a character from *Star Trek*.

'A present from Aslan,' he said, giving Xavier a small manilla envelope with something hard, about two inches square and an eighth of an inch thick, inside it. 'Don't open it now.'

'What is it?' Xavier asked, knowing the answer as soon as he'd asked the question.

'Exit One,' Droylsden said in a low voice.

'I've been fully briefed.' Packaged as aspirin; safety catch on both sides, then press the top firmly; operative period ten seconds.

'He hopes that you're – fully dressed. There seems to be a busy period ahead.'

Xavier nodded. There was something about Droylsden's attitude which made him too angry to speak; he had to put down his glass to conceal the trembling of his hand. Droylsden gave him a patronising smile, took a glass of champagne from a passing waiter and lit a cigarette. 'Is that all?' Xavier managed to say, his voice suddenly hoarse.

'I should think that's enough, wouldn't you?' Droylsden sipped his champagne. 'This is rather splendid. Far from being a naive little wine, but I like its sophistication . . . That was an attempt at a joke, my dear Xavier.'

'I'm not in the mood for jokes.'

'Well be serious then.' He lowered his voice. 'I have to make sure if you're *adequately* dressed.'

'Adequately enough. I don't like being – weighed down.'

'*Adequately* was perhaps not what he wanted to hear. Bear it in mind in future.'

'All right, I'll bear it in mind in future. Are the goods processed yet?'

'Aslan has taken over the job himself.'

'What's the origin of the goods?'

'He's not sure yet. Despite a most thorough examination.'

'Does he want me to come over? I really would feel happier if I knew more about the goods.'

'We'll let you know what you need to know. You don't really relish the sordid business of processing, do you?' Droylsden drained his champagne. 'Enjoy yourself, Xavier. I'd rather have your job than mine. And you can say that again.'

He pushed his hair away from his forehead; on the right shirt cuff was a small patch of red.

'I'm not so sure about that,' Xavier said.

Droylsden's eyes widened and he flushed, then he laughed. 'You weren't doing so badly before we came,' he said. 'We're just carrying on from where you left off.' He moved away from Xavier in the direction of the door. 'The goods smell a bit now. But someone's got to do the dirty work.'

Looking at Droylsden making his way through the crowd to the door he noticed something odd about him. He didn't shoulder anyone aside, didn't ever brush by anybody, and he didn't say *excuse me* to anybody who was in his path with their backs towards him. But somehow or other everyone made way for him, even though he was moving pretty briskly. Did normal people have some sort of instinct about people like Droylsden?

Vanessa came up to him hand in hand with the man with platinum blond hair and the Saint Laurent suit.

'Darling, Leonard wants to meet you. Xavier Flynn, Leonard Sancreed. Leonard makes films.'

'Skin flicks, actually,' the man said, putting both his hands round Xavier's right hand. 'But socially significant. That keeps you out of a lot of trouble.'

'Up the Revolution and all that?'

'Works like a fucking charm. I forgot about it with *Pink Havoc* until I'd finished. Couldn't think what to do, because I'd paid everyone and sent them home. So I put on a grey beard and wig and read bits out from Karl Marx and all those shits. Then snip, snip, snip, and shoved it in at random.'

'You're a dedicated artist, I see.' Xavier gently but firmly detached his hand.

Sancreed giggled. 'A dedicated money-grubber, love. Vanessa has never understood that.' He gave Xavier a long appraising look. 'She tells me that you're a Civil Servant.'

'I'm afraid so. Very dull.'

'You don't look dull. You smoulder, you positively smoulder. I can see that Vanessa's got hot pants for you . . .'

He wagged a long manicured finger in a gesture of warning. 'She'll destroy you, my dear. Particularly if you're the Civil Servant type.'

'Maybe I don't care whether I'm destroyed or not.'

'You will, sweetheart, you will. But you're like the rest: you can't see any further than your prick end . . .'

Vanessa yawned. 'We're going now, Leonard.'

Leonard pouted. 'I'd love to give you both dinner.'

'Not tonight, darling.' She kissed him; he stood quiescent, his hands at his side, his eyes on Xavier.

'I'm in the 'phone book,' he said to Xavier. 'Fitzjohn's Avenue.'

She punched him in his ribs. 'I hope you won't,' she said as they emerged into Kensington Square and the trees and the sunlight, still bright, but paler than when he'd gone into the house, the breeze a shade cooler.

'I assure you he doesn't attract me.'

'Have you ever been with a man?'

'What an extraordinary question. Do I look queer?'

'Lots of men I know have been. Mostly at school.'

'I went to a grammar school. We were picking up girls at fourteen.'

She smiled. 'Ah, you're the salt of the earth.' She paused beside an orange Porsche Carrera Targa. 'Did you bring a car?'

He shook his head. 'It's being serviced.'

'Unless you've got your heart set on some special restaurant, we could eat at my place.'

'That'll be nice.' He meant more than that; standing beside her in the sunlight beside nine thousand pounds' worth of sports car, her sequins now seeming to glitter more brightly, he could forget the Browning, forget the Exit One (one second and you were dead), forget the questions which had been nagging him all day, forget too his growing conviction that there was something more he had to do than obey orders.

'I had to eat a business breakfast at the Hilton today,' she said, as she manœuvred the car out from between a Bentley and a Mercedes with only about a foot to spare either way, using the masculine technique of keeping one hand only on the steering wheel and turning it full lock with the car at rest. 'And a business lunch at the Mirabelle. And Daddy's party tonight. So I'm fed up of eating in public places, and being nice to people.'

Near to her he found to his surprise that she used no perfume: there was only a faint smell of some very mild soap – Knight's Castile probably – and something very like Johnson's Baby Powder. He found it more exciting than scent; if he kept still and concentrated he'd smell her own smell, quite simply woman, perspiring now very lightly.

'I haven't ever seen a woman do that before,' he said to her as they emerged into Derry Street.

'Do what exactly?'

'Reverse properly with only one hand on the wheel.'

'I do everything properly,' she said. 'I'm very efficient about everything except personal relationships. I sometimes think that poor Leonard's the way that he is because of me. I tried to reform him, you know. Of course, before I married him, he didn't camp it up quite as much as he does now . . . Have you ever been married?'

'I never got round to it. I expect I shall.'

He didn't really want to talk; it was enough to be in an open car on a fine June evening with the wind on his face. He was glad not to be with Sally Rowmarsh, not to be on duty for once. The Porsche had an atmosphere of enormous solidity and enormous speed, as if it could fly if it wanted to; he leaned back and relaxed, only half listening to Vanessa.

'I really should get married again,' she said, almost under her breath. 'Daddy's always making broad hints about it. He wants his grandchildren to be in the business too.'

Xavier shaded his eyes against the setting sun. 'How can he be sure they'll want to be?'

'That's what I keep telling him. He doesn't bother to listen.' Xavier felt her hand on his thigh. 'You're a rather splendid specimen, aren't you? You'll have a weight problem one day.'

'I'm the product of generations of navvies and farm labourers.'

Her hand, now trembling a little, crept upwards. 'Good stock to breed from, would you say?'

'I'm not a bloody horse.' He had a disturbing sense of *déja vu*, of having been there before; and then it disappeared, engulfed by a pleasure that was delicate but full-flavoured, even rank; the thin brown hand moved upwards and he caught his breath sharply as if in pain. She took her hand away to change gear as they turned into Holland Road; he lit two cigarettes, ducking his head down to keep the match alight. As he handed her the cigarette he noticed a black Jaguar XJ12 saloon close behind them. In the front there were two young men wearing dark glasses, hair unfashionably close-cropped. There was no reason why he should, but he memorised the registration number.

'I'm not very ladylike, am I?' she asked him.

'I don't really mind.' Her hand rubbed him gently.

'It's the effect you have on me.'

'You turn me on too.' He drew in his breath sharply.

'Darling, that's the difference. Practically any attractive woman turns you on. I noticed you with that Commie bitch Sally Rowmarsh . . . She'd just have to touch you *there*, and the effect would be the same . . .' Her hand left him to change gear.

'Is she really a Commie?'

'Oh hell, I don't know. It's the effect of a day with Daddy and Daddy's associates . . . You've no idea how reactionary they are. I suppose Miss Rowmarsh is just a typical muddled Lefty, actually.'

He put his hand on her thigh; it was softer than he would have surmised. 'I only spoke to her because we have a mutual friend,' he said. The black Jaguar XJ12 with the two young men in the front was still behind them as she turned into Holland Villas Road; it slowed down, then continued in the direction of Holland Park Avenue as she went into Alton Mews on the right of Holland Villas Road.

Alton Mews was a cobbled cul-de-sac with a dozen white-painted houses – or rather, Xavier reflected, a dozen large garages with houses attached on each side. Vanessa drove the Porsche straight at the garage door of the house in the middle; with a slight hiss the door rolled upwards. Xavier pressed the release catch of his safety belt, jumped out of the car, and ran to the entrance of the mews. The Jaguar wasn't there; he went back to Vanessa, who was standing at her front door searching her handbag.

'I thought you must be fleeing temptation.'

'I was checking on something.' The Jaguar could only have turned where it did to visit a house in Holland Park Villas Road, to go into Addison Road, or to follow the Porsche. They would be back. As the Jaguar had passed the mews they would have noticed that it was a cul-de-sac, and would have had a shrewd idea that he'd be there for some time.

The kitchen was large, with a blue and white tiled floor, a pine table with four matching Windsor chairs, a huge white electric cooker, a huge dishwasher, a huge refrigerator, and pinewood shelves and cupboards which, like the table, appeared as if they had been ferociously scrubbed. The walls and ceiling were a plain and glaring white; somehow it wasn't a kitchen in which one could imagine meals being cooked. It didn't have the shabbiness of her father's house, but it had the same comfortlessness.

'I've been away,' Vanessa said, as if reading his thoughts. 'It isn't generally as unnaturally tidy.' She opened the refrigerator. 'There's a lot of cold meat and salad here. And a bottle of hock. Will that be enough?'

'That's fine.' The window was at the back of the house, over-looking – or rather overshadowed by – a ten-storey block of flats, brutally assertive in dingy concrete. There was a narrow cobbled alley and a low brick wall between the mews and the flats.

'What were you checking on?' Vanessa asked him as she put a plate of cold meat and a wooden bowl of salad on the table.

'I thought I saw someone I knew. Where does that alley lead to?'

'Addison Road. Why do you ask?'

'If I don't know these things I may live to be sorry. Or not live.' He put his arms round her waist as she was taking out a loaf from a cupboard and kissed the nape of her neck gently. It was quite smooth below the hairline with no trace of stubble. Her buttocks were unexpectedly plump, but resilient; he held her still for a moment, bemused by contentment. A woman, a plate of meat, a bowl of salad, a loaf, a bottle of wine; he couldn't really expect much more, and perhaps this moment was the best of all. There was no commitment on one side or the other, there was no satiety, no guilt and, unless you were a really inspired nit-picker, no sin.

She turned round and put the loaf down. 'Look at me and kiss me properly.'

'I'm looking at you.' Her breath tasted of tobacco and vanilla, her breasts were fuller than he had thought they would be.

'You're a strange girl.'

'You're a strange man. You looked very out of place at that party. A tiger among the tabby cats.'

'You're romanticising me, love. I'm just a Civil Servant.' He kissed her again; her arms tightened round his neck and she began to rub her belly against his. Suddenly she pulled herself away from him.

'We must eat. Sit down and have a cigarette.'

'I'm not worried about eating now.'

She touched him gently between the legs. 'I can see you're not. But there's no hurry.' She took a handful of heavy silver cutlery from a drawer beside the sink. 'May I look at your gun?'

He sat down at the table and lit a cigarette. Suddenly he felt enormously cheerful. 'It's a cigarette-lighter.'

'Show me your cigarette-lighter.'

He put the gun on the table. 'Look. Don't touch.'

Her eyes widened. 'It's so small. Maybe it *is* a cigarette-lighter.'

'It's just four inches long.'

'What's it called?'

'A Baby Browning. They used to put *Baby* on the bottom of the stock but they don't any more. It's what they call in the trade a personal protection weapon.'

'I've never seen a real gun before except in museums.' She moistened her lips. 'I've seen Daddy's sporting guns, but that's different.'

He grinned. 'How is it different?'

'*That* gun's to kill people.'

97

'That's right. If you don't kill with it, then it's not much use. It's definitely not a sporting gun.'

'Which is the safety-catch?'

'At the rear of the trigger.'

She reached over to the gun, but he put his hand over it.

'It isn't a plaything.' He put the gun back in his pocket.

She set out the cutlery and took out the bottle of wine from the refrigerator.

'It's the stuff that old Roscoe and JB can both agree upon. I like it myself. Open it, will you, pet, there's a corkscrew there.'

He went to the window and partially closed the Venetian blind. 'How much has your father told you?'

'You may as well close the blind properly.'

He went over to the window, approaching it from the side. 'How much has your father told you?'

'Darling, I'm a director of Morgate's,' She laughed. 'I'm not just a pretty face . . . He told me that you were going to do something drastic about FIST.'

'We might as well not bother with this export negotiator cover, then. But don't for Christ's sake tell anyone else. Where's your 'phone?'

'Upstairs in the next room by the window.'

'The window? That's all I needed.'

He half ran up into the next room, ducked under the window-sill, and glanced outside. A white Audi 100GL was reversing into the mews and reversing very fast; its driver was a young man with a pale face and black beard. He pulled the blinds and pulled the 'phone towards him, standing by the wall. For a second the day's code identification escaped him; he stood sweating listening to the recorded voice at the other end repeating the CED number and the request for identification. The room was large, with a newly polished parquet floor, and the furniture was dark and heavy. It was still light despite the drawn curtains.

'Drinian. Two Six Seven Beta.'

'Ninian Four Six Seven Alpha. Anything troubling you?'

'Where's Aslan?'

'Asking searching questions? I told you he'd taken over.'

'I want to speak to him.'

'I'm afraid you can't. Interrogation has reached a crucial

stage.' Droylsden giggled. 'You see, I was the villain. The heavy. Aslan is the goodie. They're now having coffee and sandwiches and talking about the meaning of life.'

There was a muted bang, in the sound range of a heavy cough, and a hole appeared in the window. He could hear a car engine but not the sound of its wheels over the cobbles. He knew that it was the Audi and he knew that he'd seen the Audi and its driver before. These were really professional; one car to do the spotting another to do the job, and possibly a third to make the getaway.

'I'm not really interested in your interrogation technique. Someone's just fired at me. I was tailed from Morgate's house. They're using a midnight-blue Jaguar and a white Audi.' He gave the registration number.

'Don't worry, old chap, it's all under control. Have you any idea what they're using?'

'Sounds like a Sten Mark 25. They're using a silencer, so it won't be an automatic.'

'Hang on a minute, will you?' Another hole appeared in the curtain. That would be what one would expect from the 25; automatic fire would soon burn the silencer out.

Vanessa appeared in the doorway. 'Did I hear a noise?'

'Stay where you are. Someone's taking a shot at me.'

'My God, how thrilling! But shouldn't we 'phone for the police?'

'Are the front and back doors locked?'

'Yes, darling. And bolted too. But we really must 'phone for the police.'

The sweat was running into Xavier's eyes; he wiped it away impatiently. 'We can be dead by the time they arrive.'

'I don't understand how they dare –'

'Don't be so bloody stupid. They're doing it, aren't they?'

He still had the telephone pressed to his ear; he jumped when he heard Droylsden's voice. 'Relax, old chap. Our boys are sorting it out.'

'Who's our boys?'

'The chaps in the Jaguar. Aslan had a feeling something like this might happen.'

'You might have told me.'

'No point in spoiling your evening. Mind you, you're rather

naughty. It's Miss Rowmarsh you should be with, not Miss Morgate.'

'I may be a hired gun, but I'm not going to be a hired prick. But what the hell is the KGB playing at? Do they want an international incident?'

'I doubt whether it is the KGB. Hang on, old chap.'

There were two sharp whip-crack bangs from the outside and the whine of high-velocity bullets. Then there was the sound of a car engine accelerating, but he couldn't be sure where it came from. Vanessa moved forward in the direction of the window. 'Keep away from that window,' Xavier said.

'But I want to see what's going on.'

'If you can see them, they can see you.' It was the old story of the amateur; she really believed that whoever had been firing at the window wouldn't fire at her because she was only a spectator. It didn't make any difference how many non-combatants were killed; people like Vanessa would continue to believe that bullets couldn't harm them. Droylsden spoke again.

'It's all right now. He's gone.'

'Why the hell didn't your boys kill him?'

'We want information in this case.'

'A lot of information can be got from a corpse.'

Droylsden chuckled. 'You *are* bloodthirsty, aren't you?'

'I don't like being the bait for a trap. And I don't like being regarded as expendable.'

'You never were in any danger, believe me.'

'Just tell me about it in advance next time, that's all. Do you want me to come to HQ?'

'If we want you, we'll let you know. Our boys will be out there looking after you. They'll pick you up whenever you're ready. See you tomorrow.'

Xavier grimaced and hung up. He twitched the curtain away a fraction from the window: the white Audi had gone.

'Is it safe now?' Vanessa asked.

He lit a cigarette. 'As safe as ever it will be.'

'I hope you realise that the place will be swarming with police soon.'

'The police have already been informed. They won't come unless we ask them.'

'Supposing it gets into the papers?'

'It won't.' He slumped into a brown leather armchair.

'Supposing, just for the sake of argument, that it does?'

'Then whoever's responsible will be very sorry.'

She came over and sat on the arm of his chair. Her eyes were very bright. They were sea-green and wide-set and almost hypnotic; he hadn't seen eyes quite like them before. 'Couldn't they be after me?'

'It's a possibility.' He stroked her thigh; the lamé had a slight agreeable roughness contrasting with the smooth flesh underneath. 'If it's FIST, I've been underestimating them all along.'

'What will you do?'

'I rather expect that I'll kill them.'

She stood up and pulled her jacket over her head, then unfastened her trousers and kicked off her silver sandals. 'You can help me with the rest if you like.'

'I'd enjoy doing that.'

As he unfastened her brassiere and gently kissed each breast, he felt strangely helpless, directed by forces outside himself. He couldn't help but be delighted with the softness of her small breasts and the hardness of her extraordinarily large nipples: the delight sent its accustomed message to his loins; but there was a part of him which remained aloof, which felt as if he were a child ordered to play with its train set whilst the adults got on with an adult job. Kneeling, he pulled off Vanessa's plain white pants and stayed kneeling for a moment, his cheek against the fuzz of fair hair, as light as the hair of her head.

She pressed his head closer to herself. 'Aren't I pretty?'

He moved his hands down from her waist to her buttocks, soft but firm, then, very delicately and lightly, between her thighs. 'I love you,' he said. It never did any harm, it might even turn out to be true and it somehow helped to keep his conscience from interfering with his enjoyment.

'It's nice of you to say so,' she said. She sighed and took hold of his hands pressing them upwards in front of her between her legs. 'Darling, how many people have you killed?'

He looked up at her sharply and realised that it wasn't only his masculinity that was turning her on.

# ELEVEN
## *4 June 1974: 5.00–5.30 Hours*

Xavier was in the middle of a crowd which filled the cobbled square. He couldn't move, he found it difficult to breathe. He was looking upwards at the building which took up one side of the square. It was old and grey, a shade darker than the sky above it. He didn't know quite what he was looking at, until he realised that it was the slender tower on the left of the building, protruding from its roof. This was the trumpeter's tower: he had to listen to the trumpeter. The black-robed figure appeared at the window, the tocsin rang out, triumphant but sad, the crowd waved, the trumpeter waved and disappeared. Xavier didn't know where he was, but it was cold and he was far from home and he had listened to the trumpeter and had learned nothing. The building with a tower on top was a church. A message had to be delivered inside the church, but what was the message? Everyone in the crowd was wearing furs, they were advancing towards him, and there was nowhere to hide. Shirley Mason was standing beside him naked, she was pointing at him, she was talking in a language he didn't know; he reached for his gun but it wasn't there and he awoke in a large brass-railed bed to pick up the 'phone, hear Droylsden's identification number and perform the necessary mental acrobatics to work out his own identification number for the day.

'Aslan wants you. Trumpkin's been found.'

'Call him Tom now. I take it he's dead?'

'Couldn't be much deader. Burned to a crisp.' Droylsden's voice was brisk and cheerful.

'I was expecting it.' He pushed the dream from his mind; just before it disappeared he identified the place: Cracow and the rotten job he was given there five years ago. 'Shall I make my own way to HQ?'

'Tweedledum and Tweedledee will collect you in twenty minutes. They'll ring three times and then signal D in Morse.'

'Most efficient. Are Tweedledee and Tweedledum their code names?'

'For the time being. They're recent additions.'

'Are you leaving anyone to take their place? The lady's rather nervous.' He looked at the sleeping Vanessa with tenderness: she lay perfectly still under the white lace coverlet, her arms at her side, her face composed in a way it was not when she was awake. It was a face under discipline, he thought with surprise.

'That's all been taken care of. I hope you've impressed it upon her not to go to the police.'

'Naturally.' Xavier yawned, and looking at his wrist-watch – 5 a.m. He yawned again.

'You've time to wash your face and say goodbye to the lady. Or even for a quickie.' Droylsden snickered and hung up.

Xavier hurried into his trousers and socks and shoes and leaned over Vanessa and opened an eyelid. She was awake immediately. He looked at her and realised what was unusual about them: the whites, so clear as to have a blue tinge, seemed entirely to be visible, not merely visible at the left and right of the pupils.

'Darling, where are you going?'

He kissed her cheek; she smelled pleasantly of perspiration and sleep. 'Something rather urgent's come up. I have to go.'

'Take my car if you like . . . If you really must go . . .'

'I really must. Transport has been arranged.'

He went over to the washbowl in the corner of the room and sluiced his face with cold water, reflecting as he did so how reliable this minor pleasure was.

Vanessa came up behind him and rubbed herself against his back. He felt her hardening nipples and an answering tautness in his loins, but did not turn round. She walked away. 'There's a razor and shaving cream on the shelf above the washbasin. Though I think you look rather nice with that blue-black beard.'

He turned towards her; she had now put on a white travelling bathrobe and was lighting a cigarette. There was a curiously domestic quality about the moment; he could have been her husband setting off for an early flight. 'The man I'm going to see now wouldn't think so,' he said.

'Dear old Cousin Piers? He's very unconventional.'

'I hadn't thought of him as Piers.' He rubbed in the Palmolive shaving cream; its clean, agreeably old-fashioned barber's-shop smell was another reliable pleasure.

'You were rather good value last night. Twice before supper, and twice after supper.' She looked at him with an amused affection and he was surprised to find that he was happy. 'I wish you didn't have to go.'

'I'm not always as good as that. It depends upon the person.' The razor was new; he was pleased to find that his hand was absolutely steady.

'I could do without you saying an Act of Contrition afterwards, though.'

He laughed. 'It's a habit, darling. Covering my bets . . .'

'Cousin Piers values you very highly.'

'That's most flattering. But I still want you to keep very quiet about what I do.'

'Don't worry. I told you I've been brought up to keep my mouth shut.' She went to the large old mahogany wardrobe and took out a white shirt. She held it out to him whilst he rinsed his face. 'Take this, darling.'

He hesitated. 'I don't really like –'

'He never wore the damned thing. Bought everything by the dozen.'

'Who's he?' He looked inside the shirt. 'My size anyway.'

'I like large men. He was my second husband actually.'

'I'm sorry.'

'Why be sorry? He was a super-sod, and that's putting it mildly.'

He put on the shirt; it was Sea Island cotton and the label was Harrods. 'I'm still sorry,' he said. 'It can't have been fun for you.'

She picked up the shirt he'd discarded the night before and held it against her face. 'I never think about it now,' she said. 'He married again. He has custody of our daughter.' She sniffed at his discarded shirt. 'It's lovely and sweaty. Do you want some coffee?'

'There won't be time. Get some sleep. There's someone keeping an eye on you.'

The doorbell rang three times, then one long, two short. He kissed her; in the loose white gown she seemed younger and more vulnerable. 'I'll see you soon,' he said.

'See you soon.' She smiled at him, still clutching his shirt.

Tweedledum and Tweedledee seemed unaffected by their vigil; they had even had a shave. They weren't twins; the one he decided to call Tweedledum had black hair, and Tweedledee had

brown hair, and Tweedledum had thinner features than Tweedledee who was slightly inclined to plumpness. They were now
wearing black anoraks and sweaters, which he didn't seem to
remember them wearing the night before. They each had the
same expression; hard, watchful, surprised by nothing, having
seen too much. They had, he supposed, saved his life: a Sten
Mark 25 would have blasted the back-door lock with one shot.
But if he'd not been absolutely certain of who'd sent them,
nothing would have persuaded him to get in the same car with
them.

'Relief arrived?' he asked them, shading his eyes against the
morning sun.

Tweedledum jerked his thumb towards the entrance of the
mews. 'Naturally, Major. We can't leave until it does arrive.' His
accent was basically Cockney, but at some time he'd sandpapered
the rough edges.

Xavier walked over to the Jaguar. There was a trace of chill-
iness in the air, but it hadn't yet become laden with carbon
monoxide, and somewhere he could hear birds singing. Settling
down in the back seat of the Jaguar, looking out at the cobbled
square with the white houses glistening with fresh paint – they
wouldn't in an area like this be allowed to let property grow
shabby – he felt for a moment a deep conviction that everything
was going to be better not only for him but for his country, that
whatever happened at HQ it would for once make sense. He said
a quick Our Father to himself and a quick Act of Contrition to be
on the safe side, and leaned well back, attempting to be as little
visible as possible.

'Any signs of activity during the night?' he asked.

'Not a thing. The bugger wasn't going to stay when he realised
there was two of us.'

'Pity you didn't get him.'

'We weren't instructed to start a gunfight, Major. Just to protect you,' Tweedledum said.

'If we'd chased his car, we might have got him. Might have got
a lot of other people too.'

'I'm not complaining,' Xavier said. They were travelling fast
down Holland Road now, with no other vehicle in sight. 'Hope
he doesn't take any more pot-shots at me, that's all.'

'It's all in the day's work, Major,' Tweedledee said, turning far too fast into Kensington High Street. He giggled suddenly.

'Yes, it's all in my day's work,' Xavier said. 'By the way, I haven't seen you two before.'

'We haven't had the privilege of seeing you before, either,' Tweedledum said. 'We'd have remembered you, Major – you have real style.'

Tweedledee giggled again. 'We don't often have the pleasure of meeting gentlemen like you, Major. You're what they call a man of distinction.'

'It doesn't really matter,' Xavier said. 'But we needn't make a meal of it, need we?' He smiled, took out his cigarettes and handed Tweedledum the packet. 'Light your own.' His hand in his pocket encountered the Baby Browning; he moved back the safety-catch.

# TWELVE
# *4 June 1974: 6.00–6.30 Hours*

Xavier felt a spasm of nausea as he looked at the large shiny print of the burned-out wreck of a car with a charred figure slumped forward in the driving seat. Its features were not recognisable.

'Are you sure it's Tom?' he asked Aslan who, spruce and rosy as ever, was sipping tea.

Aslan took out a dental cast of a large manilla envelope. The teeth the cast had been taken from had evidently been large and unflawed. 'No doubt at all, my dear Xavier. This is the one sure method of identification. Teeth are very hard to destroy. The skin on a chap's fingers and thumbs isn't.'

'I'd be grateful if you'd put it back.'

'Of course.' Aslan swept the cast back into the envelope and wiped his hands on a large white handkerchief. 'Would you like a drink?'

Xavier shook his head.

'I don't think any the worse of you for being upset, I assure you.'

'You're a trifle squeamish for our particular line of work,' Droylsden said.

Aslan went over to the walnut drinks cabinet, poured out two small glasses of brandy, gave one to Xavier and sipped at one himself. 'Drink that, Xavier, and that's an order.' He turned to Droylsden, frowning. 'I don't want machines. That's the big mistake the opposition makes. They try to turn people into machines and they break down. Or take to drink and drugs.'

'Sorry I spoke,' Droylsden's tone was surly.

'Speak by all means, my dear chap. Then I can find out what a bloody fool you are and take measures to correct it.'

Xavier sipped his brandy; gradually the nausea subsided. Aslan had said exactly the right thing; Aslan, with all his faults, had understood that one couldn't always guarantee to be blasé about violent death. 'I don't like it when chaps on our side are killed,' he said. 'The question is who killed him?'

'I'm almost certain it's FIST,' Aslan said. 'The goings-on last night virtually confirm it. But I'm not *absolutely* sure.' He smiled. 'Don't look so vexed, my dear Xavier. It's very dangerous to jump to conclusions. Unless I proceed cautiously I can find myself in the shit, to put it mildly.'

'I'm vexed, sir, because there seems a strange contrast between the way I've been looked after and the way in which Tom was allowed to bugger off on his own. When did it happen?'

'Last night, about midnight. At Hook Heath, near Woking.'

Xavier glanced at the sheaf of typescript on Aslan's desk. 'You've been quick just the same. How did the police find out it was Tom?'

'If you think for just one moment, you'll work it out,' Droylsden said. 'You must have had a very tiring night. The police were looking for Tom's car. They had the number.'

Xavier put down his brandy. 'Knock it off.' He put his hand into his pocket to rest on the Browning for a split second, then withdrew it and picked up his brandy again. 'You have a nasty tongue and you'd better watch it.'

'That's true,' Aslan said. 'On the other hand, Xavier, you have too quick a temper. If you want to live to draw your pension, you'd better learn to keep your cool. Please continue, Hugh, and kindly refrain from sarcasm.'

'As luck would have it, a police car came by soon after the explosion,' Droylsden said, keeping his eyes away from Xavier. 'The copper thought that there was something funny about it, so we got the number straightaway. We don't always, human nature being what it is. On the face of it, Drage went out of control and hit a tree. Knocked himself out, despite the safety-belt, the car blows up, he's burned to death. OK, it happens sometimes. But he hadn't struggled –'

'Just tell me how he died,' Xavier broke in. 'I've already inferred it wasn't as accident.'

'Inferred? That's a good word, Xavier,' Aslan said 'Tom died of a knife wound through the heart. It was sheer luck our finding it. And first-rate work on the part of our local chaps.'

'It seems a bit amateurish,' Xavier said.

'Indeed it is. But Tom is dead just the same. And we can't be certain how much he's told them. Which is one of the reasons for

108

no-one in the Department knowing more than they need know. And for your carrying Exit One at all times. *At all times.*'

'Rothgar is in FIST?'

'Yes, indeed. We persuaded him to tell us all in the end. He's no-one of any consequence – a lecturer in the social sciences, if you please – but quite intelligent. A little naïve; he keeps reverting to his bourgeois liberal origins. It's quite all right for him to apply force to other people, but he screams blue murder when it's used on him.'

'Did he know about what they proposed to do with Tom?'

'He had a shrewd idea that Tom was going to be eliminated. But *you* were the one he had to look after. Their general principles are sound, very sound. He doesn't really know what happened to Tom. He was given your address on Monday afternoon and full instructions. Unfortunately,' Aslan grinned, 'I mean unfortunately for them, they couldn't get hold of a gun in time.'

'He might have pulled off the job with a gun.' Droylsden said thoughtfully. 'On the other hand, a knife's much quieter.'

Aslan crossed over to the drinks cabinet and poured himself a large brandy. His step was positively springy, and he exuded a positive well-being: it was difficult to believe that he had been up all night interrogating Rothgar and sorting out Tom's death; both of which jobs, Xavier thought, were exhausting even when you extracted enjoyment from them.

'Someone in the Kensington area must have acquired information about you very quickly, Xavier,' he said. 'And your address must have been extracted from Tom pretty quickly.'

'Maybe they had it before.' Xavier stood up. 'You don't have the right to assume that.'

Aslan lifted up a large white hand. 'Calm down. Maybe they did have it before. They're very clever people and they have a lot of money behind them.'

Xavier finished his brandy. 'You don't seem to have got a lot out of Rothgar.'

'He doesn't know very much. They use the good old cell system. Very professional.'

'Not quite, sir,' Droylsden said. 'They're a mixture of professional and amateur. They were very clever about tailing Xavier and Drage on Friday and they even left somebody at West By-fleet to find out just what had happened. But the attempt to eliminate Xavier was most ill-conceived. It needed at least two people and, as I said before, they both should have had guns.'

'You needn't sound so disapproving,' Xavier said. 'I'm damned glad he is an amateur.'

'Don't be, my boy,' Aslan said. 'One generally can predict what a professional will do. Professionals know what's impossible. Amateurs don't. Sometimes they do the impossible.'

'Not very often.' A photo of Henry Kissinger and Golda Meir, arm-in-arm, their faces idiotically cheerful, obviously about to sing a duet, had replaced the photo of Hitler: suddenly he didn't find it, or the other photos, amusing.

'Often enough to worry me. Rothgar's strategy – or let's say FIST's strategy – was excellent. Their tactics were rather sloppy. It was all left to Rothgar.'

'Even then he could have been lucky,' Droylsden said.

'But Xavier has had the experience and he hasn't. So now Xavier is alive and well and having it off with young ladies, and John – we've become very close – is meeting another villain. In the shape of Wanda. He won't expect her to be rough with him. But she will. My word, yes, she'll sort him out . . .' He smiled. 'Force, Insurrection, Sabotage, Terrorism. He'll find out all about force . . . By the way, Xavier, Hugh tells me that you were a shade, well, uppity about our interrogation methods. However briefly, you mounted a moral high horse. I wouldn't like to think that it could become a habit. And I do hope that you'll take your little pills if ever the occasion should arise.'

'Don't worry, sir,' Droylsden said. 'I'm sure he'll be able to find a tame Jesuit to produce unanswerable arguments in favour of this particular pill.' There was a sneer in his voice.

'I'll never try to prove how good I am at bearing pain. Is that enough?' With an effort Xavier kept his tone neutral.

'I'm sure that you'll be sensible about it, dear boy. Should you ever be in that position.' Aslan's voice was soothing.

'But you're still squeamish about really efficient interrogation,' Droylsden said.

'I'm not keen on using torture.'

'Neither am I,' Aslan said. 'Any fool can use torture. Either you go so far that you kill them or you frighten them so much that they tell you whatever they think you want to hear. But you're alive because we persuaded Rothgar to tell us he was in FIST.'

'There's something you should know which you're not going to like very much,' Droylsden said. The sneer had left his voice. 'We think that FIST knows a good bit about you.'

'How much?' The room suddenly oppressed him. Despite the tea and the brandy and the professional camaraderie which Aslan always managed to generate, he felt as if under interrogation himself.

'That's what we're working on. Some of the things they know they're welcome to know. Like the location of this establishment. I mean, everyone knows that the CIA's at the Pentagon and the KGB at Number Two, Dzerzhinsky Square, but what good does that do them?'

'We needn't advertise ourselves, just the same,' Xavier said. 'Sir Geoffrey knows too much. His daughter knows too much. I'm wondering who else knows too much. And why you bothered to provide me with any cover.'

'You *do* believe in being frank, don't you, Xavier? As for cover – it's insurance. It still can be useful. But Sir Geoffrey and his daughter – and his son, whom you haven't had the pleasure of meeting – must know who you are and what you are.' Aslan grinned. 'You're on close terms with the daughter already, aren't you?'

'You weren't told to be, incidentally,' Droylsden said.

Aslan held up his hand. 'He wasn't indeed, but it does no harm. A great deal of information can be acquired between the sheets. I'm sure that he can manage a closer acquaintance with Miss Rowmarsh too.' He laughed. 'Just close your eyes and do it for England, Xavier,' he said. 'Not that you need close your eyes. She's not at all bad looking.'

'Putting that matter aside, what do you want me to do at Morgate's?'

'I want you to take your instructions from Sir Geoffrey.'

'Frankly, I think he's a bit of a nutter.'

'Most successful business men are. You'll clear all his instructions with me, of course. But basically I want you – with help, naturally – to eliminate all the key members of FIST.'

'My concern is with Soviet illegals.'

'You're not going to discontinue that, my dear chap. Our information now is that there's a link-up.'

'It's too vague, it's too indiscriminate –'

'I decide that, Xavier.' He frowned. 'Christ, what's up with you? We're talking about an organisation which has made two attempts to kill you in one day. It isn't a debating society.'

Xavier had been increasingly feeling tobacco-hunger – a causeless irritability, a very faint dizziness, a sensation of vision and hearing being a shade too acute, an intimation of depression. He gave in and lit a cigarette.

'All right,' he said. 'I just want to make it understood that I'm not a Mafia hit man. Whatever the bright boys say, we're not just the same as the other side.'

Aslan smiled. 'I agree with you absolutely, Xavier. Let's have another very small brandy, we deserve it.'

He poured one out for Droylsden this time; and as Droylsden raised his glass Xavier noticed a spot of blood on the other cuff of his shirt.

# THIRTEEN
## *5 June 1974: 8.30–9.00 Hours*

Peter Dykenhead rinsed the two plates, two cups and saucers, two knives and two spoons and put them in the Miele dishwasher which stood beside the sink. It wasn't worth the trouble of putting in the detergent. The Robinsons were coming for dinner that evening and Lorna would be able to refuse Sue Robinson's offer of help with the washing-up in her usual phrase – No need, darling, *we've got a mechanical slave*. It always gave her a kick; though one would have thought that by now the Robinsons would have known that they had a dishwasher.

It didn't seem so long ago that it was loaded twice a day and every flat surface in the kitchen was littered with used plates and mugs and empty Coke tins and jars with their lids off. He put away the pot of Frank Cooper's Oxford marmalade and the toast-rack in the appropriate cupboards, the butter dish in the refrigerator, and wiped the orange Formica top of the kitchen table. With the orange Hygena units, orange and white tiles, orange curtains, the white ceiling and walls, and the white refrigerator and spin dryer and new split-level gas cooker, it looked like a picture from *Homes and Gardens*. Lorna didn't have enough to do now; he had virtually forced her to go back to her old job in London to save her sanity.

He didn't have to rush; he sat down at the kitchen table and lit a cigarette. To the left of him he could see the front garden and the three oak trees which had given the house its name. The house stood at the end of a narrow lane off the Guildford Road between Prey Heath Road and Saunders Lane; it had no neighbours, which was the reason for him buying it originally, but now more and more, particularly in the evenings, he wondered if he'd made the right decision. Though they were so near Guildford and Woking, he felt somehow or other out of the main current of life. He crossed over to the Golden Labrador lying by the back door. She rose and nuzzled his hand; he patted her smooth head, then opened the back door. She ran out into the sunlight, scampered round the garden, then urinated at her favourite spot by the weeping willow on the right. This was part of his daily routine; she was let out into the garden as soon as he left the house. Sometimes he and Lorna worried about her being lonely, but there was plenty of space for her in the garden and she had a kennel in case it rained. But it wasn't the same as having Lorna there all day.

The garden looked marvellous, he thought; the lawn had become or at least was becoming really sleek; which was what happened when it was mown and rolled and watered regularly and not used very much. The dog stiffened and growled; he heard a car engine and saw through the front window a black Ford Granada estate car. The doorbell rang.

Two men stood at the front door, both large, at least six inches over his five foot eight. One was middle-aged, with a pale sagging face and a tired expression: the other was in his early twenties, with a thin deeply-tanned face which didn't seem to have any expression at all. Both wore grey suits, white shirts and brown leather gloves; for some reason Dykenhead found this disturbing. The dog, suddenly beside him, growled deep in her throat.

'Be quiet, Goldie.'

'Mr Peter Dykenhead?' the elder man asked.

Dykenhead nodded.

'This is my warrant card. Sergeant Chambers. Thames Valley Police. This is Constable Brown. May we come in?'

'I'm just going to my office, Sergeant –'

'We won't take long, sir.'

Somehow he found himself in the sitting-room, Goldie still growling beside him, Chambers and Brown facing him.

'Oh my God,' he said, 'is it my wife?'

'No, no, sir, nothing to worry about at all. Nothing to do with your wife.'

'Or your sons,' the other said.

Dykenhead caught sight of himself in the mirror above the fireplace: a grey-haired man with a lined face, too lined even for fifty-three, thin, neat, a sedentary worker, a small helpless figure beside the two policemen. He glanced at the Granada outside.

'Why aren't you in a police car?'

A gun appeared in Brown's hand.

'You'll have to come with us,' Chambers said. 'Please don't try

114

anything. *He* likes shooting people. I don't.' He took Dykenhead's arm, gently but firmly; 'Come on, Mr Dykenhead.'

Goldie leapt at Chambers; there was a sharp crack and a smell of cordite and her forehead seemed to disintegrate into a mess of white and grey and pale yellow, and her jaws were forced apart by a high-pitched whine. There was another sharp crack and her writhing subsided. The grip on Dykenhead's arm tightened.

'You filth,' he said. 'You dirty murdering filth,' and threw himself at Brown only to be stopped short by a shattering blow in the kidneys.

'Shame about that,' said Chambers. 'Only natural for the dog to behave as she did. I'd sit down if I were you, Mr Dykenhead. You'll be better in a moment. Ronnie, you'd better get some of that PVC sheeting from the car and take the dog with us. In fact, take it now.'

'Jesus, the fucking thing'll weigh a ton. You might give me a hand.'

'I'll have to stay with Mr Dykenhead.' He held out his hand to Dykenhead. 'Give me your car keys, Mr Dykenhead. And the garage keys. Thank you.' He put the keys in his pocket and frowned at Brown. 'Do what I say, Ronnie. I won't tell you again.' He sat down opposite Dykenhead; as with the younger man, it appeared as if his gun actually grown out of his hand. Brown picked Goldie up. 'When you come back, Ronnie, you'll have to clean up that carpet,' Chambers said. 'There's blood on it.'

Dykenhead stared at him. His face was absolutely placid: emotion was no more to be expected from it than from the gun in his hand. In situations like this you were always supposed to feel that it was some horrible dream, but he knew very well that it wasn't, that for no reason at all violence had come into his life, had taken over his house, that there was blood on the carpet and cordite mixing with the smell of furniture polish and that there was no help and no hope of help.

'You've made a mistake,' he said. 'I haven't any money. I haven't any involvement with politics –'

'We're all involved in politics,' Chambers said. He glanced into the garden. 'You've some lovely iris there, Mr Dykenhead. You do right to keep it together. Is that Blue Shimmer there in the centre?'

'Look, what the hell do you want? I've got absolutely nothing to give you. You've made an awful mistake –'

'You're Peter Dykenhead, age fifty-three, height five foot eight, grey hair, regular features, Deputy Manager of the Export Department at Morgate's? Of course you are. I've come to fetch you.'

'About what? To see whom? Are you mad?' Dykenhead's voice rose to a scream.

Brown came back, breathing heavily.

'Get a damp rag from the kitchen and wipe up that mess, Ron,' Chambers said. 'And be quick about it. Take away the rag with you. When Mrs Dykenhead returns, we don't want there to be any trace of our visit. He's a good boy, Mr Dykenhead, but he's like all his generation. He isn't thorough.'

'What will it take for you to let me go? You can always say I wasn't in –'

Chambers shook his head. 'No, no. Not for a million pounds, Mr Dykenhead. We wouldn't live to spend it. It's not just that, either. It's like this – do you remember *Great Expectations*, Mr Dykenhead? Of course you do –'

Dykenhead fished in his pocket for a cigarette.

'What are you doing?'

'Getting a cigarette.'

'I don't see why not. Now, I want a smoke myself – I always have one about this time. But I mightn't smoke the same brand as you, and I might forget the stub. And somebody might notice.'

Brown came into the room with a rag and a bucket and knelt down, still scowling. 'I don't see why I always get these fucking rotten jobs.'

'Because you're a young ignorant shit and I'm ten times cleverer than you. Shut up and get on with it.' The tone was suddenly cold. He turned smiling to Dykenhead. 'He'll learn, won't he, Mr Dykenhead? But then you have sons yourself . . . Well, in *Great Expectations*, this convict, Magwitch, escapes and he makes the little boy Pip bring him food and so on. And he says words to this effect.' He leaned back, the gun still pointed at Dykenhead, but with an expression of quiet enjoyment: ' "You may think I'm a hard man, but I have a young man with me compared with whom I am a werry angel" – of course I can't do the accent. And he tells the boy that if he informs on him that that young man will tear his heart and liver out and eat them . . . Wonderful stuff, Mr Dykenhead, wonderful stuff! To cut a long story short, Mr Dykenhead, that's how it is with us. Ron and I are horrible, let's face it, Mr Dykenhead. But we're angels compared with the people who employ us. If we don't deliver you, there won't be any excuses. In fact, if we couldn't deliver you, we'd shoot ourselves.'

Dykenhead suddenly had an impulse to cry. He found himself thinking of Lorna and his sons and the tears weren't for himself but for them. 'I don't see why you can't tell me what this is all about.' His voice, he was surprised to discover, was quite steady.

'It isn't my concern, Mr Dykenhead. We deliver, like the post office. But we're rather quicker. Though to be fair, we're much more expensive . . .' He scowled at Brown. 'Do bloody well get on with it, Ron. And wash out the bucket and put it back exactly where you found it . . . Just take your coat off and roll up your right sleeve, please, Mr Dykenhead. Cover him, Ron.' His voice was now crisp and impersonal. He got up with surprising speed and came over to Dykenhead, a hypodermic in his hand. 'Don't be alarmed, Mr Dykenhead. This isn't fatal and it isn't addictive –'

Ron snickered. 'That won't be a problem for him.'

'Shut up, Ron. Or *you'll* have some problems when we deliver. It won't hurt, Mr Dykenhead, just a pinprick –'

There was no means of resisting and no sense in resisting, only the pain of the needle, much more than a pinprick, and a sensation of heaviness and coldness and a distortion of vision, the room suddenly enlarging and the sunlight dazzling unbearably then a sudden descent, the pale weary sagging face above him liquifying, the light dwindling to a point, then darkness and voices speaking in a strange language in the darkness and the sound of a car engine and the smell of tarpaulin and petrol and blood.

# FOURTEEN

## *5 June 1974: 10.30–11.30 Hours*

The walls of Brian Morgate's office were oak-panelled to waist
height and plain white above, except for the side facing the desk,
which, rather incongruously, was almost entirely taken up by a
huge picture window. The red carpeting was of the same pattern
and texture and degree of shabbiness as the carpeting which
Xavier had noticed in Sir Geoffrey's London house. The furniture was dark, Victorian, and solid. There was a large coloured
print of the 1974 Morgate 1200, a large sepia-tinted photograph
of Everard Morgate, the founder of the firm, who looked like Sir
Geoffrey with mutton-chop whiskers and a high stiff collar, and a
group portrait of the Board of Directors. On the faces of ten of the
twenty directors (among whom he was amused to see Vanessa,
trim and demure in a dark dress with a white collar) could be seen,
whether young, old or middle-aged, male or female, the unmistakable Morgate cast of feature – thin, fierce, with a trace of
humour. When Brian Morgate came forward to shake Xavier's
hand, Xavier saw, with some irritation, that he stood four inches
above him. He was Xavier's age but, Xavier reflected, looked
older; he had about him an expression of strain. His father's
features were all there, but diluted, softened, blurred, not ef-
feminate but not strongly masculine; his hair, razor-cut and
brushed straight down in a fringe over his forehead, gave the
impression of being pale because of lack of vitality rather than
positively fair. The light-grey silk suit, like the broad blue striped
linen shirt with the large chunky gold cufflinks and the gleaming
casuals in a brown so dark as to be always hovering on the verge
of black, was obviously made to measure; the wide silk tie was an
exact match for the worried blue eyes.

'Do sit down, Major Flynn.' His voice was deep and rever-
berant, as well it might be, Xavier thought, with a chest measure-
ment which must have been at least forty-six inches. It matched
his size, but didn't seem to belong to him, as if assumed to give
him authority. 'There are cigarettes at your elbow.'

'I'll smoke my own.' Xavier lit a Silk Cut King Size. 'They don't kill you quite as rapidly.'

'Don't you believe it. We've an old chap on our estate – used to be our chief gardener – and he's fit as a fiddle. Smokes forty Capstan Full Strength a day. Got the hell of a cough, though . . .'

He drew a sheaf of typescript towards him. 'You want to see Dykenhead in Export, don't you? Of course, you know your own business, but I can't really see why.'

'It's something which he may be able to clear up. A minor point.'

'In that case, see our indispensable Mrs Alvaston.' There seemed to be a note of resentment in his voice. 'Nothing she doesn't know. You could even try me.' Now the note of resentment was unmistakable.

'He saw Tom Drage on Friday night. I want to know what he saw him about.'

Morgate took out a cigarette from the silver box, tapped it on a manicured nail – Xavier noticed small white flecks on the nail – for an unnecessary forty-five seconds. 'Dykenhead knows nothing about FIST, Major.' He lit the cigarette with a tortoise shell and gold Dupont lighter. 'He is a sound, reliable chap, been with us twenty-five years, but keeping the exports flowing is his *only* concern. He's a bit of an old woman, actually. One wouldn't want to frighten him.'

'He must have had something to tell Tom Drage.'

Morgate flipped through the typescript. His hand seemed to be trembling. 'Nothing about it here. I must say I'm not very pleased about it. Why not see me? Or my father? Or any of the other directors?' His tone was not so much angry as petulant. 'Really, Major, you should wait until my father comes in.'

'I'd rather see Dykenhead now, if you don't mind.'

'Very well, then.' Morgate lifted the 'phone. 'I'd be much obliged, Miss Stevens, if you'd put me in touch with Mr Dykenhead. What? I see. Thank you.' He put the 'phone down. 'He hasn't turned up.' He frowned. 'Very odd. If he were ill, he'd have let us know. He's very much that sort of chap. Conscientious. But I'm not pleased with him. Why not come to us? We're not unapproachable.'

'He must have had his reasons, which Tom Drage would have known.'

'It's terrible news about Drage. Terrible.' Morgate sighed. 'He's not the first young chap to miscalculate with a fast car and he won't be the last.'

'He was the original boy racer. I like the MG V8 myself, but it's unforgiving if you don't use your brains.'

'And so it goes. But we've got to carry on . . .' He sighed. 'I only hope that nothing's happened to Dykenhead. Probably had a breakdown and he's fuming miles away from a 'phone.'

'He lives on the Guildford side of Woking. He shouldn't be very far from help wherever he is. How late is he?'

'Forty-five minutes now. Really not like him at all . . .'

'What is like him?'

'If he were ill, he'd have 'phoned. If he'd been delayed for any reason, he'd have 'phoned. Not that the occasion has ever arisen. I don't think that he's ever been late.'

'You'd better get in touch with the police straightaway. Give them this number for authorisation' – he gave Morgate a six-figure number slowly and distinctly – 'and his wife's office number, then tell them to check at his home and put out a general alarm.'

Morgate gave him an aggrieved look and picked up the 'phone again. Xavier didn't bother to listen to what Morgate was saying on the 'phone; the tiny tape-recorder sewn into the lining of his breast pocket would take care of it anyway. What was Aslan playing at? Couldn't he see that whatever information Dyken-head had must be valuable to whoever killed Tom? What was the old fool trying to do? Prove that FIST really meant business?

Morgate put the 'phone down. 'Must say that that number worked like a charm. Everything's in hand.' He cleared his throat. 'I think we ought to be frank with each other, Major. We don't really want you to investigate. Your superiors don't want you to investigate. The Cothill Detective Agency is already doing just that. And we own a piece of the action in that agency. In fact, we own it. We have undercover agents working in this factory and in other factories within the Group. And in FIST itself. Look behind you, Major.'

Xavier glanced over his shoulder through the picture window.

'Ten acres of buildings, Major. Five thousand workers. We have a subsidiary in Birmingham, and we have associates who supply us with all our needs. If FIST attacks anywhere else we're

120

in trouble, but this is the heart of the business. The acts of sabotage which have taken place already could have set us back very badly, but we have damned good workers and we're also renowned for paying cash on the nail for any jobs which are done for us. So we've survived: but FIST isn't going to let us survive if they can help it. Once the 1200 ceases to be delivered, the Japs and the Italians and the Germans will leap into the gap. My God, it doesn't bear thinking of. They'll murder us, they'll ruin us –' He pulled out the white silk handkerchief from his breast pocket and wiped his brow. There was for a moment the smell of fear above his expensive cologne. 'Everything gone for nothing –'

'I'm perfectly aware of the situation,' Xavier said impatiently.

'Major Flynn, Cousin Piers says that you're first-rate at your job, and that's enough for me. But, after all, you've been paid by the Government all your life. All right, you've earned your pay. But it comes in every month regular as clockwork. You're secure. You can't see it as we do – a continual struggle. Even for us.'

'There isn't any need to tell me all this, Mr Morgate. I've taken a course in elementary economics long since.'

'The fact is that we haven't time to deal with FIST through Special Branch. Which is why my father went straight to Cousin Piers. Which is why we've kept quiet about the sabotage. You must understand. We could be in deep trouble so easily –'

The 'phone bleeped. Morgate picked it up. 'Show them in, will you, Miss Stevens. And forage for some coffee, will you?'

He took a deep breath and seemed to recover himself as he put the 'phone down. Droylsden, Vanessa and a stocky middle-aged man whom Xavier hadn't seen before came into the room. As she passed his chair Vanessa laid her hand caressingly on Xavier's shoulder; Morgate saw it and smiled faintly. Xavier glanced at him speculatively: he wasn't the man his father was.

'Please sit down, everybody. This is strictly an informal meeting. No records are being kept and I do assure you that the room isn't bugged. Major Flynn, you've met everyone except Roy Cothill who's the Chief Executive of the Cothill Detective Agency. Mr Cothill is Acting Head of our Security Department.'

Cothill nodded briefly at Xavier. He had iron-grey hair, worn very short, a light-blue suit and, unexpectedly, black suède shoes and a gold Omega Constellation. The blue spotted handkerchief in his breast pocket was silk. His face was deeply lined, the mouth pulled down at the corners. Xavier decided that he didn't like him, but resolved not to show it.

'My father sends his apologies for not being with us today, but has given me full authority to act for him in his absence,' Morgate said. 'My sister will confirm that. Full authority.' He seemed slightly anxious, as if assuming too much; there was a pause and then Vanessa nodded. The sunlight through the big window caught the faint down on her face, dusting it with gold; Xavier felt a spasm of unaffected happiness, then put it out of his mind, turning his attention to Morgate.

'As Mr Cothill has predicted from the beginning, FIST means business,' Morgate said. 'Its business is to *destroy* us. Destroy us utterly.' He thumped his fist upon the desk. 'FIST is not under the illusion that destroying us will mean the end of capitalism in this country, but it will be a good start. They will go on from there.'

'Darling,' Vanessa said, 'I'm not really bothered about what they do *after* they destroy us. What do we do to stop being destroyed?'

'Mr Cothill will tell you that.'

'We already have seven names of FIST members,' Cothill said. His voice was harsh but low-pitched. 'Two are employed in this factory. Here are their photos.' The two small colour prints each showed an unlined, unformed face, medium-length mousy hair, shirts with long points, suits with broad lapels and flared trousers; they might have been twins, except that the one called Benson had a slightly thinner face than the one called Simmons, and had also a heavy crop of acne.

'They look very young,' Xavier said, handing the photos back.

'Benson is twenty, Simmons twenty-one. They work in the Stationery Department along the passage. What has their age to do with it?'

'The IRA uses children,' Droylsden said. 'You'll find full details in the report. Simmons is Humility and Benson is Chastity.'

'I wouldn't have thought he'd have had any other choice with all those spots.'

Vanessa giggled: Morgate frowned.

'We could look at the report now,' Cothill said.

I want to form my own opinion, and I can't do that when you're there. I'll come back to you later if necessary.'

'We don't want you to do anything about Humility and Chastity without telling us,' Cothill said.

'Their code names?' Xavier asked.

'The others are Liberality, Temperance, Brotherly Love, Diligence, and Meekness.'

'The Seven Cardinal Virtues – how odd. I'd like to have a look at Humility and Chastity.'

'The Stationery Department is on the way to your office,' Cothill put the photos in his pocket. 'The five other members of the cell are all employed in this area, with the exception of Diligence, who is employed in Whitehall. We've checked and double-checked them. We've had assistance from your Department, Major. Otherwise we couldn't have done it.'

'Why can't you just give these names to Special Branch?' Xavier asked.

'They haven't any criminal records. They have no association with any political party. What can Special Branch do about it?'

'Are you sure they have sabotage in mind?'

'That is their declared purpose.'

'And you want my Department to stop them –'

The light above the door glowed red and Miss Stevens came in with a tray of coffee. For the first time Xavier noticed that she was a tall blonde in her twenties with full breasts which joggled slightly under her short blue dress. Vanessa grinned at him and raised a finger as if in reproof; he grinned back at her.

The light above the door went out as Miss Stevens left the room; Cothill took a gulp of black coffee, wiped his mouth and said to Xavier, as if there had been no interval in their conversation: 'Yes, we want you to stop them.'

'It's been explained to you already,' Droylsden said. 'I'll take care of clearance with Aslan. We don't want the Board or any of the staff involved any more than is strictly necessary. Necessary, that is, to maintain our cover. No-one outside this room must know what we're here for.'

'We propose to stand above the struggle,' Vanessa said. 'We are not going to enquire how you stop them.' She looked at Xavier. 'Every facility will be given you, Major Flynn.'

123

'I think it might be as well not to use my military title,' Xavier said. 'If we're given the necessary information, Mr Droylsden and I can plan the necessary action.'

'I have the material here,' Droylsden said.

'Nothing must be done on the premises,' Morgate said. 'Is that understood? It's a tempting notion, but it just isn't on. And we don't want any publicity. Whatever you do, we don't want any connection with Morgate's to be established.'

'That will be entirely up to you,' Xavier said. 'Not only must you be most discreet, but you mustn't ask us any questions.'

Morgate flushed. 'We're not stupid, you know: only frightened. And hoping to God' – his voice became waspish – 'that you act more quickly and ruthlessly than the usual Government department . . .' His voice trailed away. 'Sorry, that wasn't very nice of me. But it *is* a matter of survival –'

'Isn't it for us all?' Xavier said. 'Is there anything more?'

'That's it.' Morgate looked suddenly tired. 'There's an office for you down the corridor. Miss Stevens will show you.'

Xavier stood up. 'Mr Droylsden and I will adjourn then.'

He nodded to Morgate and Vanessa and Cothill and went out, followed by Droylsden. The red light came on and the door opened to admit Miss Stevens. He followed her without speaking, reflecting that there was something more he should have said, but Vanessa's cool acceptance of the whole project had shocked him in a way that he hadn't before thought possible. For she knew how FIST would be stopped, he saw it in her eyes.

Miss Stevens preceded them along the narrow cream-painted corridor, her hips swaying slightly, her high heels noisy on the dark brown linoleum. He tapped her on the shoulder. 'I want some stationery,' he said.

'There is all that you'll need there, Mr Flynn.'

'I want some graph paper and some coloured pencils.'

She nodded. 'We'll call in.'

The Stationery Department was a large down-at-heel office with four plain birch desks each with a tattered red swivelling typist's chair and a large plain table and a plain Windsor chair. In the corner stood a new electronic calculating machine which with its glittering chrome and white paint accentuated the shabbiness of the office. A large white jug, a white bowl of sugar, and

124

four white cups and saucers stood on the table amongst a litter of forms. Xavier focused his attention on Humility and Chastity, who were giggling together with a fat middle-aged woman in a sheer white blouse and a thin young girl in a black dress, and after a second he turned to stare out of the window, assuming a bored expression.

He followed Miss Stevens out of the office and down the corridor again, fixing the faces of Humility and Chastity in his mind. She stopped at a frosted-glass door. 'This is your office, Mr Flynn,' she said. 'If there's anything you need, just pick up the 'phone.'

Xavier put his hand under her chin. 'You're very pretty,' he said. 'What we really need is a direct line to London.' Looking at her more closely he revised his estimate of her age to thirty, if not a year or so more.

She returned his gaze, her eyes calm. But there was a consciousness of his signal having been received. 'We've made provision for that, Mr Flynn.' She went inside the office. 'Just pick up the white 'phone to speak to me. The red 'phone gives you a direct line to Exchange. It's a different number, and calls made to that number don't pass through our switchboard.'

'That's fine,' Xavier sat down behind the desk. It was a plain office desk in elm, with an ink-stained and cigarette-scarred top. 'You don't go in for luxury at Morgate's, do you?'

'It isn't the policy of the firm to spend money on frills.' Miss Stevens's voice was noncommittal. 'Will that be all, Mr Flynn?'

'Yes, thank you. Except for your 'phone number.'

She smiled. 'Ask me again tomorrow.'

Xavier grinned. 'Don't worry. I will.'

'I know you will, Mr Flynn.' Her hips were swaying slightly as she left the room.

'I want that frosted-glass door replaced by a steel one – with a mortice lock, and I want Morgate either to change his office or change that window,' Xavier said to Droylsden.

'It's three floors up,' Droylsden said. He was sitting opposite Xavier and had already opened his briefcase – large and battered in brown leather with a crown and BOARD OF TRADE stamped on it in tarnished gold letters – and was taking out a thick sheaf of typescript.

'So is that building opposite three floors up,' Xavier said. 'Though I'm chiefly concerned with my own security. As far as I possess any.'

'I'll arrange it,' Droylsden said. 'Why didn't you bring it up at the meeting?'

'Because I wanted the meeting over with as soon as possible. The less anyone outside the Department knows the better.'

'I should imagine that they know all about it already,' Droylsden said in a bored voice. 'Let's act on the assumption that they don't. *We* are handling the matter. That's all. Let's get on with it.' He slammed the typescript down on the desk. He went to his brief-case again. 'Here's your copy. We get down to the nitty-gritty at page sixty.'

Xavier did not look at his typescript, but stared at the plain yellow distempered walls, blotched slightly with damp, the coconut matting, the wooden filing cabinet, the wooden bookcase crammed with out-of-date *Who's Whos*, *Kelly's Merchant Manufac-turers and Shippers*, the worn brown linoleum and a brand-new Sony portable tape-recorder on a table by the desk. 'I keep wondering what has happened to Dykenhead.'

'The police are making enquiries. Nothing more *we* can do.'

'There might have been if you'd been a little less rough with Rothgar.'

'He got so damaged that he wasn't worth keeping. I made that clear to you this morning.'

'He puzzled me. His hair and his clothes weren't right. They were OK for the majority of ordinary teachers, possibly OK if he'd been in engineering or chemistry. But not quite trendy enough for the social sciences . . .'

'Christ, maybe *you* ought to be in the social sciences, lecturing about class differences. We've got seven people to deal with now, and we have to do it quickly. Because after that there'll be more people to deal with. At least thirty. FIST will then cease to function.'

'Because the survivors will be terribly discouraged, and the links between the cells will be destroyed.' Xavier sighed. 'It sounds so simple. OK, let's work it all out.' He flipped over the pages of the typescript and stopped at page sixty. 'All very re-spectable and bourgeois. Of course, that's what makes the organisation so effective . . .' His eyes widened, and he brought the typescript closer to him. 'Jesus!' He was very pale. 'There's been a balls-up here.'

'You mean Diligence, I expect. That little star means that he's been checked by D15 too.'

'D15 gave Cothill the lead?'

'Through us, naturally. Gathering information is their *raison d'être*, after all.'

'So it goes,' Xavier said bitterly. 'I could do without their bloody information –'

The room was being slowly shaken, there was a diagonal crack in the frosted glass of the door, it was torn away from its hinges with an impossible slowness, to be suspended ten inches above the ground, staying there for a full fifteen seconds, there was noise and smoke and the smell of sulphur and burning paint and the sound of women screaming rising through it, the noise as if expanding inside the head, then only the screams and the door dropping to spray glass over the room and then, for less than a second but seeming longer than a second, absolute silence and the sun through the window at the side of the room opposite the door seeming unnaturally bright. Xavier stood up from behind the desk and bent over Droylsden who was curled up in a foetal position beside his chair.

'Are you OK?' He had a strange feeling of release and calm: this was what it was all about; he was going into action.

Droylsden stood up. 'The bastards,' he said. 'The dirty murdering bastards.' His smooth face was disrupted with anger; he stamped on the floor in unselfconscious rage.

Xavier was already speaking into the white 'phone. The screaming continued; it now seemed more animal than human.

'I'll kill them all!' Droylsden screamed, stamping again.

Xavier smiled at him, feeling for the first time something like fondness towards him, as he recognised that he had, after all, the proper professional reactions: there was anger but no fear.

'We will, Hugh, we will,' he said and spoke again into the telephone, wrinkling his nose at the smell of burning flesh that was now creeping into the room.

# FIFTEEN
## *5 June 1974: 11.30–11.45 Hours*

Dykenhead felt a crushing pain inside his head, then a dazzling light forced his eyes open and he was lying in bed with Chambers sitting at his head in a shabby beige armchair, a gun in his hand. The room was large and smelled faintly musty. The floor was bare; around the walls ran the edging to which the fitted carpet had once been attached. The two large windows were boarded up, but overhead shone an unshaded 150-watt bulb, and beside Chambers was an oak-based standard lamp with another unshaded 150-watt bulb burning.

He stared at Chambers. There didn't seem anything to say or, rather, there seemed too much to say, more than there'd ever be time to say. He didn't know where he was: the faded red and blue wallpaper, the plain pine table on the right of Chambers, the shabby beige armchair and sofa matching the armchair in which Chambers was sitting, lined up in a row on the left, gave him no clues. He had not expected them.

Chambers lit a cigarette; the familiar smell of tobacco was for a second reassuring, then added to his terror. His mouth was very dry.

'Give me a drink.'

There was a decanter of water, a bottle of Martell brandy, and two tumblers on the table. Chambers poured him a glass of water. He drank it thirstily; halfway through he stopped, visualising the glass thrown at the eyes of Chambers, the gun dropping, the feel of the gun, the terror in the eyes of Chambers as he shot him like a dog. Like a dog – and Chambers rose with extraordinary speed and he felt the gun in the centre of his forehead.

'Continue drinking, Mr Dykenhead,' Chambers said. 'Please don't see yourself as the hero of a thriller. James Bond might get out of this situation, but you won't.' He took the gun away from Dykenhead's forehead and sat down again. 'I'm now aiming at your hand'. The result of your throwing that glass that your hand will be very painfully damaged. I have no instructions to kill you yet.'

'I've finished now,' Dykenhead said. 'Take the glass.'

'Just put it down on the table, Mr Dykenhead.'

'I think I'm going to be sick,' Dykenhead said.

Chambers smiled. 'And who shall blame you? Just be sick on the floor. This is Liberty Hall.'

Dykenhead suddenly looked down at himself, his mouth dropping open in shock. 'Where are my clothes?'

'That's a silly question,' Chambers said.

'I'm on a bare mattress. A bare mattress. Are you mad? Jesus, what is this all about?'

'I can't tell you, Mr Dykenhead. I only wish that I could. The fact is that I don't know.'

'What's the idea of taking my clothes?'

'My guess would be that it's because there's an imperative need to demoralise you quickly. So that you won't hold anything back. Particularly for a man like you, nothing could be more humiliating. It even makes you feel – with no good reason – a deep guilt.' Chambers poured an inch of brandy into the glass and sipped it with enjoyment.

'You're not an ordinary criminal, are you?'

'That's most percipient of you, Mr Dykenhead. I was an elementary school teacher originally. Then the cost of living grew higher and higher and my salary didn't increase with it. I am now a traveller – I hate the word representative – for a firm connected with education. That is, as far as my wife and family are concerned.'

'Listen. I don't care how much money you want, I'll get it for you. I give you my word –'

Chambers held up his hand. 'I've told you before, Mr Dykenhead, I can't let you go. Apart from any other consideration, I'd have to kill Brown first. It wouldn't be easy, and there'd be consequences arising from that. Personally, I've nothing against you. You're just another job as far as I'm concerned . . .' He handed Dykenhead a packet of Rothman's King Size and a box of matches. 'I wasn't told that you couldn't smoke. For that matter, you can have some brandy if you like. It'll settle your stomach.'

Dykenhead lit the cigarette, surprised to find his hand steady. He took the glass of brandy that Chambers handed to him. As he sipped the brandy he was overtaken by a numbness of the emotions: there was no hope any more but neither was there fear. This bare room with the boarded windows and the glaring lights was where he had always been.

The door opened: he looked towards it and dropped his glass. 'Oh, God, it can't be you –'

'Pick up his glass and give him another drink, Mr Chambers,' said the man at the door. He sat down. 'We're going to have a good old chin-wag, aren't we, Peter?'

Dykenhead stared at him and then leaned over the side of the bed and vomited.

# SIXTEEN

## *5 June 1974: 12.15–12.45 Hours*

The tangle of metal and plastic which had been a new electronic calculating machine still emitted heat and an acrid smell of paint and cordite: the desk on which it had stood was as if sawn up into separate pieces. On top of the large steel filing cabinet at the far end of the office a typewriter stood on its end. A huge lump of plaster rested on top of a table, in the exact centre as if it had been deliberately placed there. Half of the large room was a litter of broken glass and upended chairs and desks and scattered pieces of paper: the other half, furthest from the calculating machine, was untouched. There were large patches of blood on the wall by the calculating machine and a pool of blood on the floor in the untouched part of the room.

'They're all different, aren't they?' Xavier said to Droylsden. 'You can never be sure about any explosion.'

'It isn't our job to speculate,' Droylsden said. 'And not to speculate conspicuously. We'll get a report later.'

Mrs Alvaston came over to them from the undamaged part of the office where she had been talking in a low voice to Cothill, Sir Geoffrey, Brian Morgate and a young lean man with a sun-tanned face, large RAF moustache, short hair, and a black blazer, who had been introduced to Xavier as Rory Clonmell, the Deputy Security officer. Near the calculating machine a fireman and a middle-aged man in a dark-grey suit were scribbling in identical small black notebooks. Two Morgate security guards, large young men in peaked caps, dark glasses, white shirts, black ties and navy-blue trousers, stood by the door on the right, looking self-consciously tough.

'Sir Geoffrey would like to see you at about three o'clock,' Mrs Alvaston said. 'I've arranged new accommodation for you in Room 27 on the second floor.' Nothing in her speech and bearing indicated that she was standing on the spot where three-quarters of an hour previously two men and two women had died and one woman had been seriously injured.

131

The middle-aged man standing by the calculating machine put his notebook in his pocket and came over to them.

'We've not been properly introduced, have we, gentlemen?'

'Mr Flynn and Mr Droylsden are from the Department of Trade and Industry, Inspector,' Mrs Alvaston said.

'I'm Inspector Robinson.' He looked at Xavier and Droylsden, a faint smile on his face. It was a round cheerful face with a high colour and a large mouth; only the grey eyes were hard and watchful, seeming to belong to another face.

'Mr Flynn and Mr Droylsden are here in their capacity as Export Negotiators,' Mrs Alvaston said. 'They were in the small office along the passage when the explosion occurred.'

'So I've already gathered, Mrs Alvaston. These two gentlemen acted with great presence of mind.' He took out his notebook. 'That young lady – Miss Stevens. You saved her life, Mr Flynn, by applying the tourniquet so quickly.'

Xavier grimaced. 'When she wakes up to find her face blown away, she won't thank me.'

'Terrible, terrible. But you did your best, you can't do any more. There's blood on your hand, Mr Flynn. You aren't hurt, are you?'

'It's not my blood,' Xavier said. 'We shall be here the rest of the day, Inspector, if you want us.'

'I'll let you know if I do.' He looked at them directly with an oddly appraising look. 'If I were you, gentlemen, I'd have a good stiff drink. The shock'll hit you afterwards.'

'We'll take your advice, Inspector,' Xavier said. 'God, what a mess . . .'

'Too true, Mr Flynn. I've to go through this office with a fine tooth-comb, then ask hundreds of questions . . . Hundreds?' He laughed. 'Thousands. All futile, or nearly all. That's the only way to do it, though.'

'I'll take Mr Flynn and Mr Droylsden to their office,' Mrs Alvaston said.

'Do that,' said the Inspector. 'I mustn't keep you, gentlemen. Life must go on, mustn't it?' He went over to the wrecked calculating machine.

As Xavier went out, he found Clonmell's eyes upon him, hard and appraising as the Inspector's had been. He stopped at the entrance to Room 34; the door, torn off its hinges, lay on the floor in a litter of broken glass.

'The briefcase and all the documents are in Room 27, Mr Flynn,' Mrs Alvaston said. She handed each of them a tagged Yale key. 'I have another key. A mortice lock will be fitted soon.'

'You're very efficient,' Xavier said.

'We try to be, Mr Flynn. If you don't keep yourself busy at times like these you go mad . . . We may as well not bother with the lift . . .'

They followed her down the steps and along a shabby corridor virtually a duplicate of the corridor on the floor above, into an office which was virtually a duplicate of Room 34 except for its plain-fronted door.

'You can wash at the end of the corridor,' Mrs Alvaston said. 'If there's anything you need, just pick up the white 'phone. Direct to Exchange on the red. Places are reserved for you in the Staff Canteen in the building opposite, but just ask if you'd prefer coffee and sandwiches to be sent in. And now if you'll excuse me –'

'I was wondering what you did in the War, Mrs Alvaston,' Xavier said.

'Oh!' Her hand went to her bosom; for a second she looked young and defenceless, the softly gleaming auburn hair adding to the illusion. 'I was in the WAAF. Why do you ask?'

'Curiosity. Where were you stationed?'

'Biggin Hill, then the Far East. Actually, I got round quite a lot. But that's not relevant now, is it?'

He looked at her thoughtfully: her mask had slipped for a moment and now he was not sure who she was.

'We ought to be returning to what we were doing before the explosion,' Droylsden said.

'I was just thinking how admirably self-possessed Mrs Alvaston is. The scene just after the explosion wasn't pretty. She must have seen service, as they say.'

'We've all seen service,' Mrs Alvaston said. She turned sharply, the mask on again, almost as if she had just saluted Xavier, her plain white linen blouse and navy-blue skirt heightening the military impression, and went out.

'There's a cool one,' Xavier said. He waved towards Droylsden's briefcase. 'We can now cross Humility and Chastity off the list.'

Droylsden took the two sheaves of typescript from his briefcase. 'Are you surprised?'

'Not really. It's the classic technique. FIST would use these chaps purely to deliver information. They'd 'phone in the information. They wouldn't be told when the bomb would go off – or they'd be told wrong. Credit side, one successful operation. Debit side, two silly kids.'

Droylsden yawned. 'I can see that it would tidy things up for FIST. I can also see arguments against it from FIST's point of view . . .'

Xavier lit a cigarette, then looked in revulsion at the blood on his right hand, a darker shade now, but still sticky.

'Wash your hands, for Christ's sake,' Droylsden said sharply. 'And then let's get on with our job instead of playing detectives.'

Xavier crushed his cigarette out in the large glass ashtray on the desk and walked out of the room and down the corridor, slamming the door behind him. Unbidden and irrepressible, the picture of a red dripping mask – raw flesh with the bone showing through – filled his mind; through the incredibly large opening in the lower part came the high-pitched scream and above the mask, the most telling detail of all, the excruciating pay-off of the black joke, was the long, glistening blonde hair that it would be a pleasure to touch. He felt a hand on his shoulder and saw that it was Sally Rowmarsh, walking along the corridor to the Stationery Office, looking slightly dazed.

'I heard the explosion,' she said. 'What happened?'

'A bomb. Four killed. What are you doing here?'

'I was on the floor below. I'm doing a series on Morgate.' She moved away from him, but he took hold of her arm.

'They won't let you in there. Where've you been?'

'I took a day off. Let me go –'

'You didn't tell anyone where you were.'

'I took the day off, then I changed my mind. I wanted to come on spec. I hate having everything laid on . . .'

'I have bad news for you,' he said. He paused. 'Christ, I'm not very good at this sort of thing.'

'What sort of thing?' Her hands were clasped together.

'Something's happened to Tom.'

She gasped, but said nothing; he took her into Room 27, where Droylsden was speaking into the red 'phone.

'Yes, he is being rather tiresome –' He looked at Xavier and Sally Rowmarsh and frowned. 'I'll 'phone you later.' He hung up.

'This is Miss Rowmarsh,' Xavier said. 'Tom Drage's friend. My colleague, Hugh Droylsden.'

Droylsden nodded in Sally Rowmarsh's direction, then put the two sheaves of typescript into his briefcase. 'I'd better leave you to yourselves. I'll see you in about a quarter of an hour, Flynn.' He stood up. 'My sympathies, Miss Rowmarsh.'

There was a thirty seconds' silence after he had left the room. Sally Rowmarsh slumped into a chair, then sat upright, gripping the arms of the chair tightly.

'This will be a shock to you.' Xavier's voice was gentle. 'Tom is dead.'

'It isn't really a shock. That's funny, isn't it? How did he die?'

'A road accident. At Woking. Very late last night or very early this morning.'

'What the hell was he doing at Woking?' She took out a packet of Gauloise Bout Filtre from her large suède shoulder-bag; Xavier lit it for her. 'I keep trying to give it up.'

Xavier lit a cigarette himself. 'I keep thinking about it too.'

'Were there any other cars involved?' Her voice was without emotion, a professional journalist's voice.

'Not that I'm aware of. He crashed into a tree at high speed. He must have died instantly.'

'Are you doing the same job here as him?' As he was asked the question he was aware of danger, aware that she had become an interrogator, suddenly cool and composed in a high-necked beige trouser-suit, not bright enough for someone of her colouring but exactly right for a professional woman doing a professional job.

'Roughly speaking. Hugh and I were to give him a hand anyway.' It was best not to look away from her, but instead to look straight back which, even under the circumstances, was enjoyable, her eyes being large and well-shaped and wide-set, and so dark a brown as almost to be black.

'Roughly speaking? You're very strange, Mr Flynn. Just as

135

Tom was strange. He never told me much about his job. I lived with him off and on for four months and I can't remember him ever going into any detail about it. I'm not going to now, am I?' She started to weep; Xavier crossed over to her and gave her a handkerchief.

'If you're too upset, I'll arrange transport home for you.'

She shook her head. 'I've got my own car.' She wiped her eyes. 'There's a job to do. If they'd let me . . .' She looked away from him. 'I don't get official sympathy, of course. It was just a casual affair, I keep telling myself . . .'

'That doesn't stop you from loving him,' Xavier said gently.

She winced. 'Christ, don't do that! All of a sudden being a decent human being. I can't cope with that . . . I don't know whether I loved him or not. I'm going to miss him, though.' She stood up. 'I'll see you later.'

'You don't have to see me. Not that I wouldn't enjoy it.'

'I want to. But not here. I've got to try to find something out about the bomb. If I don't, I'm in trouble.' She blew her nose. 'I'll give you your hanky back . . . How is it you're still in the building, by the way?'

'I might ask the same question of you.'

'They evacuated the building – I sneaked back and hid in a loo.'

'I wish I could have hidden in a loo. But we were practically next door, so we had to try to help.'

'There's blood on your hand.'

'It's not my blood,' Xavier said wearily.

'Just what has happened? I'll find out anyway.'

'Two young men dead, a girl and a middle-aged woman dead. And there's a pretty girl who isn't a pretty girl any more. You'd better ask Mrs Alvaston.'

'I have a notion that that won't do me much good,' she said. 'It doesn't make any difference, I've got to try.' She walked out, still clutching Xavier's handkerchief.

Xavier picked up the red 'phone and dialled. 'One Five Zero Nine, Drinian,' he said, yawning.

'Aslan. How are you, dear boy?'

'Tired. It's been a long day.'

'*You* should complain. I've had just two hours' rest since the goods were brought in last night.'

'It seems rather a shame that the goods aren't, so as to speak, around any longer.'

'In their no doubt praiseworthy enthusiasm I'm afraid that Wanda – and others – damaged the goods past repair . . .' Aslan's voice assumed a note of irritation. 'Is there any special reason for this call, Xavier? Because I now am looking forward to returning to the bosom of my wife and family.'

'Sally Rowmarsh is here. I've just been talking to her.'

'Tom's little friend? But why shouldn't she be there? She's doing a series on Morgate's.'

'I told her what had happened to Tom.'

'You could have checked with me, but it doesn't really matter.'

'Do you still want me to see her?'

'If I didn't, I'd have told you. I'd still like to know what he found out – or what he thought he'd found out – at Morgate's. It's just possible that he may have told her something.'

'There's still no word of Dykenhead. Don't you find it significant?'

Aslan sighed gustily. 'I do continue to emphasise – and I'm sure Hugh does – please don't go stumbling into the labyrinth. We have other people in the Department whose job it is to investigate. Which they are doing, with might and main. You, my dear chap, are the Minotaur rather than Theseus.'

There was silence. Xavier grinned to himself. 'All right. Very neatly put.'

'Thank you, Xavier. But let me spell it out. Just do what you're told. You can, I think, acquire some useful information from Miss Rowmarsh, but not with your brain. With a quite different organ . . . Don't concern yourself with the use that is made of that information. And now I am, as they say, signing off. Reepicheep will take over.' He hung up.

Droylsden came in as Xavier was replacing the 'phone.

'Were you speaking to Aslan?'

'It's about time that I did.'

Droylsden opened his briefcase and took out two thick red folders. 'I got these covered. Miss Rowmarsh was trying to read the title pages. Amidst her heartbreak.'

He took out a silver flask and two small metal cups. 'Vodka? Not Bison, I'm afraid.'

'As long as it's alcoholic.'

Droylsden handed him the vodka. 'You're rather disturbed, aren't you, Xavier?'

'I've good right to be. I'll accept six of the seven names on that list. They don't seem likely FIST members to me but I take your word for it.'

'Not my word. Not Cothill's word. But Aslan's word.'

'All right. But there's one I can't accept.'

'Because you know him. Because he's a friend of yours. And that is why you're the best man for the job.'

'There's been a mistake.' Xavier drained his cup at one gulp.

'That's what you want to believe,' Droylsden said. 'Of course, we could always get someone else to do it.' He held out the flask. 'Another little one?'

'No.' He put the cup down. 'I'll do it. But if there has been a mistake, I'll kill you.'

'You can try,' Droylsden said cheerfully. 'You're welcome to try, old man.'

# SEVENTEEN
## 5 June 1974: 18.30–21.45 Hours

The moustached gentleman – for so he assuredly would have described himself – plying the décolletée young woman with champagne, was very obviously alone with her and she very obviously wasn't his wife or fiancée, and after being persuaded to drink a few more glasses she was going to sleep with him; the message of the drawing was that if the champagne were Louis Roederer this was the sort of situation in which you would find yourself.

'I like it,' Xavier said to Sally Rowmarsh. 'There's lots of very satisfying detail, but the line's beautifully clear, no fuss at all. Though it's a con trick really –'

'All advertising's a con trick,' Rod Deveron broke in. He emptied his glass of white wine: his large red face perceptibly grew even redder and he loosened the collar of his flowered shirt.

'Like that whisky advert with the chap alone with the beautiful bird,' Xavier said. 'You know the one? There she is, showing nearly all she's got, ready for it, and the bottle of whisky in a prominent position. Well, drinking whisky may get you into that sort of confrontation, but a truthful advert would show horror and dejection on the girl's face and bitter shame on the chap's face.'

Sally Rowmarsh giggled.

'You're very smooth,' Rod Deveron said and went over to the bar, managing to lurch slightly in the two strides it took him to get there.

'And you're bloody rough, mate,' Xavier said under his breath. 'Let's go and eat, Sally.'

'He'll go away soon,' she said. 'This is my local, and he's a friend of mine. I'll need him before I need you. Have you any friends?'

'Not many. I know a lot of people.' There was Father Kevin, but could your confessor be your friend? Render therefore unto Caesar the things which are Caesar's – but Caesar had become more and more demanding. It was best not to think of Diligence. If he did, he'd begin to feel sorry for himself. His stock of friends was running low. There had been friends at school, there had been friends in the Army; but since joining the Department he'd lost touch with them. The nearest he'd come to friendship was with Nat Weiberg. He could relax with Nat because he was in the same line of business, but not working for the same masters. In CED there never could be the same cosy camaraderie that Sally Rowmarsh would find in this long, narrow, comfortably old-fashioned room.

'You're miles away,' she said. 'You deliver a set piece, then return to your own thoughts. Why don't you have friends?'

'Because he's a Fascist shit,' Rod Deveron said, returning to the table with two glasses of wine in one hand, and one in another. Xavier noticed with a feeling of revulsion that his fingernails were black-rimmed.

'That word doesn't mean much any more,' he said calmly. 'Those who make their living by using words ought to respect words.'

'I agree with you,' Deveron said surprisingly. 'One gets into bad habits. Just the same, you're a rabid reactionary. I can smell it a mile off.'

'Don't be such a bore,' Sally Rowmarsh said. 'He's a friend of Tom.'

'Tom's a rabid reactionary too. With bouts of bad conscience from time to time. God knows what about.'

'Tom's dead. Road accident.' He scrutinised Deveron's face for signs of embarrassment; he would have enjoyed his being discomforted, even in the smallest way. But Deveron's expression didn't change.

'Sorry to hear it, Sally. Not that I liked him. Still, I'm not you, am I? You're bound to feel differently.'

'What was he guilty about?' Xavier asked casually.

'I haven't the faintest idea. Only met him about half-a-dozen times, generally in a crowd. He didn't fit in particularly well, though.' He rummaged in the breast pocket of his suède jacket and pulled out a long pale cigar, a shade darker than cream with a curious greenish tinge. 'American. I rather like them . . . Yes, Tom didn't fit in, any more than you do.'

'I think you're trying to needle him,' Sally said. 'I wouldn't if I were you.'

'Oh, I know he's tough. But he keeps a low profile. Like Tom.' Deveron's voice had the actor's quality of instant projection; the three middle-aged men chatting at the bar showed no signs of having heard him, but Xavier knew from their sudden and almost imperceptible change in posture that they were noting every word. Deveron's cigar had a sweetish, rank, damp smell, like dock leaves and elderberry; it was a foreign smell in a way that Havana would not have been.

'I'm just a very ordinary Civil Servant,' he said. 'Like Tom. And I'm rather hungry.' He turned to Sally. 'I did promise you dinner.'

'It's early yet,' Deveron said. 'Sally's handed in her Morgate piece. You're at Morgate's, aren't you?'

'For the time being.' Deveron's shirt was scarlet, his tie – broad but narrower than the now outmoded kipper width – was pale green. Xavier momentarily had a picture of his hand grasping it, shaking Deveron until his face went as scarlet as his shirt, then mottled blue.

'So was Tom. And now Tom's dead. It's all rather significant.'

'Your imagination's running away with you, Rod. There's nothing significant about a road accident.'

'Or about a bomb? Four people killed?' Deveron's pale blue eyes were watching Xavier's face intently.

'He was in an office only a few yards away. He behaved with great presence of mind.' She smiled, but not with her eyes. 'You've never really recovered from that series being turned down, have you, Rod?'

'You can't win 'em all,' Deveron said. 'Don't be such a rotten little cunt, Sally. It doesn't suit you.'

Sally stood up. 'We have to go now.' It was as if she had not heard Deveron. 'I'll see you, love.'

Xavier rose with her and as he passed Deveron, gave his tie a tug as if playfully, but pulling uncomfortably tight and jerking Deveron's head sharply forward. Deveron gasped. 'They wouldn't let you wear a tie like that in the Civil Service, old man,' Xavier said. 'You must tell me about your series some time. Ciao.' He clapped Deveron on the back, hard enough to hurt, but assuming an expression of absentminded geniality.

In the taxi, they sat in silence, he with his hands folded in his lap, she with her gaze fixed towards the road. Xavier let his eyes close, glad to relax, not to be on his guard, enjoying the cool air through the half-open window, happy not to be driving, happy, as long as Sally was silent, not to be obliged to take even the smallest decision. He was taking a pretty girl to dinner on a fine June evening, and now that there was this moment of stillness he could at last properly appreciate her smell—faintly of sweat, faintly of linen, more strongly of an expensive perfume, amber-gris not spirit-based, pepper and lemon verbena and roses as near as he could identify it, but, pleasant as it was, no more than the fancy wrapping around her personal smell, which was always what excited him the most about a woman: the moment of its recognition was the moment that a relationship began.

Going into Sloane Square she broke the silence.

'Are you asleep?' She tugged his hair gently.

He opened his eyes and smiled at her.

'I'm just relaxing. It's been far too exciting a day.'

'You are rather a relaxed person. You were very relaxed with poor old Rod.'

'I think that poor old Rod can manage very well. What was the series about?'

'The Enemy on the Right. The Fascist pigs of the Special Branch and the Secret Service and the Monday Club and so on. Rod swears that it was turned down because it was too hot to handle.'

'More likely because it was too boring.'

'He's a very good journalist, even if he is pissed out of his mind most of the time. He's nosed around quite a lot.'

'That's no guarantee that his stuff won't be boring.' The taxi made a U-turn in a gap in the traffic of one second's duration and two cars' length: the motor-bike behind it continued for a hundred yards and then came to a stop at the kerbside. Its rider bent over the handlebars and began to fiddle with the brake lever. Xavier could not see his face, but noted automatically his white crash helmet, waterproof jacket in roadworker's orange, and red trousers. The bike was a Morgate 1200, unmistakable, even if he hadn't seen so much of it recently, because of its completely covered engine and deeply valanced mudguards. Xavier helped Sally out and paid the taxi-driver, his eyes still on the Morgate 1200.

'Nice bike, that, Guv'nor,' the taxi-driver said, following Xavier's gaze. 'Only water-cooled bike on the market. Heavy, but nice, and quiet and smooth.' He was young, with a smooth tanned noncommittal face, which Xavier found reminiscent of Droylsden's; his accent was as if deliberately roughened.

'It's something that it's British,' Xavier said. 'I'll buy myself one for Christmas. Cheerio.'

The taxi-man saluted him in the odd gesture, part a farewell wave from equal to equal, part a parody of the tug to the fore-lock, used by the self-employed and drove off towards Sloane Square. A young man in a cream suit standing at the kerb further on held his hand up; the taxi went past him. Xavier filed the information in the instant retrieval part of his memory and took Sally Rowmarsh's arm as they went into Daisy's.

'The entrance is skilfully concealed, isn't it?' she said as they went down the steep narrow steps.

'Most people can find it. It's British food. You don't mind, do you?'

She laughed. 'It makes a change.' She deepened her voice to impersonate Xavier. '*It's something that it's British* . . . You're about thirty years behind the times, Xavier.' It was the first time she'd used his Christian name; though it didn't matter these days he knew that for her and with him it was significant.

He smiled. 'You couldn't have said anything which pleased me more. It's never been *my* ambition to be trendy.'

The long low-ceilinged room was half full, the lighting muted but not so muted that one couldn't read the menu or distinguish the faces of the other diners. And the waist-high partitions between the tables could have their uses; nothing was more unlikely than a restaurant in England suddenly becoming a battleground, but he had always to remember that the unlikely could happen soon and that if he wasn't prepared for it he could within a second become a corpse or, far worse, his one private fear, a living vegetable fed through tubes in a hospital bed.

'It's never been mine either,' she said fiercely. 'To be trendy I mean . . . Why do people like you always think that?'

143

'It was just a casual remark, darling.' He touched her hand.

'Don't call me darling. It doesn't suit you. I have a name. And don't take your hand away. Leave it for a moment.'

He put his hand over hers. It was trembling for a minute, then was still.

'You're such a bastard. Worse than Tom. I don't know why I'm here.'

He stroked her hand. 'I expect because you want to talk about him. Do you want a drink?'

She shook her head.

A glass of wine with the meal, that's all.' Her hand started to tremble again. 'There's a bit in Boswell's *Life of Johnson* when Johnson says, "Sir, Panizzi" – or whatever his name was – "is going to be hanged tomorrow, and we all love him dearly, yet there's not one of us will eat one slice of plum-pudding the less . . ." I can't remember the exact words, but that's the message.'

'Fried mushrooms and then fish pie for me,' Xavier said to the waitress. 'I'd recommend that to you too, Sally. Unless you have other ideas. And a bottle of the house rosé and to hell with the connoisseur lark.'

She nodded. 'I'm too tired to choose.' Her hand was still trembling.

'Take it easy now,' Xavier said, as the waitress went away. 'You don't have to talk about Tom.'

She took her hand away and fished in her shoulder-bag. 'It's mixed up with Morgate's.' She brought out a packet of Gauloise and shook it. 'Christ, I've been smoking like a chimney. Like the old, old joke, my favourite old, old joke – she doesn't have periods, she has falls of soot.'

Xavier put two cigarettes in his mouth, lit them, and handed her one.

'That's sexy,' she said. 'Cary Grant style, but he doesn't smoke any more, so they say.' She inhaled. 'Too damned mild. If I'm going to be poisoned, I want to make a proper job of it. You want to find out something about Tom, don't you?'

'He was doing a job at Morgate's and he left a few loose ends. Nothing very important.'

'I have a feeling that – oh hell, I don't know. Yes, I do. Something is going on there. They didn't tell me everything.'

Xavier shrugged. 'Nobody ever does tell anyone everything.'

'Tomorrow morning the public won't be told *anything*. Don't you find that strange?'

'It happens all the time. Or so I understand.'

'The editor doesn't frighten easily. But he was a frightened man. Somebody had leaned on him.'

Xavier tried to think who'd be available for leaning on Fleet Street: if the editor had really been frightened, Reepicheep must have decided to go. Reepicheep was just four foot eight and had large blue eyes and a doll-like face – a china doll's, an old-fashioned doll's with a determined asexual sweetness, not one of the modern ones with a King's Road Carnaby Street pertness and availability. He himself found Reepicheep frightening, which was quite a thought . . . He smiled at Sally Rowmarsh. 'Probably Sir Geoffrey had a quiet word with someone and they had a quiet word with your editor.'

'A quiet word? That's just as bad. Where do the quiet words stop?'

'Don't ask me, love. It has nothing to do with me. I've told you, I'm just an ordinary Civil Servant –'

'You're not. Tom wasn't. I've met men like you before. I interviewed Mike Hoare once – you know, the mercenary. Very soft voice, gentle, good manners, most civilised. But I had the feeling that he was like – a loaded gun. One second – less than one second – and he'd be in action . . .'

Xavier poured her a glass of rosé. 'As the high-class connoisseurs say, a young wine, an adolescent wine, but not without a certain gawky charm . . . No doubt you're right about Mike Hoare, but not about Tom. Did he ever talk to you about his job at Morgate's?'

The fried mushrooms had arrived; he took a bite purely for pleasure, savouring the contrast between the bland crispness of the batter and the earthy meatiness of the mushroom, then the next bite out of hunger.

'I can't remember,' she said. 'He didn't talk much about his work. But he did say that something odd was going on. You know he was an accountant once?'

That wasn't quite true: Tom had done two years in a chartered accountant's office, landed himself in various sorts of trouble

145

because of his violent disposition, and had ended up in the Army, where Chuck Eustace had spotted him. But it was near enough; Tom had a definite ability with figures. 'He wasn't at Morgate's to audit the accounts,' he said. 'But he might well have spotted something. I wish he'd told you what.'

'I've a good mind to find out.' She was eating greedily now, something he always liked to see in women.

'I wouldn't worry if I were you. They're very sound.'

'I've heard that said before. The next you hear, the firm's in Carey Street.'

'Were you with Tom a long time?' he asked, determined to keep the conversation in the proper direction.

'We met in January. At the American Embassy.'

'One of our few perks. What attracted you to him?'

She pushed aside her empty plate and stared at him. 'What attracts me to you. What attracts most women to you. It's just physical.' In the half-darkness her eyes were black.

'I'm very spiritual too. Not just a beautiful animal.'

'You're not beautiful exactly. You're built for a purpose. Tom was, but he wasn't always happy about it. He had bad dreams; he'd wake up trembling and sweating . . .'

Two men and two women entered the room; Xavier moved back in his seat a little, tensing himself. Middle-aged, Harrods and Fortnum & Mason's, nothing flashy, in good spirits but not noisy, gentle, gentle, sleepwalking British bourgeoisie – no danger, all clear, but watch it, watch it. 'It happens to us all,' he said lightly. The waitress cleared the plates away.

'You could describe these people who've just entered to me now,' she said. 'To the last detail.'

'You really will have to write that novel. Did Tom live with you all the time?'

'Just off and on. He had a place of his own. He didn't like to be tied down. He took great pains to tell me that.' Her voice had a bitter tone.

'He didn't bring any papers home from Morgate's?' The waitress brought the fish pie in a large deep earthenware dish.

'If he did, I've never seen them . . . Is that fish pie as nice as it looks?'

'It's superb. All sorts of fish, all piping hot.'

'At school fish pie was cod and mashed potatoes all mixed up. I've never had it since.'

'You don't go in for English cuisine, you see. This is the *authentic* fish pie . . .' The waitress divided the crust neatly and spooned the pie on to their plates, almost filling each plate up. The pie smelled of herbs and the sea rather than the fishmonger. Xavier guiltily remembered that he'd forgotten to say grace before a meal which deserved it, then classified the sin as venial, put it in storage for his next Confession, and concentrated on the pleasure of eating; for the time being there had been enough interrogation and it was enough to punctuate the meal occasionally with small talk and compliments which would, if he'd interpreted her attitude and her words correctly, direct them both naturally in a friendly way, with no strings attached, into her bed. She wasn't his sort of person and sooner or later she was bound to say something which would both shock and frighten him because of its sheer crapulent stupidity – there'd been a girl at a Hampstead literary party once who believed that revolutions were spontaneous mass uprisings. But her face, when she let it slip into contentment, and her body, slim but with no concave lines, no harsh angles, would guarantee him oblivion: a simple animal happiness before and during the act, sleep after . . .

'Where are you?' he heard Sally Rowmarsh say from a distance.

He smiled. 'Making love to you.'

'You weren't looking at me. Why the hell don't you look at me? You're with me, aren't you? I'm a person, aren't I?'

He had heard that complaint before; but Vanessa was amused, and Sally Rowmarsh was making a complaint.

'I won't take my eyes off you the rest of the evening. You're well worth looking at.'

'No-one would think it. God, I really am a sex object to you, aren't I?'

He found himself thinking again of Miss Stevens's wrecked face, at which no-one could look with desire again. 'You're you,' he said. 'A human being.' He put his hand on hers. 'Relax and be human.'

'We don't live in a very human world, do we? Bombs in offices, people killed for no good reason –'

'That's very human, alas.' He took a mouthful of rosé and then a forkful of fish pie, but the meal now had become the background to the interrogation which she hadn't to be aware was taking place.

She drained her glass of rosé: automatically he poured her another. 'They're talking about the IRA, of course. What would they do without the IRA?'

'The IRA does tend to go in for planting bombs,' he said gently.

She drained her glass again. 'Order some more wine, will you?'

He gestured to the waitress.

'Another bottle of rosé? Or half a bottle?'

'A bottle. And for Christ's sake don't look so shocked.'

Xavier held up the empty bottle and smiled at the waitress; Sally Rowmarsh looked at him coldly as the waitress took his order.

'I wouldn't be served so quickly,' she said. 'You're a great big beefy charmer, aren't you?'

'She happened to be there,' Xavier said.

'You're not looking at me again,' she said. 'Tom was the same.'

Xavier smiled his thanks at the waitress as she brought him the bottle of wine. 'I'm sorry I had to spring it on you like I did.'

'There wasn't any other way, was there? Funny, I never really knew much about him . . . I told you he didn't live with me all the time.' She lit a cigarette and pushed aside her plate. 'He didn't keep any of his stuff at my flat. Just a shaver and shirts and underwear. He hasn't left any mementoes. He wasn't a man for mementoes. He came and he went and one day he went . . . I'm an unlucky girl, wouldn't you say?'

'Car accidents happen all the time.'

'So they do. But you know what? I'm going to make some enquiries about this accident. You know something else? I'm not going to get very far.' She leaned forward and pinched his arm with surprising strength. 'Aren't you drinking?'

He shook his head. 'I've had enough.'

'Now you're really behaving like a Civil Servant. Controlled and temperate and sensible. But you were in the Army, weren't you, Major?'

'It's no secret. I left because I was bored. Too much paperwork.'

148

'So you became a Civil Servant? Never mind, Xavier, I won't cross-examine you. I'm sure you have all your answers ready.' She lifted her glass to her lips then put it down. 'I've had enough. Do you want to take me home?'

Outside, the King's Road was still crowded; the passers-by seemed to be all young, slim, in jeans or long skirts, in heavy sweaters or tank tops, in black and mud-brown and hodden-grey and faded blue and very occasionally dusty pink, all sober, all quiet, all empty, all composed, all curiously purposeful: Xavier felt suddenly out of place, in a hostile country. A taxi coming towards him from the direction of Sloane Square suddenly made a U-turn and stopped beside him. At the wheel was the driver who had taken them to Daisy's. Xavier's hand went to his jacket pocket; his finger was on the trigger of the Browning when he saw Reepicheep get out of the taxi. He was wearing a navy-blue silk suit, a white shirt, a spotted blue bow-tie and black suède shoes instead of his usual light-coloured clothes. A black scarf would cover the shirt; as Xavier looked at him he knew that Reepicheep was going into action, would have known it from the almost palpable cheerfulness which emanated from him: Reepicheep loved his work. Reepicheep gave the taxi-driver a note. 'Seventy? No, no, keep the change. And here's another fare for you, you lucky man.' He gave Xavier and Sally the briefest of social smiles with no sign of recognition for Xavier, and strutted off towards the entrance of Daisy's.

'By the way, Guv,' the taxi-driver said, 'you dropped something earlier. May not be important, but you never know.'

It was a visiting card with Xavier's name and address. Under the name, in Aslan's small regular handwriting, was the number 46921, and *11.00 Hours HQ*, and on the bottom right, **PTO** for *personal message*. Turning the card over, Xavier read: *Remember it's for England, and don't spare yourself. Love, Aslan.*

He smiled and the taxi-driver smiled back. He put the card in his pocket: it would be torn to shreds by the end of the journey. He had kept the card out of sight of Sally Rowmarsh, who was now giving her address to the taxi-driver; but as he put it in his pocket he had a momentary sense of her somehow having read it.

# EIGHTEEN
## 5 June 1974: 21.46–21.59 Hours

Temperance took off his glasses, sighed, and said: 'Time for a breath of air.'

'Surprise, surprise,' his wife said.

'I don't know what you mean, dear.' His eyebrows went up, corrugating his forehead so as to momentarily make him appear much older than his thirty-five years.

'We've been married for ten years now and every night at about a quarter to ten you say that it's time for a breath of air. What about something else, for a change? Something we'd both enjoy?'

He put his glasses in their case, put the case in the breast pocket of the old fawn tweed jacket which he always changed into on coming home, and stood up. 'The twins aren't asleep yet.'

'Yes they are.' Her grey nylon dress, though fully cut and knee-length, had, apparently through no conscious effort on her part, worked its way up almost to the groin. Her legs were bare, which always excited him. They were long well-shaped legs with a very fine down, ash blonde like her hair; she had never needed a razor or depilatory cream.

'I really do need a breath of air,' he said, and smiled at her. The smile made his thin dark face suddenly younger.

She frowned and picked up her knitting, an aubergine crew-neck sweater to replace the sagging and threadbare fawn sweater which he had had ever since they were married and which, she had decided, was going to be lost in the near future. Her dress, without her touching it, seemed to go down to her knees again.

'Have your damned breath of air,' she said. 'And your little think.'

'A man in my position does have to think,' he said mildly.

'I don't see why you can't think here.'

It was impossible to explain to her, much though he loved her, that the parquet-floored lounge with the matching white and pink floral wallpaper and curtains, with the new hi-fi and 26-inch colour TV, with the suite with the pink and orange Liberty loose covers – spotless and neat despite seven-year-old twin boys – wasn't the place for what he had got into the habit of thinking about at this time for the last ten years. He needed to be outside for that, smelling the grass and the trees, walking, not sitting still, but walking along paths which he knew so well that he didn't need to make any conscious note of his direction. He looked again at fundamental principles on these walks or, rather, this walk, renewed his vows, reaffirmed his loyalties.

His wife noted with sadness as he got out of his chair that already his mind was away from her, away from the children, the house, and even, she felt sure, his job.

'Victor,' she said as he was at the door, 'have you another woman?'

He turned, honestly surprised. 'Good God, Margaret! I've enough on my plate with you!'

'I wish you had, that's all. Or that you were – in trouble. Normal trouble, like fiddling the books or taking backhanders. Or drunken driving. I wouldn't even mind dope . . .'

'I do wish I knew what you meant.' He laughed. 'Honestly, darling, I'm not in any sort of trouble. Never have been. I'm a very respectable, mundane sort of fellow, I'm afraid.'

'You may be respectable, but you're not mundane. I do think you're in trouble.'

'I thought that that was what you wanted.'

'I said *normal* trouble. *Understandable* trouble. I've lived with you for ten years, Victor, and I know when you've had a good day at work or a bad day at work and I know when you feel randy and when you feel dog-tired and I know when you've a cold coming on and I know when you're in trouble.' Her tone was impersonal, unemotional, the voice of the old woman of the tribe, the oracle of the shrine with the parquet floor and Liberty loose covers.

'All right,' he said. 'I'm in some mysterious trouble. So I'll have a walk to sort it out. To find out what it is, because I'm damned if I know . . . I won't be long, dear.'

He closed the door behind him, not with a bang, but harder than was his practice. His wife got up and walked over to the sideboard and poured herself a glass of brandy. She took a mouthful, coughed, then found herself weeping. 'Always the same words,' she said aloud. '*I won't be long, dear.* And it's always an hour, no more, no less.' She wiped her eyes, then went back to her armchair with her brandy. She sat very still, sipping the brandy slowly.

Outside, leaving Cyprus Close – *an exclusive development of 4-bedroomed Georgian-styled houses, 2 bathrooms, full gas-fired central heating, double garage, landscaped garden* – Victor had already put her out of his mind. To marry her had been a decision which he had taken before his thinking had fully matured, before he had realised the shattering truth of the statement that the function of philosophy was not to interpret the world but to change it. Because of that thought having been formulated, the big house of Sir Henry Segrave on his right now no longer was a private residence and he, the son of a plasterer, lived in a new house in what was once part of Segrave's garden, with a Cortina shooting brake and a Fiat 500 in the garage; and now, because he'd understood, some nine years ago, what the old monster Marx meant, the kind of living represented by Cyprus Close was on the way out. He had never regretted his marriage: he was a human being, he needed to love and to be loved. He would be powerless to change the world if he didn't go along with the world for as long as was necessary: his sacrifice was to conceal his beliefs; his continuing reward, when with his comrades, was to think and talk only in terms of concrete action.

He glanced at Broomcroft Close on his right, an earlier development, with which Cyprus Close was virtually identical. The first houses in Cyprus Close had first of all cost more than the first houses in Broomcroft Close; and now their value was falling and inflation was increasing. The system was falling apart but the process had to be hastened; it had been hastened today though the deaths had not been part of the plan. Deaths were part of the plan, but they hadn't to be inflicted by mistake.

There had presumably been a fault in the timing mechanism; Brotherly Love was brilliant but slapdash. But as they could hardly examine it now and as the police would almost certainly say that the timing of the explosion had been deliberate, it could only be resolved to discipline Brotherly Love and to be more careful next time.

152

There was a lot more to be thought about tonight. He looked with pleasure along the tree-lined road – not one of the great roads and with nothing of especial charm or architectural merit along it, but pleasant, civilised, open country beyond it, the daylight still lingering. The coolness wasn't seasonable, but he liked it better than the warmth which would have been seasonable: the night smelled cleaner, almost more austere. He brought his mind back to what he had come out for: the replacement of Humility and Chastity at Morgate's and the question of Peter Dykenhead. He stopped opposite Pyrford Common Road to look left, look right, and look right again; at this time traffic was fast-moving, and he could spare five seconds to safeguard himself.

But at the entrance to Pyrford Common, on the patch of ground by the roadside left of the playground, he took no notice of the young man and the young woman 'kissing in the black Marina. He walked on into the woods, keeping to the footpath; when he had disappeared from sight the young man broke away from the young woman and picked up a telephone from a socket under the dashboard. 'Edmund. Clear this end. Target on his way. Over.' He replaced the 'phone and embraced the young woman again, unbuttoning her blouse.

'Sod,' she said, and slapped his hand. 'This is business.'

'We've got to look as if we mean it,' he said, laughing. The laugh changed into a grunt of pain as her hand went downwards quickly.

Temperance walked further into the woods, bearing leftwards in the direction of Pyrford Court. A young man in a navy-blue suit and black sweater and, what was strange for the time of year, strange at any time, black rubber gloves, came over the crest of the slight rise just before the tennis courts, walking briskly towards Temperance. Temperance felt a slight apprehension, an atavistic fear, then dismissed it firmly. When he and the young man were nearly touching Temperance moved automatically to the right to let the other pass; the other moved in the same direction, then his hand flickered and Temperance felt a sting in his left hand, a pinprick, an irritation, a wound, an agony, his mouth was pulled wide open to scream but he could make no sound, both arms jerked upwards over his head as if to denounce the whole heartless world, his body went upwards, he

153

was on tiptoe, his hands now curling as if to climb over a high wall; he stood immobile for five seconds, apparently holding on to the wall, then fell straight forward on his face, his hands still above his head. The young man bent down, picked something up from the ground, and walked on briskly towards the Pyrford Common Road without a backward glance.

# NINETEEN
## *5 June 1974: 21.59–22.02 Hours*

Reepicheep stood by the door, breathing deeply and slowly, perfectly relaxed. The door opened inwards, with the handle on the left; the light switch was six inches to the right of the handle. Standing where he was, he could hit the target immediately; the trouble was that you couldn't always be sure of how the poison would work, and the subject might fall backwards out of the room, or roll along the landing curled up like a hoop and down the stairs. He'd known that to happen, just as he'd known them to scream their heads off; Susan had to cook up each batch of the stuff as it was needed, since what made it undetectable – she had explained it to him once, using a great many formulae and diagrams – also made it unstable to a certain degree. It was better to allow the subject to get into the room and close the door; he moved into the cover of a mahogany tallboy to the left of the door handle. The flat was on the top floor, there was no-one at home in the two flats below, the walls and the door were thick. The heavy red velvet curtains over the two large windows – good quality like everything in the flat – very effectively cut out all the illumination from the street lamps outside, but his eyes were used to the light by now, and in any case he knew the layout of every room in the flat before he had even entered it.

His walkie-talkie bleeped. 'Meekness is downstairs opening street door. All clear. Message over.'

Reepicheep smiled, showing small white regular teeth. The object in his hand was black plastic with no brightwork, with a three inch muzzle and a plain cylindrical butt. There was a trigger and a guard, but it appeared somehow flimsy and toylike, not like a weapon at all.

Reepicheep heard the door open. The light came on. He stayed perfectly still, a small black figure, the black silk scarf tucked into the front of his jacket. He continued to breathe slowly and deeply; only amateurs held their breath, which could leave you slightly dizzy and in need of oxygen and which would inevitably result in an audible exhalation. The woman closed the door and came forward towards the fireplace, not looking to her right. Reepicheep came up behind her and aimed at her hand; she gasped, half turned her hand up to her face very slowly as if it had suddenly become heavy. She turned round very slowly, still holding up her hand as if to inspect the tiny red mark there.

Her eyes behind the blue harlequin glasses widened, then closed, her face convulsing; she sagged forward on to her hands and knees, then brought up her head with a great effort. 'God, oh God!' she said thickly, then rolled on to her side.

Reepicheep picked up the dart, put it in a plastic envelope, felt her pulse, and let her hand drop to the floor. A Senior Civil Servant in the Department of Education and Science would have had a fatal heart attack at her Chelsea home; heart attacks were something which frequently happened to sedentary workers on the executive level, particularly when they were forty-five and weighed twelve stone but only stood five foot two. He put the weapon away in his shoulder holster; he would be very glad to hand it in at HQ. There was nothing better for this kind of job but you could never have the same affection for it as you could have for a gun. He shrugged his shoulders and went out of the flat, closing the door behind him very quietly. As always after a job he felt an enormous contentment, a craftsman's pride, marred only by the knowledge that it would have been greater still had his target been taller.

# TWENTY

## 5 June 1974: 22.30–23.00 Hours

There was a moment, kneeling above her naked body, when he felt an odd sort of remorse: lying there with her legs together, her arm across her eyes as if to shield them, her dark hair spread out over the pillows, she looked young and helpless and somehow virginal. And yet there was the breeze blowing in through the open window, stirring the pink curtains, bringing in the smell of the Heath, and there was the sharp smell of her excitement and there was no hurry. He was in a strange bed, the hundredth strange bed, high above London and the smoke, so that, gratefully, he could hear silence too, silence that allowed him to enjoy the rustle of grass and trees, the sound of her breathing, the hoot of an owl; allowed, too, the hope that this might be the last bed, that love might begin. He kissed her nipples, feeling them harden, then her belly; very gently he parted her legs and stroked her, lightly and slowly, resting his face against her thigh. He felt her hand stroking his hair then pressing his head down against her thigh. 'Don't stop, don't stop.' She ran her hand over his cheeks. 'Oh God, men are so nice . . .'

Keeping his hand between her legs, stroking more quickly now, he moved up beside her and kissed her.

'I only want to give you pleasure.'

It was true; there had been a time when he'd only wanted to stick it in, to get his ashes hauled, to give a rousing fuck; but now, whenever he found the quality of helplessness in a woman, the capacity of being hurt, which he had so suddenly found in Sally, it was the woman that mattered, his pleasure came through the woman's pleasure, and time expanded and pushed away Aslan's world, pushed away the picture of Tom's blackened body, pushed away the memory of Shirley Mason's contorted face, pushed away the thought of what he had to do very soon and to whom he had to do it; his fingers explored warm responding softness now, he heard the owl hoot again from outside, very near, and a tiny scream, and then her hand went downwards and then he was drawn into her, wishing more urgently than ever before for love, approaching closer to love, with each thrust, hearing her moan, gasping himself, his heart hammering, approaching still closer to love, nearly there and then into ecstasy instead, into complete abandonment, the charge into the sun, the warmth tingling through his whole body and lying spent and weightless beside her, grateful certainly, satisfied certainly, but no nearer love.

They lay still beside each other in silence, then he touched her gently between the legs.

'Is it all right?'

She laughed. 'Why don't you say it? I've come, darling. It wouldn't matter if I hadn't. I'm quite happy.'

'Just a minute.' He got out of the bed and knelt down, his lips moving.

'What on earth are you doing?'

He got back into bed. 'Saying an Act of Contrition.'

'You are the end, Xavier, you really are. Supposing you sin again?' She switched on the small table lamp at the bedside table, took out two cigarettes from the packet there, lit them, and handed one to Xavier.

He inhaled gratefully. 'If I sin again, I'll say another Act of Contrition.'

She smiled. 'But you're OK for now? If you die, you'll go straight to Heaven?'

'There'll be a long stretch in Purgatory first. With my record, about a billion years.'

'Supposing you're struck dead in the act? It has happened, you know.'

He kissed her. 'There might be just time to repent. Dying always takes a certain amount of time, even if only a split second.'

'You should know.'

He looked at her sharply.

'Why should I know?'

'You've been a soldier, haven't you?'

'That was a long time ago.' He yawned. 'God, what a day it's been.'

'Better at the end than the beginning.' She stroked the thick black hair on his chest. 'Where you're not hairy, you're very

158

white. I've never seen such a white skin . . . I didn't want to go out with you tonight, actually. I keep telling myself that you're not my sort of person.'

'I think we do rather well together.'

'That's just our bodies. They were friends from the start.'

Xavier yawned. 'Isn't that enough?'

'I find you fascinating from a professional point of view.' He recognised the look of appraisal in her eyes; it was not exactly a cold look but love, or even affection, was not there.

'I haven't any stories for you.'

'I wondered if you could use your contacts at Morgate's for me.'

'Such as they are, I will. I can't promise you anything.'

'I'll do something for you if you do something for me.' Her hand went downwards. 'Messages are going through very slowly now, but soon communications will be re-established . . .'

There was a faint pleasure in his groin but he paid no attention to it: what fully occupied his mind now was the FIST list and the one name he'd looked at to the exclusion of all the others; if he didn't do the job, he'd never be any good to the Department again, and if he did do it, he'd never be any good to himself again. But here in this room with the pink roses on the wallpaper and the pink curtains and new biscuit-coloured carpet with the girl beside him he couldn't do anything about it; there was nothing to be done until eleven o'clock tomorrow, and anything might happen tomorrow.'

'Let's have a drink,' he said.

'I've only whisky.'

'That's fine. Nothing with it.' He stubbed out his cigarette and lit another as he lay waiting for her to come back.

When she brought in the whisky they sat up in silence sipping it. He felt its warmth in his stomach and ceased to think of the list. He found his eyes closing, stubbed out his cigarette, and drained the whisky. He lay down gratefully; she slid down beside him and put her arms around his neck.

'It's turned cold, Xavier. Keep me warm.'

'I'll look after you,' he said, as he would have said to a child. 'I'll take you on my black ship.'

'Your black ship?' Her voice was drowsy.

'Sometimes when I'm just drifting off to sleep, I imagine I'm at the quayside waiting for a black ship. A sailing ship. Black ships are the only real ships. I board the black ship, and she sails away . . .'

'Where does she sail to?'

'Just a trip round the bay.'

And as sleep overcame him his last thought was that the black ship was designed for the open seas and long voyages; his eyes closed, the breeze through the open window was a high wind, the sails of the black ship filled and she strained at her anchor, the gulls crying overhead.

# TWENTY-ONE
## *6 June 1974: 10.00 Hours*

IGOR MAKLEVITCH, DIRECTOR, SCIENTIFIC AND TECHNICAL DIRECTORATE, KGB, TO MIKHAIL KOTOLYNOV, DIRECTOR, ILLEGALS DIRECTORATE (DIRECTORATE S).

It is now twenty-eight years since I took over Operation X, put into cold storage for the duration. It has run like a dream. It's a classic of its kind, as well it might be, since its originator was Lenin himself. He handed it over to Nikolai Bukharin, taking great pains to present it in such a way that Bukharin came to think of it as his own creation. That was always the way with Lenin: he didn't tear down his colleagues, he built them up.

And now, Comrade Mikhail, the time has come for us to review Operation X. There is no need to analyse its benefits: they exceed our greatest expectations. The gain to the USSR is far beyond what was hoped originally – and so too the damage to the UK and, through the UK, to the capitalist Powers. The actual administration of the operation has been, until now, trouble-free. In one sense, it is the most economical operation that we have ever mounted. In another sense, and a most unacceptable sense, it is the most expensive.

I am not for one moment suggesting that we should recommend that the operation should be terminated. What I am suggesting is that you and I should meet at the earliest opportunity to have a very serious and thorough discussion. What is in my mind first and foremost is its cost. In our present positions, it's all too easy to forget this. Easy for us; but not so easy for people in the field like the unfortunate Pletnev.

Secondly, there is a matter of principle involved. You know me, dear Comrade Mikhail: I've always been fundamentally a pragmatist, which is why the Boss chose me to run Operation X in the first place. And yet, as a good Marxist, I don't like it.

I remember my reactions when the Boss explained it to me.

I think that they showed, because he looked at me with those strange yellow eyes and asked me: 'Does Operation X shock you, Comrade?' I thought hard and quick. 'Yes, it does, Comrade. That is not a reflection on its merits –'

He cut me short. 'Good, good,' he said. 'It shocked me at first. So did the NEP at first. But the NEP was necessary at the time, and so now is Operation X. Operation X is a whore whom we use until we can afford to marry our true love . . . But don't ever fall in love with a whore, Comrade.'

I'm wondering if we haven't done just that. Moke too: isn't he lavishing expensive gifts upon the whore, spending, so as to speak, other people's money?

I hasten to add that this is no criticism of him. There is no doubt about his sheer brilliance, his absolutely incomparable efficiency.

But let us for once anticipate a problem. And let us also discuss three problems which now seem minor, but which I feel in my bones are going to increase in importance. The first is the question of reopening communications with Yuskevitch. The second is the question of the future relationship between the British agent Flynn and Yuskevitch, and tied up with this inseparably will be our attempt to ascertain the precise status of Flynn in CED. The third is the question of FIST, which I personally see as being a matter of comparing its value to us with the value of Operation X.

These three questions are one question. I have no evidence for this – or at least none which would stand up to an official enquiry. I only know that the connection makes sense to me and I have a shrewd idea that it makes sense to you.

Do nothing impetuous, take no action. But put everything else aside and *think* about Operation X for an hour. And then see me. At our age, it wouldn't do for us to fall in love with a whore.

# TWENTY-TWO

## 6 June 1974:
## 11.30 Hours–12 Noon

The Conference Room was adjacent to Aslan's office, a small room oak-panelled to waist-level with plain brown fitted carpet of the same shade as the oak panels. Almost the whole of the room was taken up by a long mahogany table with four matching dining chairs at each side and a carver at each end of it. On the wall behind Xavier, who sat next to Bunty, who was at the right of Aslan at the head of the table opposite the steel door, was a large diagram of the KGB organisation. Facing him were charts of the CIA organisation, the FBI organisation and the British Intelligence and Counter-Espionage Services. Despite the steel door and the charts, the room always gave the impression of a Victorian dining-room, the dining-room of a gloomy and puritanical Nonconformist family – if not a lunatic's family who would put arsenic in the Brown Windsor soup. There was a vase of white and gold and blue iris on the centre of the table; when he looked at them more closely, there was blue mixed with the white and maroon with the gold, and the blue was a soft grey-blue, gentle and warm.

Aslan looked up from his agenda and smiled at Xavier. 'They're very pretty, aren't they, Drinian? Gathered by Bunty's fair hands from her own garden. This damned room needs cheering up.' He lit a cigarette. 'Not but what I aren't very cheerful. Edmund, Digory, Jill, Reepicheep, I'm very pleased with you.'

Edmund and Digory, two slim young men whom Xavier found difficulty in telling apart, stiffened and seemed somehow as if saluting; the girl, pert-faced and blonde, coloured slightly. They were nice young people, Xavier thought, in their early twenties, with clean fingernails and clean hair and clear skins, the bright young executives at what might have been any business meeting, the hope of the future. Reepicheep smiled faintly. Susan, middle-aged and dumpy with a muddy skin, remained impassive.

'I agree, Director,' she said in her surprisingly musical, completely unaccented voice. 'It's the first time for the young people and they put not a foot wrong. Speaking for myself, I'm glad there were no problems with Exit Two.'

'No indeed, Susan. It worked like a dream. There might, there just might, be a problem about the mark left by the dart. It's only a pinprick, and Exit Two neutralises after half an hour, which is the beauty of it. But I'd like you to get together with Wanda – Polly, I mean – and Cornelius on this. Bunty will arrange it.'

Susan grimaced. 'You know that Wanda and I are not always – *en rapport* – Director.'

Xavier restrained his smile. Susan had come to CED from East Berlin with a sheaf of KGB formulae and an anti-Nazi record documented up to the hilt; the trouble was that Wanda liked Germans no more than she liked Russians. Aslan looked at him mutely; Xavier got up, walked round the table to Susan and put his hands on her shoulders. 'I'll have a word with Polly, *mein Liebling*,' he said. 'Just to please me, be friendly with her. You know we can't do without you. You work well together even if you do hate each other's guts.'

'Very well, as long as you promise, Xavier,' Susan could never remember the code names, which were always used at official meetings. 'We must all make sacrifices . . . Through blood and night to light . . .'

Aslan wagged his finger. 'Naughty, naughty, Susan, you'll shock the young people.'

Xavier squeezed Susan's shoulders gently and went back to his chair.

'I think that that wraps up the first two items on the agenda,' Aslan said. 'You'll note, Drinian, that we've all been busy whilst you've been enjoying yourself.'

'It was all in the line of duty,' Xavier said lightly. 'But I agree with you about last night's operations. There's only one thing. I still feel that we might consider bringing them in for interrogation.'

'In some instances we will. But that's for the future. What

164

works best now is for swift and ruthless action. Last night we put the boot in twice. So twice we've said to them loud and clear that we know as much about two of them as we need to know. Otherwise, they'll reason, we'd have taken them in for interrogation. So now they'll have to reorganise. Over and above that interrogation is a long and chancy business –'

Bunty coughed. 'You have a luncheon appointment with the Chairman of the Council at one o'clock, Aslan.'

'Good God, yes. Sorry, Drinian, I can't discuss this any longer. Not now, anyway. Which brings us to Item Three. We've got your written report – can you summarise it very briefly?'

'As I said to you originally, Miss Rowmarsh is a typical woolly-headed liberal. She wouldn't be of much use to FIST or the KGB either – except unknowingly, because she's bright enough. She doesn't know any more about what Trumpkin was looking into than we do. She's curious about Morgate's, though. I'm aware she's doing a long piece about them, but she seems curious beyond the line of duty. And she's a bit too curious about me.'

'Um. I think that Miss Rowmarsh is becoming a nuisance.'

'She's easily enough dealt with. Just forget about her. She can't do any harm.'

'I disagree with you. She's clever and muddle-headed and inquisitive – she can do a great deal of harm without even meaning to . . . But we'll leave the matter in abeyance for the moment and get on to Item Four, which is actually 4 on the list on the tasteful pink paper before you. You have put ticks after 1 and 2. Within the very near future I want you to put a tick after 4. I'd like you to have a word about it with Ninian. It would be nice then if later in the day you both would have a discussion with my babies' – he smiled at Edmund and Digory and Jill – 'about it. A sort of seminar. That's the only way for them to learn the job, apart from them doing it.' He stood up. 'I now declare this meeting closed.' He walked out of the room, closely followed by Bunty, who gathered up the litter of papers in front of her at the head of the table, assembled them together in one neat pile with no protruding edges and put them in her briefcase in what was apparently one swift movement. All the other papers on the table were left where they were; only Bunty could take any material away. The concealed cameras automatically operated as long as anyone was in the room. Edmund, Digory and Jill followed Bunty, chattering like children let out of school; Susan and Reepicheep stopped beside Xavier, who sat doodling on his notepad.

'Through blood and night to light,' Susan said. 'It's just the colours of the German national flag, when Germany was unified. Red, black and white. It had nothing to do with the Nazis, it was a long time before the Nazis.'

'I know, love,' he said gently.

'Xavier, when the Nazis made the Munich *putsch*, or rather tried to make it – in 1923, I think – if only the authorities had shot Hitler and say half a dozen others, there would have been no Nazi movement. If Kerensky had shot Lenin and, again, just half a dozen others, there would have been no October Revolution. You are surely aware of this lesson of history?'

'I am aware of this lesson of history, Susan. I am also aware of other things. Which is what I personally feel about – Diligence.'

'You've spoken to me about him,' Reepicheep said. 'I know what you feel.'

'He's part of my life,' Xavier said, in a flat voice. 'They don't leave you much, do they?' A nerve in his cheek suddenly twitching, he began to copy out the diagram on the wall facing him: the box for the Government, the line underneath it for the Ministry of Defence, the lines from there to D15 and D16, the line from the Home Secretary to the police, the line from there to Special Branch, the line from the Government to the Internal Security Council, the line from the Internal Security Council to CED, the line from the Internal Security Council to the Internal Security Committee. He put a question mark halfway up the line from the Government to the Internal Security Council, then crossed the diagram out savagely, tearing the paper.

'You don't want to do the job because Diligence is your friend,' Reepicheep said. 'You think it's a betrayal. Hasn't he betrayed you?'

He had never heard Reepicheep speak so seriously before. 'All right,' he said wearily. 'I do appreciate what you've said, but I don't need to be told my duty.'

'Just to be coaxed a little,' Droylsden said from the door. Xavier looked at him, unpleasantly startled; how long had he been standing there? Then he realised that it didn't matter; Droylsden could hear what had been said as easily from outside as from inside.

'I won't keep you two,' Droylsden said to Reepicheep and Susan. They nodded coldly at him and left the room. Droylsden sat down opposite Xavier, his feet on the table.

'Reepicheep and Susan are senior operatives,' Xavier said. 'They're entitled to a little more respect.'

'All right, I'll give them a little respect. Actually, they were both talking good sense. We're dealing with FIST in the only possible way. Incidentally, you seem to forget that they've tried twice to knock you off.'

'I wondered why you were giving me cover last night.'

'It was Aslan's idea, not mine. We wondered if Miss Rowmarsh might not be arranging something for you . . .'

'You're not going to be able to give me cover indefinitely.'

'Just so. Which is why, for your own sake, we've got to press ahead. It's your friend Diligence who's keen on knocking you off. Doesn't that alter your feelings towards him?'

'I'd like to be sure of that. Not knowing anything of the source of the information, I can't be.'

'You're not going to know anything about the inside man. I needn't tell you why.'

'Fair enough.' But a sense of unease, a sense of being pushed out of the main stream of events, increased; he couldn't put his finger on it, but what was happening now seemed to be dictated by office politics, by Droylsden's advancement, rather than by operational necessity.

'These two chaps who were blown up,' he said. 'Benson and Simmons. It was a bit risky using them.'

The writhing trunk that had been Benson had screamed a lot before it was still; Simmons had died instantly, the back of his head blown off.

'It worked, didn't it?'

'But was it meant to go off when it did?'

Droylsden shrugged. 'Who can tell? But now two of their top people have been eliminated. An eye for an eye, a tooth for a tooth, and all that. It won't be good for their morale.'

'There's one thing which keeps bothering me, which is this

167

chap Dykenhead. He disappears into thin air, and no-one seems to care.'

'I assure you that they do. But it's no skin off your nose, is it?'

'It was skin off Tom Drage's nose,' Xavier said bitterly.

'We'll sort it all out, I promise you. Now can we get on with some serious work?'

'The sooner the better.' Xavier felt a spasm of nausea; he breathed deeply, and it passed.

'When's sooner?'

'Probably this week-end. He has a cottage in Yorkshire. Goes there most weekends in the summer, but I'll check on it.'

'Is he a hard man?'

'You mean violent? Not that I know of. A very kind man. Gentle and loving, I would have said.'

'So would everyone else. He's built up a marvellous cover.' There was a note of professional admiration in Droylsden's voice.

'A marvellous cover,' Xavier said sadly.

'All these years it's just been a marvellous cover. What isn't a marvellous cover? What can we depend on?'

'Ourselves,' Droylsden said. 'We've nowhere to run to.' He laughed. '*Whom God abandoned men defended and saved the sum of things for pay* . . .' He looked away from Xavier, suddenly subdued. 'What a bloody theatrical hackneyed thing to say . . .'

'I would have said it if you hadn't.' For a second Xavier felt strangely happy, no longer alone.

# TWENTY-THREE
## *13 June 1974: 11.30–12.15 Hours*

Sir Geoffrey Morgate's office was evidently very recently redecorated and refurnished, some forty feet by thirty, with a picture window taking up almost the whole of one wall and reaching nearly to the ceiling, thick fitted yellow carpet with a tinge of maroon, and yellow Venetian blinds, now half closed against the bright sunlight. The leather-topped desk behind which Sir Geoffrey sat, the long noteboard alongside the wall facing the window, the glass-fronted bookcase, the round coffee-table to the right of Sally Rowmarsh, were in a dark teak which effectively contrasted with the carpet and the blinds and the long tan-coloured buttoned leather sofa, and two large armchairs, on one of which she sat facing Sir Geoffrey, who held the microphone of her portable recorder gingerly.

It had all been done regardless of expense. Under the 26-inch colour TV in the far corner was a cassette TV recorder; they were only recently on the market, in the region of six hundred. The Bang & Olufsen hi-fi taking up the wall opposite the noteboard wouldn't be so far off six hundred, either; and the large Sony portable radio on the desk was the kind that could get ship-to-ship messages from the other side of the world, and the box of cigars was Romeo y Julieta and the silver cigarette box was, as she knew, filled with Benson and Hedges Luxury Length. The room reeked of money, of conspicuous expenditure, in a way that the other offices that she had visited did not; sonething about it set her teeth on edge, gave her a sense of corruption.

Sir Geoffrey smiled at her, his bright eyes lingering for a second on her legs in their black Dior tights. Her red linen dress wasn't mini, but it revealed what she knew were very pleasantly rounded knees; she smiled back at him, because he looked scrupulously clean with his dazzlingly white hair and white teeth which obviously weren't false but probably were transplants — which would cost at least three thousand – and the white shirt and the cream linen jacket. It was an old jacket but recently pressed and laundered; he looked as if he didn't give a damn about his clothes, even though he kept a valet. His smile was rather disconcerting; the enjoyment of her legs which it was displaying was not only frank but rather savage, but his thin large-nosed face was rather savage, come to that.

'Very agreeable to talk to a pretty girl on a fine morning,' Sir Geoffrey said. 'Even though I've been talking about business rather than her . . .'

'That's very kind of you, Sir Geoffrey.'

'Always tell pretty girls they're pretty. They never object to it.'

'They'd be odd if they did.'

'Gets you into trouble, though. That's why I've divorced three wives. Or rather why they've divorced me . . . Married to the Morgate 1200 now.'

'Why does it sell so well?'

'Said it often enough before. Not that I mind saying it again, if you want to give us a free advertisement. It sells for the same reason as the Jaguar. Powerful, smooth, terrific value for money. And in addition we don't change for the sake of change. We've had bright boys who wanted to make it air-cooled. My father stood against it and I stood against it. That's another reason for it selling. The engine's covered, you don't need special clothes. And it's quiet . . .'

'How is it that you've kept afloat – to put it mildly – and so many other British motor-cycle manufacturers haven't?'

'We own all our component manufacturers for one thing. No-one's ever kept waiting on the assembly line for components to come through. And we don't change for change's sake, but we do get new machinery. And we're a family business. No financial whiz-kids from outside to muck us about.'

'Your finance is in the hands of a sound conservative family bank. Van Norden's.'

He nodded, suddenly wary.

'Which you own? Or rather in which, through her nominees, your daughter has a controlling interest.'

He laughed. 'You *have* done your homework, young lady. My daughter actually has more money than me. Her mother, my first wife, left all her fortune to her. It's not exactly a secret about Van Norden's, but we haven't broadcast it either. You've been busy as a little beaver, haven't you?' He smiled, but his eyes did not change expression.

To her annoyance, she felt something very like fear, then dismissed it. It was no secret, as he said. 'It's my job, Sir Geoffrey. But I'm on your side. I think that Morgate's is an example to all British manufacturers. I'd like you to tell them your secret.'

The door opened and a young girl came in with a tray with a silver coffee-service and two white and gold Royal Doulton cups and saucers, put it down on the desk, not looking at Sir Geoffrey or Sally, and scuttered out.

'Nervous little thing, that,' Sir Geoffrey said. 'But she'll soon settle down. I'll have a word with Mrs Alvaston about her: I don't like anyone to be frightened of me. And that's another reason for our success. We're interested in each and every one of our employees.'

'You've never had any labour trouble at all, Sir Geoffrey?'

'Never, right from the beginning.'

'That rather surprises me, knowing your political opinions.'

'What are my political opinions, Miss Rowmarsh?'

'It's said that they're extremely Right Wing.'

'Black or white, Miss Rowmarsh?'

'Black, please. No sugar.'

'Extremely Right Wing . . . I wouldn't say that . . . I'm an orthodox, strictly orthodox Conservative, actually. Which I admit is unusual these days. I get on very well with my work-people because that's what the majority of them are. I treat them well because it's in my interest to treat them well.'

'Your hatred of Communism has been expressed in very strong terms, Sir Geoffrey.'

'They're all traitors, and all should be hanged. That's merely a statement of fact.'

'Feeling as you do, how is it that you trade with Communist countries?'

'I haven't much option. The Government twisted my arm.'

'I thought that the Russians manufactured motor-bikes themselves.'

'They do. They're the worst motor-bikes in the world. No-one who knows anything about motor-bikes would be *paid* to ride one. And when we trade with the Russians one of the bonuses is this:

they're admitting that Communism doesn't produce the goods, that it simply isn't efficient . . .' He stopped. 'I'm afraid that you'd better keep that off the record.'

He looked at his watch, a gold one, but obviously old, with Roman numerals and a worn leather strap. 'I have an appointment in a quarter of an hour, Miss Rowmarsh. Do you think you've got enough?'

'I'd like to fill out the question of your labour relations. It doesn't seem to me that your explanation is sufficient. There must be something else.'

'There is. Making motor-cycles is still, basically, a craftsman's job. You have job satisfaction. You're making something you can be proud of. We've never cut corners, we've never skimped to get a few shillings extra profit. We make a quality article – a luxury article, and the British working man's a frightful snob. God bless him. And of course we're one of the last of the family firms. We're personally involved at the top – Morgate's *means* Morgate's. Our subsidiary firms stand on their own feet, but they're run on the same principles.'

'And you've really never had any labour trouble at all?'

'I thought I'd made that clear. We've never had any labour trouble.' Sir Geoffrey put down the microphone, took a cigar out, and cut it with a gold cigar-cutter.

'Reluctantly, we must part, Miss Rowmarsh. Perhaps in the near future you'll brighten my life again with your pretty face . . .'

'That's very nice of you.'

Sally Rowmarsh switched off the tape-recorder, and put it in her battered leather shoulder-bag. 'And thank you very much for all your help, Sir Geoffrey.'

'You'll let us see the proof?' Sir Geoffrey asked.

'Of course, Sir Geoffrey. My editor's most particular about it in such instances.'

As she was at the door Sir Geoffrey said, 'You mentioned Van Norden's. They're very discreet and old-fashioned, and there won't be much of a story there. But ask my son, and he'll put you in touch with the right people.'

'I'll do that. Thank you again, Sir Geoffrey.' He was smiling, but this time his eyes had an expression of excitement – not quite lust, but something near it.

A minute after the door had closed behind Sally Rowmarsh, Mrs Alvaston came in, glanced at Sir Geoffrey, went to the sideboard and took out a bottle of Talisker and two glasses. She poured out two large measures and took a glass over to Sir Geoffrey and sat on the desk at his right hand, lighting a cigarette.

'She's a nosey little bitch,' he said.

'Why did you see her? Why are you giving her the run of the place? And why are you sending her to Van Norden's?'

'Because, my dear Stella, it'll look odd if I don't.' Her skirt was riding up; he put his hand on her knee.

'You fancy her, don't you?' She gasped as his hand went further up.

'You know who I fancy.' His hand continued to explore her thighs. 'You're an old-fashioned girl, that's what I like about you. There's nothing like suspenders . . .'

'She's too inquisitive altogether.' She raised herself from the desk and tugged downwards under her dress; there was a rustle as a garment dropped to the floor.

'That's nice,' he said hoarsely. 'That's very nice.' He pushed his chair back. 'Stay there, stay there . . .'

'Yes,' she said. 'A little more.' She stroked his hair. 'Yes, yes.' Her back arched and she cried out.

'I was too quick,' he said, moving away from her. 'I'm worried about that damned girl.'

'Stay there for a moment, darling, it doesn't matter . . .'

'I'll be better next time . . . Something will have to be done about Miss Rowmarsh.'

'You'll think of something.'

He moved away from her and sat down, buttoning up his fly. 'I have already thought of something,' he said.

# TWENTY-FOUR
## *14 June 1974: 1.00–1.20 Hours*

TAPE RECORDING. SOVIET EMBASSY. KENSINGTON PALACE GARDENS. VSEVOLOD ZELENSKY, IN WHOSE OFFICE THE RECORDING WAS MADE, IS 38, OFFICIALLY DESIGNATED AS A COMMERCIAL ATTACHÉ. HE IS ACTUALLY A SENIOR SCIENTIFIC AND TECHNICAL DIRECTORATE AGENT. LEV ULRIKH IS 26, OFFICIALLY DESIGNATED AS A CULTURAL ATTACHÉ, AND IS ACTUALLY A JUNIOR DIRECTORATE S. AGENT.

VZ: Is this what you've hauled me out of a deep sleep for, Comrade? A perfectly straightforward directive?

LU: Excuse me, Comrade, that it isn't. It raises several most disturbing issues. It's addressed to your department but also concerns mine. But to whom should it be addressed?

VZ: That's a rhetorical question, Comrade. Because you're going to tell me.

LU: Directive V. Obviously it's a wet job. And that is why – and I make my profoundest apologies again, Comrade – I had you hauled out of bed.

VZ: Oh, cut out the apologies. You did quite right to call me. You're quite wrong, though, to assume that it's necessarily a wet job.

LU: Surely the intention isn't just to give this British agent a joyride?

VZ: I don't know. The message orders, in no uncertain terms, that a specific object – that is this British agent – be delivered to certain people as soon as possible. Think of him as an object rather than as an enemy, and you can't go far wrong.

LU: Do you mean, Comrade, that this man who has to our certain knowledge killed at least fifty of our agents, is *not* our enemy?

VZ: Of course he is our enemy, my dear young fire-eater. But that is not what the message is about.

LU: But if it is, then it's directly contrary to our policy. Except in the most exceptional circumstances –

VZ: These might be exceptional circumstances. The agent in question might well be doing us an absolutely unacceptable amount of damage. I'm damned sure he's not, though he's good enough at his job. But I don't know the whole story – only the little bit of it I need to know.

LU: I don't understand, Comrade. With the utmost respect, I'm compelled to say that you appear to be contradicting yourself.

VZ: Oh, cut out all this with the utmost respect stuff and get yourself a drink from the cupboard over there. Pour me a Scotch and have what you like yourself.

LU: That's very kind of you.

VZ: I'm a very kind man. Besides, you're young and ambitious – you'll go places with the proper guidance. And as the saying goes, always be nice to people on your way up. You may meet them again on your way down. What I'm telling you, my dear Lev, is that it isn't for us to question the wisdom of the Centre. They're human, of course, they make their mistakes, but that's no skin off our noses. Not if we stick to the rules.

LU: It's been heard of for people to be in deep trouble for being too rigidly bound by narrow legalistic considerations.

VZ: In theory, my dear chap, and at a level far higher than ours. Actually, that particular charge is another way of saying that somehow or other the power has slipped from a chap's hands . . . You will now arrange for that message to be forwarded to the correct destination and then you'll put it out of your mind.

LU: I can't put Operation X out of my mind.

VZ: Between you and me, neither can I. I'm far more bothered about the fate of Flynn the Fearless Fucker.

LU: (*laughs*) Your pet name for him, Comrade?

VZ: You've got to have your little jokes in this job, otherwise you'd go dotty . . . I've looked up the record of this Flynn chap, and I'm not sure why the Centre's suddenly making all this fuss about him. Personally, I think he's just a psychopath. (*Scratch of a match, an interval, a cough.*) I ought to give up these damned

175

things, but if I do, I'll probably take to something worse . . .
(*coughs again*).

LU: That's a nasty cough you have, Comrade.

VZ: Thank you for telling me, that's really cheered me up . . .
Yes, on the whole, I think Flynn's a psychopath . . .

LU: Not like us, Comrade.

VZ: No, Comrade, not like us. Not like us at all.

# TWENTY-FIVE
## *15 June 1974: 8.00–8.30 Hours*

On the moment of awakening, the large mahogany wardrobe, the brass-railed bed with the white lace bedspread, the mullioned window, were everywhere and no known place, all the strange bedrooms he'd ever slept in; and then, fully awake, it was Vanessa's bedroom and this was the fourth time he'd slept here, he was at home in the room, he was at home with her, and from the kitchen he could smell toast and coffee. He closed his eyes for a moment and imagined himself married, at the beginning of two days of leisure. From outside he heard the sound of children's voices: he went over naked to the window, parted the curtains by half an inch and saw down in the mews a young man and a young woman, a boy of about three and a girl of about four getting into a bright orange Citroen 2CV. They all wore faded blue jeans, but the father's sweatshirt was fire-engine red, the mother's bright blue, and the children's white with CHARLOTTE in large black letters across the little girl's and JEREMY in large black letters across the little boy's.

'They're a very trendy couple,' Vanessa said from behind him, gently pinching his bottom, then moving her hand round to his groin. 'Why don't you wave them goodbye with this?'

'I'm tired of that word. What does it imply in this instance?'

'They're bisexual for one thing. At least she is. Invited me in for coffee one morning and tried to touch me up . . . My God, it leapt up then . . . That proves something kinky about you.'

'I can see they're depraved,' he said absently. The Citroen's engine coughed three times then started with a roar; the car moved off slowly, its exhaust a blue haze in the sunlight. 'The bastards,' he said. 'For their tomorrow I give my today.'

Vanessa pulled him round to face her and pulled him across to the bed, shedding her white towelling bathrobe on the way; he seemed to fall into her rather than enter her, and almost immediately they were both crying out together, trembling for a moment then lying still together, their limbs spread out as if in absolute exhaustion.

'Look at me,' she said after a moment. 'Why don't you look at people?'

'I am looking at you.'

'You're looking at the person you'd like me to be.' She poured him a cup of black coffee from the table on her side of the bed and passed him a plate with a slice of thinly buttered toast. He bit into the toast.

'What's she like?'

'A good Catholic wife and mother. Which isn't *me*, is it?'

The coffee was scalding hot and strong, one of the minor pleasures which he was beginning to enjoy so much that it was becoming a major pleasure.

'I'm afraid not, darling. It wouldn't be a sin for *you* to marry me, because you don't know any better. But it would be a very grave sin for *me*. Much worse than simple fornication . . .'

She ran her finger along the scar across his belly. 'At your age you should be married.' She scratched his belly with her finger-nail suddenly; a few flakes of skin came off. 'I could always bribe someone at the Vatican.'

'I'm in the wrong job to marry anyone. I don't much care what happens to me now, but I'd care too much if I had a wife and children.'

'You enjoy your job too much, don't you? You don't want anything to get in the way of it . . . And I know just what you enjoy about it. It's risking your life. It gives you a kick . . . It's real gambling. And for whom do you risk it? The Government? With each one worse than the one before? The people? Christ, they're in a perpetual trance; they honestly believe that everything's going to continue just as it always has done. Everything's getting worse, and they can't see it. Five years from now, or even less, they'll be lucky if they even get enough to eat . . .' She laughed. 'I sound just like Daddy in full spate . . .'

He put his coffee down. 'Just what is all this leading up to?'

'I'll get you a job, a decent job. We can even leave this wretched country . . . I'm beginning to fall in love with you, God knows why. I expect one reason is that you really like women. And another is that you're so wonderfully old-fashioned. A relic of the

178

past, but in perfect working order . . . I want to slap a preservation order on you . . .'

'I think it's too late for that. You don't resign from my department.' For the first time the image of the black ship came to his mind in the daylight, the longing to be in it grew.

'Cousin Piers will listen to me.' There was a note of absolute assurance in her voice.

'Cousin Piers, even Cousin Piers, has to listen to other people. He's under orders, and not from the Government. Governments change, the people who give him his orders don't. They don't change, and they don't change their rules. I don't resign. They don't believe in resignation.'

She grasped his hand tightly. 'Go on. Who are *they*?'

He shook his hand free and got out of bed. 'It's time for me to go.'

'You won't ever tell me,' she said resignedly. 'But think about my offer. Cousin Piers *will* listen to me . . .' She drew in her breath sharply. 'God, what a wonderful body you'd have for a navvy. It's not a Seventies body at all, really. Too heavy for that . . . You haven't said your usual Act of Contrition, have you?'

'I said it to myself . . . I'm going to Confession today, anyway . . .'

'God, Xavier, you're the absolute living end!' She began to laugh helplessly, the brown slim body – with no white modesty marks – rolling diagonally across the bed. She sat up and poured herself a cup of coffee. 'If you look in the left of the top drawer in the dressing-table, you'll find a small Tiffany's box,' she said. 'Bring it to me.'

The drawer smelled of sandalwood and was full of neat piles of brightly-coloured underwear, its lack of creases and deep lustre – as if from inside each thread – the sure proofs that it was real silk. It must have been bought on an impulse and never worn: he knew that her underwear was invariably plain white cotton.

'Your bottom drawer?' he asked her as he brought the small black box over.

'In a manner of speaking. Wedding gifts.' She took out a gold cross, an inch and a half in height, on a heavy gold chain. 'Bend down.' She fastened the chain round his neck. 'I hope it doesn't make you feel like a gigolo.'

He touched the cross gently: it seemed smooth with a living smoothness like mink or ermine rather than with the cold slickness of baser metals. He had never seen gold of such purity before. 'I'll always wear it,' he said. 'I've never had anything like this before.' He kissed her cheek very gently.

She lit two cigarettes and handed one to him. 'You mustn't sell it and give the money to the poor. Promise.'

'Certainly not.' He grinned. 'The poor you always have with you.'

She sat up suddenly, spilling the coffee over the bedspread. 'Oh no, darling. Don't say that, please don't say that.'

# TWENTY-SIX

## *15 June 1974: 10.00–10.10 Hours*

He'd been on the M1 for twenty minutes, holding the Mini at a steady fifty in the middle lane, the sunroof open, when he became aware of the blue BMW 2500 coming up fast in the outside lane. For a second he was tempted to let it pass – he was in no hurry to reach his destination and it was pleasant to feel the sun and the wind on his face, pleasant too to drive the Mini at half its potential, aware of power in reserve – but instinct and caution made him press the button to close the sunroof, snick into fourth gear, and put his foot down.

By the time he moved into the outside lane he was over the hundred mark and the BMW was still on his tail, the distance between them narrowing, and he could see that the driver of the BMW had a black suit and a peaked cap, that one of his passengers, a middle-aged man in a grey suit and white shirt, was sitting beside him, his head bent down, his hands busy with something out of sight, and that the younger man – also in a grey suit and white shirt – in the rear seat was yawning; he'd never seen the three men before, but he'd seen before – changing up, the needle going to 110 – that kind of face, the hard man's face, the killer's face.

A Cortina shooting-brake with a man and a woman and three children, was ahead of him well on the left of the outside lane, its roof-rack piled high; he sounded his horn but could tell from the sudden angry stiffness of the driver's attitude that he wasn't going to move over; he flashed his headlamps and left-hand indicator, keeping his foot down, and passed the Cortina on the middle lane, his nearside wheels occupying a quarter of the slow lane, an articulated lorry with a load of girders coming up on the nearside lane, passing the articulated lorry – now blaring its horn angrily – with precisely one inch to spare and moving over, tyres screaming, on to the middle lane to pass a Hillman Avenger and then into the fast lane, lurching suddenly, a skid beginning; a cold feeling in his stomach, then warmer in his groin, almost sexual, his foot off the throttle, the car righting itself; and then the BMW still coming up behind, its headlamps flashing, the road clear but it wouldn't be for long at this speed, and even if it were to be clear all the way, there was no substitute for litres or weight or for the design of the BMW, which was expressly to hold it as if on rails at over a hundred, hour after hour with no effort; the Mini was a marvellous job but sooner of later something would blow up or he'd hit something or he'd go off the road, and there wasn't going to be the chance to get the Smith and Wesson out of the briefcase beside him, and it wasn't on to have gun duels on the M1, he hadn't ever killed an innocent person and he wasn't going to start now; and then he saw the man beside the driver hold up a large white placard, pointing with a stubby forefinger: CED DRINIAN 697 BETA, and he found himself trembling and suppressed it and pushed the button to let down the right-hand window, flashed his left-hand indicator, and moved into the middle lane, the slow lane, the hard shoulder, giving the slow-down signal. He let the Mini roll to a stop on the hard shoulder, switched off, and put on the hand-brake. The BMW stopped behind him; the driver stayed at the wheel, his passengers got out. Xavier in the Mini, taking the Smith and Wesson out of the briefcase and releasing its safety-catch. The sweat was stinging his eyes; he took off his sunglasses and wiped the sweat away with the handkerchief from the breast pocket of his navy-blue jacket. He noticed for the first time that it was monogrammed X and had a laundry mark; he should have changed it for one of the new ones he'd put in his brief-case.

The middle-aged man stopped beside the Mini. He smelled strongly of sweat. 'Major Flynn? I'm Mr Tumnus.' He waved at the younger man, who was still yawning. 'This is Mr Beaver. He's not notable for his exquisite good manners . . .' If he had had an accent it would have been Cockney, Xavier thought; he rummaged his memory for the two names and found nothing.

'I haven't seen you two before,' he said.

'We haven't seen you, Major,' Mr Tumnus said. 'But then we're new boys. There's an emergency. Aslan wants you to come back to HQ with us.' He crooked his finger at the BMW. 'Donald the Demon Driver will take your car back.'

'I'd like your identification number,' Xavier said, his finger on the trigger of the Smith and Wesson.

'It's 721 Gamma. I've been told you've got a gun, Major. Smith and Wesson 9 mm automatic. Here's my authorisation for it.It'd be better if you put it in the briefcase, and leave the brief-case in your car.' He mopped his face with a large yellow silk handkerchief. 'We can't hang about here all day, Major.'

Xavier put back the safety-catch of the gun, stifling an impulse to shoot Mr Tumnus. If the operation was postponed, it was a relief, he was glad of it; but it was like postponing a dental ap-pointment, you merely delayed the evil day, the pain was still in wait for you. He got out of the Mini slowly and reluctantly. 'It's a five-speed gearbox,' he said to the driver, who had taken off his cap, got into the Mini, revved up noisily, and drove off, moving into the fast lane almost instantly.

'*He*'s not notable for his exquisite manners either,' said Mr Tumnus as he waved Xavier towards the back seat of the BMW, which was purring smoothly in neutral. 'Mr Beaver will drive. The lad will quite enjoy himself, he loves driving. He's a rough diamond, Major, but he's only young and he's got to learn.'

'I'm sure that you'll teach him, Mr Tumnus. What is your name, anyway?'

'Chambers. Though I rather like Mr Tumnus. One of my favourite Narnia characters. I read each one as they come out, Major. I've got firsts of them all. Worth a bit now . . . I'm a great reader, always have been. Takes your mind off things.'

'That's what we all need from time to time.' The warnings were coming through now unmistakably: Chambers certainly was a professional killer, every line of his face was weary with the knowledge of killing, though not, strangely enough, quite coar-sened with it. And his companion was a killer, but a killer whose mind was a blank, who killed because it was as easy a way as any to make a good living. And their proof of identification could only have come from one source. Yet there was something that wasn't right about the whole incident, that didn't fit in; and if that were true, he'd better say a very good Act of Contrition.

'Why didn't Aslan radio me?' he asked, keeping his tone casual.

Chambers shrugged. 'He tried. Couldn't get through at all. Maybe you weren't switched on. Maybe there's something wrong

183

at your end, maybe at his. I don't know. None of my business, Major.'

Xavier decided to say the Act of Contrition anyway, the words running through his head as he spoke. 'You were trained by the Department?'

Chambers laughed. 'Oh yes, Major. Started off as a freelance then got so much work that they decided it was cheaper to put me on the strength.' He lit a cigarette and offered the packet to Xavier, who shook his head.

'It's a dreary six months at Bleak House,' he said, his eyes on Chambers. 'Still, you never forget it . . .' *I am resolved by the help of Thy grace never to sin again* . . .

'It's just like going back to school again, Major . . . Funny thing, I was a schoolteacher once. Just didn't make enough to live on. A shame, really; it's a worthwhile job. Our present occupation isn't really creative, is it?'

Xavier smiled. Chambers was a character to treasure, and there was no mistaking the tone of affection with which he'd spoken about the Narnia series. 'Do you have any idea of what this is all about, Mr Chambers?'

'Calormen is up to its tricks again.'

Calormen: the dark country, the evil country, the enemy of Narnia . . . It was easy to perceive what was in the mind of Chambers; it was obvious that the fool was even pleased with himself. A feeling of bitter regret almost overwhelming him as he did so, Xavier put his right hand into his jacket pocket; Chambers, who was sitting on his right, brought out a Baby Browning with amazing speed. The BMW kept up a steady seventy, giving the impression of being much slower; with one part of his mind Xavier tried to work out where he was, then gave it up within two hundredths of a second; the motorway didn't seem a real road and made even the landscape bordering it seem unreal, and where he was was now irrelevant. What was relevant was that the door to the right of Chambers hadn't been closed properly; he moved the safety-catches on both sides of the Exit One container, then kept his hand still, the fingers spread out, as Chambers put out his left hand to examine the pocket.

'It's only aspirin,' he said. 'I don't quite understand why you should draw a gun on me, Mr Tumnus.'

184

The driver half turned his head.

'Look to your front, Ron,' Chambers said sharply. 'I'll handle this.'

The driver grunted something under his breath and unfastened his safety-belt; the car slowed down and moved over into the middle lane; Xavier was breathing deeply and slowly, ready for action, and the moment for action, the moment when time was measurable by hundredths of a second (and when it wasn't he had better retire) was nearly upon him.

'I really do have a splitting headache,' he said, assuming a mildly petulant tone.

'My sympathies, Major. Just take your hand out of your pocket slowly and show me those aspirins. I've got some whisky in my flask to help wash them down.'

He took out the Exit One in the Bayer tin, holding it by the edges, passed it over into Chamber's outstretched left palm and pressed the fat stubby fingers down over it, grasping Chambers's right wrist with his left, wrenching quickly and up with his shoulder, the brakes screaming and the front seat suddenly striking him hard in the belly, a crack of bone, the sound of the Browning, hurting the ear savagely in that confined space and a choking smell of cordite and the smell of sweat and urine and now death – all in succeeding one hundredths of a second, and Chambers's hand going to his belly, the pale sagging face blotchy red and tautened; the Browning was dropping to the floor, the car had lurched into the slow lane now, in the gap between two furniture vans, the tyres squealing as it was held two inches away from the van in front, the sound of horns and brakes, the smell of rubber and diesel oil, a London sign coming up, the information rejected, catching the gun, the driver standing on his brakes now, Chambers going backwards, his mouth open, not so much screaming as wheezing in a high key, the door swinging open behind him, then closing, the fat body, now dead, but the wheezing continuing, falling towards him, pushing him back against the left-hand door, the left arm coming up to hit his face, the right arm staying still, and all that mattered now was to have enough time to bring himself and the gun upright before the driver, the car having now almost stopped, could turn and shoot him; he had turned his head, his left hand still on the steering wheel, the muzzle of the gun was coming up, when Xavier fired. The driver's eye turned into an ooze of red and he screamed, a high scream which curiously unconvincing, too thin for a grown man, too theatrical, like a child pretending to be hurt, and then it kept on unbearably, the mouth wide open, and Xavier, convulsed by pity, emptied the magazine of the Browning, and the driver slowly slumped forward, quiet at last.

# TWENTY-SEVEN
## *15 June 1974: 11.30–11.40 Hours*

'My old Dad loved to reminisce about his experiences in the Great War,' Aslan said, stretching out his legs to rest his feet on the jump seat. 'The Great War was a time of almost unalloyed felicity for him, as the Second World War was for me . . . You see, Xavier, I like killing people and blowing things up, and that's what I was paid to do during those happy years . . . Even now, when the little ones have gone to bed and I'm digesting my dinner, I like to sit by the fire getting gently pissed and listening to Vera Lynn records . . . However, to return to my old Dad, one of his favourite anecdotes, if so it may be termed, concerned the visit of HRH the Prince of Wales to a trench where there'd just been a lot of hand-to-hand fighting. HRH, who with all his faults was a lad of spirit, had always wanted to be where the real fighting was, and for the first time he saw what it was like. Blood and guts everywhere, lots of corpses, and lots of unfortunate chaps who, the state of medical science being what it was in those days, would soon wish they were corpses . . . HRH surveyed the melancholy scene, shook his head slowly, and then said, *Well, this is a bit of a bugger, isn't it?*'

Xavier closed his eyes, and leaned back, feeling suddenly tired. 'A lovably human reaction,' he said, wondering when Aslan was going to get to the point.

'That's what I said to myself when I looked at these two corpses,' Aslan said. 'This is a bit of a bugger. We have not the services of the Disposer, and week-ends are always difficult. I had a great deal of 'phoning to do and no-one was pleased.'

'I'll let them kill me next time. I wouldn't want to cause anyone inconvenience.'

'That's why it's all a bit of a bugger. I don't feel that they really did intend to kill you.'

'You may well be right; if Chambers had shot me as soon as my hand went to my pocket – or as soon as I got into the car – there's not much I could have done about it.'

187

Aslan patted his shoulder. 'My dear Xavier, I'm not condemning you for wishing to preserve your valuable life. What I'm wondering is who wanted you and what for.'

'And from where there's a leak.'

'That's bothering me rather . . . Among other things. There's talk of Yuskevitch being exchanged . . . For whom?'

Xavier laughed. 'They'll pick out some poor harmless British national with a pin. You're familiar with the technique . . .'

'Indeed, I am, Xavier. Unfortunately, it's a technique which might well work with the present Government. Unless, of course, Operation X is somehow tied up with the deal . . .'

'Operation X? It's not so long since you were doubting its existence.'

'Well, it still isn't my pigeon, or yours, come to that. It has been indicated up till now that it was typically fiendish, along the lines of a chemical to make all our balls drop off . . .'

'I was under the impression of that having already happened to the last Government.'

Aslan snorted. 'Christ, they didn't *have* any to drop off . . . Seriously, though, that sort of thing just isn't on, for the simple reason that it can backfire. But there is something afoot, and it certainly isn't for the benefit of the United Kingdom, if United is what we may term it.' He took a silver flask out of his hip-pocket and passed it to Xavier, who shook his head. 'No? Of course you're on duty.' He took a swig of whisky and replaced the stopper. 'I wish I had more chaps like you around me, Xavier.' There was genuine affection in his voice. 'The hell of a lot of them got killed in the War. Intelligent patriots, chaps who loved their country and who had read a book or two into the bargain. Chaps who could actually think for protracted periods without smoke coming out of the tops of their heads.' He passed the flask to Xavier. 'I'd like you to have this, Xavier. As a gift. My father gave it to me. My initials are on it, but you can have them changed . . .'

Xavier took the flask; for a moment he found it difficult to speak. 'I won't have the initials changed,' he said. 'Thank you very much.'

Aslan coughed. 'Have a good swig after you've gone off duty tonight.' He glanced out of the window at the green well-tended fields under the sunlight. 'A lovely day, let's go out and kill something, as the old joke goes . . . But I'll now go home, get gently pissed, and do some thinking. Gets me out of weeding the garden.'

He was wearing a threadbare once-white tennis shirt, yellow with washing, old and patched grey slacks frayed at the turn-ups, dingy white tennis shoes and no socks, to which ensemble he managed somehow to give a suggestion not only of the South of France and large private yachts, but also of an old family manor, strawberries and cream on the velvety lawn, croquet and cricket and, as always, power.

'The older of those two chaps told me they were once free-lances,' Xavier said. Chambers was a superior sort of hit man. But Brown was pure thug. You could see that he was scarcely human. Actually, Chambers got a bit too clever, poor sod.'

'That makes a nice change these days.'

'He'd actually read the Narnia series and he called the Op-position Calormen. Which we don't.'

Aslan lit a cigarette. 'First today,' he said. The smell of Turkish tobacco – almost too sweet, suggestive of the Twenties, its texture crêpe-de-chine rather than the coarse linen of Virginia – filled the Rolls. 'I think that I may change all the names soon,' he said. 'We ran out of Narnian names a long time since, anyway. The Chairman has never approved. Not only is he so stupid that, to adopt a famous saying, he can't chew gum and walk straight at the same time, he's also illiterate. Not that it ever mattered. I could always get my own way with him. And now my old pal Nigel's taking over, any day now . . . Goodbye King Log, hello King Stork . . . We're going to see changes, Xavier.'

'I hope not.' He had a strange sensation of being near to Aslan, of understanding what made him tick; it was not a feeling of affection, but nearer veneration. 'Aslan suits you.'

Aslan was silent for a moment. 'I'm grateful for that, Xavier. All the more so since you've never been a creeper. It also says what – despite all the rather sordid things we have to do– CED is there for . . . Do you still want to carry out the job tonight? You will be given extra cover, but I shall understand if you don't want to.'

'Better that I do. I might find out a bit more. Wouldn't it be advisable, though, to bring him back?'

'We've got all the information that we want. Let's just carry on smashing up the machine.'

'All right. What about transport?'

'You'll pick up an MGB – the V8 model, I think – at Scatchington motel. There's a briefcase inside with all that you'll need. Just give your name at the counter. By the way, did Chambers or Brown mention the Opposition at all? Or Operation X?'

Xavier shook his head. 'Not a word.'

'I didn't really expect it. They seem from your account to have been typical removal men. Probably used because they were expendable.'

There was, Xavier was surprised to note, something like relief in his voice. 'As you said, it's not our business.'

'No, Xavier, it isn't. We only investigate as much as is necessary for our main purpose. And we know what that is on a fine sunny day like today. And there are times when I'd sooner you than me, but you don't have to believe that . . .'

'I do believe it,' Xavier said, absurdly touched.

# TWENTY-EIGHT
## *15 June 1974: 11.45 Hours*

YURI VLADIMIROVITCH ANDROPOV, CHAIR-
MAN OF THE KGB, FOR THE SPECIAL AT-
TENTION OF IGOR MAKLEVITCH, DIRECTOR,
SCIENTIFIC AND TECHNICAL DIRECTORATE,
AND MIKHAIL KOTOLYNOV, DIRECTOR, IL-
LEGALS DIRECTORATE (DIRECTORATE S).

It is imperative, Comrade Ivanova, that this reaches its destination immediately, and that it is acknowledged and acted upon
immediately, and I don't care if it does ruin their week-end,
because they've already ruined mine. I have been already, the
matter being so urgent, in touch with the First Secretary of the
Party and with Deputy Chairman Tsvigun. We'll consider what
further steps are to be taken after I've seen your transcript.

This memorandum should, strictly speaking, be addressed TO
WHOM IT MAY CONCERN, for it vitally concerns other senior
personnel besides those to whom it is specifically directed. In
short, this is a pie into which many grubby fingers have been
poking. I am going to smack those fingers hard. And if they don't
take heed of the smack, they'll be cut off, and I mean that. I was
given my present authority and I have survived to the age of
sixty, because I know how to be ruthless and when to be ruthless.

The action concerning the British agent Flynn which was
directed late last night – fill in the details, Comrade Ivanova –
was completely misguided in itself, in that the value of its object
is debatable. It is at least a year – check on that, Comrade Ivanova
– since we considered Operation X, for the very simple reason
that it hasn't, until very recently, given us any trouble. Leave
well enough alone is my motto, as long as one is quite sure that
it's well enough.

And I agree with you that Operation X is becoming more and
more expensive and, whilst being simple in itself, raises more and
more complex questions. Nothing in our profession is simple, and

to make it even less simple, there's always the overriding necessity for security. The less information our agents have, the less information can be extracted from them should they fall into the hands of the enemy.

There is yet another factor to bear in mind. Naturally we have a relationship with the clandestine organisation known as FIST, and have given them substantial help whenever it was advisable and possible. Such organisations serve the interests of the Soviet Union – whether in some instances they desire it or not – or even intend it. But whatever benefits may accrue to the Soviet Union as a result of their activities must be thought of as fringe benefits. Our relationship with them is avuncular rather than paternal. They cannot be depended upon where anything of real importance is concerned.

I will admit, however, that I am most favourably impressed by the efficiency of the organisation of FIST and by its exemplary discipline, its ability to bide its time, to wait for the right moment to strike. It is a genuine clandestine organisation, each member has a virtually impregnable cover and, above all, knows better than ever to become involved with any other Left Wing organisation. But it is still amateur, it still has a long way to go. Only a few days ago – insert the date etcetera, please, Comrade Ivanova – a job was bungled. It could be argued, I'm well aware, that the bombing was a successful act of terrorism, and terrorism is one of the main purposes of FIST. This doesn't alter the fact that the bomb didn't explode when it was planned that it should. And the reason wasn't circumstances beyond the control of FIST, but simple technical inefficiency.

What's that? Yes, I'll take it. (*Break here.*)

I have just learned that the Flynn operation was unsucessful, which is just as well. If it had gone as it should, the result would not have been the end of Operation X; I would have seen to that, and I have reason to believe that certain members of FIST would have assisted me – as far, I repeat, as members of such organisations could be of assistance. It would have meant a great deal of trouble, though; trouble which you may be sure I should pass on to you. I am essentially a quiet, retiring man, content to serve the Soviet Union without fuss; I'm not flamboyant, and I don't use flamboyant words. So when I use a neutral all-purpose word like *trouble*, just think for a moment about all its meanings. *All its meanings.*

There is the question of Flynn. There are some KGB officers who consider him to be of some importance. Others have the opposite view. What action has been taken, or not been taken, is something about which I have no precise information, but I shall look into this in the near future.

Finally, I shall consult the First Secretary again and then call a meeting on the subject of Operation X. It will not be easy for me to smooth him down. He is going to be very angry indeed. He is very much in favour of Operation X; it is pre-eminently suited to our present policy of what for convenience's sake we call *détente*. He also esteems Moke most highly and has been known to compare him with Victor Serge. Here I would remind you that Moke is not only concerned with Operation X. It is even possible that the First Secretary might decide that he can do without you, Comrades, before he can do without Moke. Mull *that* over . . .

I can't be sure, of course. His feelings may have changed. You do have a strong argument against Operation X; its high cost is undeniable. And Yuskevitch, who shares your views, has friends. But in your shoes, I should be sweating, just the same.

Finally, you will not mess about with Operation X any more. Leave it to me. Keep right out of it. Frankly – though I do appreciate that your motives are of the highest – you simply don't realise what damage you can do. In the immortal words of the Boss, you're like puppies whose eyes have not yet opened.

# TWENTY-NINE
## *15 June 1974: 22.00–22.15 Hours*

Xavier held the MG on the clutch for a second as he took the corner to the right at Dick Hudson's pub on the corner, noting that the corner was so sharp – the T-junction of two narrow moorland roads – and sloped so steeply that care would be necessary even when turning to the left. It wasn't planned for him to return this way, but things didn't always work out as planned; he drove on at a steady thirty along the road to Basildon, memorising the landmarks which he had already spent two hours memorising on the Ordnance Survey map that afternoon. If he had to leave in a hurry there wouldn't be time to look at signposts. He translated the blackness all around him – a blackness which for a second seemed the blackness of emptiness rather than that of night – back into the map, identifying the string of lights below in the valley as the lights of the main Leeds–Otley road to the north. He could see it now even in the darkness – the wild country, the Scythian country, the sheep and curlew country where you could walk for thirty miles and never see another human being; looking around him even from inside a moving car he felt a sense of exultation, promised himself to return here, and then, as he saw Droylsden's BMW 2002 parked on the verge beside the reservoir on the right, knew that he never would.

He pulled up behind Droylsden and got out. Droylsden wound down his window. 'Five minutes to go. Tweedledum and Tweedledee are at Point B.'

'I wonder why you don't send in tanks,' Xavier said. 'And Edmund's at Point C, I take it, and I can see for myself where you are.'

'I'll take over if you like,' Droylsden said. 'It's all the same to me.'

'We're not changing horses in midstream.' He took a deep breath of cold air. 'God, that's wonderful. It's so clean . . .'

'The object of the exercise is to stop your friend Diligence breathing it,' Droylsden said. 'Make sure that there's no-one else along who has the same idea about you . . . About three hundred yards further along to the left – Reva Hill Lane. It's hellishly rocky, but you can just make it.'

'I know,' Xavier said.

He lit a cigarette and stood in silence, his eyes on his wrist-watch. He stamped the cigarette out, turned to return to his car, then turned back. 'Hugh,' he said, 'you're a shit, but I trust you.' Droylsden looked at him in amazement, smiled, and held out his hand. Xavier shook it, and went to the MG.

As he drove away, for a moment he was tempted to put his foot down, to go past Reva Hill Lane, on to the main road, on to the M1, to keep on travelling, to see what the MG would do and to hell with it if he got killed; it was a car that had to be driven, but it wasn't viciously unpredictable as the more modern designs; as long as you kept to the rules it would go wherever you pointed it and you'd not be frightened of that big, lightly-stressed engine blowing up either; he'd go past Reva Hill Lane and on to the M1 and, if he didn't kill himself, take Vanessa up on her offer of a job and to hell with Aslan and to hell with CED and to hell with the United Kingdom.

The map unreeled itself in his head; he turned left at Reva Hill Lane, a narrow track between five-foot-high drystone walls, and pitched and rolled for half a mile, the springs groaning, the ex-haust more than once scraping stone until suddenly he saw Reva Hill Cottage, a small whitewashed cottage with a patch of level ground in front of it where the lane ended. To the right of the cottage at the end of the patch of level ground was a wooden garage, the doors open. He went quietly to the garage, his hand on his Smith and Wesson: there was only a black Morris 1000 tourer there, its top down. He knew it well, had ridden in it when it was new, had cleaned it more than once; it was part of his youth. 'Jesus,' he said aloud, 'Jesus, help me. Oh Jesus, what shall I do?'

Over to the south a green light flashed three times; he went up to the MG, took out the big Pifco signal lantern and flashed back three times. He put the light away, went to the gate, and opened it. He stood still for a second. The garden was tiny, but crammed with flowers, bordered by a white palisade fence. He shut his eyes for a second, half hoping for death, half hoping that Droylsden and the others had made a mess of it, that an explosion would come out of the darkness to take him into darkness and then, if what the owner of the Morris 1000 had told him was true, from darkness into light. He opened his eyes, walked to the door and banged the knocker. The light was on inside the room to the left of the door and he could hear music.

The door opened and Father Adrian—it was useless now to think of him as Diligence – answered it, peering at Xavier over the tops of gold-rimmed bifocals. The thin, gentle face, the close-cropped grey hair, seemed to Xavier never to have changed since he first saw Father Adrian at St Raymond's twenty-four years ago; the face had gathered a few more furrows, had grown a shade redder, an increasing stoop had brought his six foot two down to six foot, and the thin body sagged a little; there was the beginning of fatigue, the muscles slack instead of taut. But this Xavier saw as a trained observer, a CED agent; as a private person, a human being who loved Father Adrian, at sixty he had not changed.

Father Adrian held out his hand. It was cold but dry, with a firm grasp. 'How wonderful to see you, my dear Xavier! I'd been expecting you somehow.'

'I didn't tell you that I was coming.'

'No-one told me that you were coming. But I wasn't surprised to see you. Sit down here and have some Irish, the real McCoy.'

The room was small, with white plaster walls, and the ceiling low with black oak beams overhead. There was a wood fire in the big stone fireplace, and a scent like cinammon overlaying the smell of cigars and whisky. There were white-painted bookcases on each side of the fireplace, and on each of the other walls, a cream Indian carpet on the stone floor, a marmalade-coloured Chinook dog rug with black eye-markings by the hearth. There was a shabby leather suite with high-backed chairs and a three-seater sofa, and a coffee-table with the bottles of whisky, rum, and brandy, a drum of Wills' Panatellas, four wine-glasses, four high-ball glasses and four small tumblers in the centre of the room. Beside each chair at the fireplace was a small round table. The music was coming from a small portable radio on the drinks table; Father Adrian switched it off. 'I can't resist Mozart,' he said. 'You remember what Lenin said about music.'

'It softens you; it makes you want to pat all sorts of horrible people on the head . . . Or words to that effect.'

'Or words to that effect. It was Beethoven, but it doesn't matter now.' Father Adrian picked up his cigar from the ashtray beside him and motioned towards the table. 'Help yourself to a cigar and a drink, Xavier.'

'I want you to hear my confession.'

The black thick eyebrows, so oddly in contrast to the grey hair, lifted. 'You've come a long way for it.'

'That doesn't make any difference, Father.'

'Very well, then. It's the last time, anyway. Kneel down there.'

He sat down in the armchair he had just left; Xavier knelt beside it.

'Forgive me, Father, for I have sinned . . .' He listed the usual sins mechanically, scarcely hearing them: lust, anger, neglecting his morning and night prayers – once – blasphemy, pride. Father Adrian, his fingers together, listened with a bored expression. 'Sloth,' Xavier said.

The black eyebrows shot up. 'Explain yourself, my son.'

'There is something I should concern myself with that I haven't really concerned myself with. It's a matter of making enquiries about something which I know to be wrong. I don't have to investigate, but my conscience tells me that I should, that I've been having it too easy for a long time.'

'It might be lack of ambition that you're really accusing yourself of. That may be a fault in some people's eyes, but it isn't a sin. Still, sloth it is . . . Make a good Act of Contrition and say for your penance three Our Fathers, and Three Hail Marys . . .'

Xavier bowed his head for the words of absolution, feeling, though it wouldn't last, the familiar lightening of the spirit.

As he got to his feet Father Adrian took his collar and jacket off and put on a white polo-neck sweater which gave him a strangely raffish look. 'My last clerical chore, my dear Xavier. Now you can have a drink. Look, I'll pour some into my own glass and take a mouthful – so.'

Xavier accepted the glass, sat down, lit a cigarette, and took out the Smith and Wesson.

'I thought that you used poison.'

'It depends on the circumstances. In any case, it's unwise to use any weapon exclusively . . . Oh God, never mind that.' The heat of the fire was making him sweat. 'Tell me it isn't true, that's all, and I'll cancel the operation. I don't care what story you make up to explain it.'

'You've always had a kind and a loyal heart, Xavier, but it's no use denying the facts. You have colleagues in the vicinity, and they'll do the job even if you won't.'

'I can get you out of here.'

'There's nowhere for me to go, Xavier. Others are involved. There has been a split in FIST, and now it's going to be resolved. I've been a Marxist since I was thirty, Xavier, and helped to set up FIST some six years ago. And now they're dropping the pilot . . . How much time have we got?'

'About five minutes. Do you want to say a prayer?'

'I can put up with being killed, but not with being insulted. I repeat, I am a Marxist. Everything in the universe is material –'

Xavier smiled. 'Does that include the idea that everything is material.'

'I haven't the time to argue, Xavier. I became a Marxist because of what I learned from history, which is that what everyone is really after is power. Richelieu and Père Joseph, for instance, believed in the non-material world, believed too in what Lenin calls an eternal morality, a fixed morality. But not in their capacity as statesmen, dear me no.'

'I remember you bringing out this very issue.'

Father Adrian looked at him with affection. 'I always regret not having persuaded you to go to university. You might even have been working with me in FIST now.'

'I doubt it – Father.'

'You needn't hesitate about calling me Father. I wouldn't really feel happy about your calling me Adrian, and I'm too fond of you to like the notion of being Mistered by you. But on second thoughts, I think that you're right in what you say . . . The university wouldn't have changed you, Xavier. You'd still be on the same side, even if it were proved to you it was the losing side. As it is. And the Church has had the death-wish for a long time; not that any organisation could survive a drivelling idiot like Pope John . . .'

198

He poured himself a full glass of whisky. 'You're not drinking, Xavier.'

'Not on duty.'

'You'll go far if you live, Xavier. I taught you well in my capacity of Father Adrian. In case you feel upset about what you have to do, remember this: if we had a Marxist Government now, I should do to you exactly what you're going to do to me.'

'You're a brave man,' Xavier said, glancing at his watch. He heard in the distance the sound of a car engine.

'A revolutionary is at the best on holiday from death, as the German said . . . Once you face the fact that when you die you go into nothing, there's nothing left to fear, and all your acts have value, they are acts for their own sake, not to qualify for future reward or avoid future punishment. That is the great gift of Karl Marx to the human race –' There were three short knocks and a long knock at the door, followed by three short blasts and one long blast of a car horn. 'Is that the signal?'

'Yes,' Xavier raised the Smith and Wesson.

'Make a thorough job of it. Even with a ·38, one shot isn't enough. Goodbye, Xavier.' He smiled, looking at Xavier with a genuine affection. 'Fire when I raise my hand.' His hand went up and Xavier squeezed the trigger twice.

# THIRTY
## *16 June 1974: 4.00 Hours*

---

'You've had a long day, son.' Xavier's mother said, pouring him a cup of tea. 'Are you sure you won't have another sandwich?'

'Sure, Mother.' Xavier sipped the strong tea and leaned back in his chair. 'You shouldn't have stayed up for me, I could have got something for myself.'

'Your father couldn't sleep and he wouldn't let me sleep either.' A small plump woman with only a few strands of grey in her thick black hair, she looked ten years younger than her age of sixty; her skin was fresh and rosy, almost unlined, and her blue eyes were clear and alert.

'It's a wicked lie,' said his father. 'She wanted to be up to look after you herself. She's a great one for looking after people, is your mother.'

'I don't know why he doesn't come here to be looked after properly,' Xavier's mother said. 'Chertsey's no distance from London.'

'The boy needs to be on his own, woman, not to be fussed over by you.'

'I know what he wants to be on his own for. It's high time you were married, Xavier.'

Xavier smiled. 'All in good time, Mother. Perhaps when I get promotion and keep more regular hours.' He knew the conversation by heart, and found it soothing as he found the atmosphere in the big yet overcrowded room – crammed with ornaments and china – two glass-fronted display-cases full – and furniture – three large armchairs, two three-seater sofas, two smaller armchairs, three coffee-tables, two small occasional tables, a cocktail cabinet, a small bookcase – not to mention a 26-inch TV, a Grundig radiogram, and, he was sure, at least one new object that wasn't here on his last visit. The colours of the room were predominately brown and grey; neither of his parents had any colour sense, so they played safe.

'I thought that Civil Servants always kept regular hours,' his father said, relighting his pipe. He had a look of Father Adrian, Xavier reflected, but his face was not so gentle; it appeared as if he were always about to erupt into a fit of temper, but he almost never did. And he was more heavily built than Father Adrian, and at five foot ten a little shorter. *You go into nothing*; there was a brave man.

'They mostly do, Father,' he said. 'But not those who have to deal with businessmen.' His father's hair was grey, but lately he'd taken to wearing it longer, not really long in the accepted sense of the word, but if it grew another two inches he'd look like an old woman, particularly in that long dark grey woollen dressing-gown, almost identical in colour and cut to his mother's.

'Must be rather irksome, dealing with these fellows,' his father said. 'Seeing them live it up, trying every fiddle . . .'

'There's nothing else can be done, taxes being as they are,' Xavier said. Idly looking round the walls – two Madonnas, the Flight into the Wilderness, his mother and father's Papal Blessing, the First Communion certificates of himself and of Clodagh, a large black crucifix – he saw a reproduction of the Dali Crucifixion.

'It looks more as if Our Lord were going to take off into space than to be crucified,' he said.

'It's art,' his father said. 'You're conservative in more ways than one, Xavier.'

'We don't have any politics in the Civil Service.'

'You don't seem to have a union, either,' his father said. 'They're working you to death.'

Xavier stifled an impulse to burst into hysterical laughter. 'I don't think that my Chief is a trade-union type,' he said.

'Sorry to hear it. Never mind. Did your business go well today?' his father asked.

'The contract was signed,' Xavier yawned. 'I think I'll go to bed.'

'Your room's ready for you,' his mother said. 'Can't you talk about the contract or whatever it is tomorrow, Pat? The boy's tired to death.'

'I don't mind. Why shouldn't he be interested?' He got up, went over and kissed his mother and laid his hand on his father's shoulder. 'Good night, Mother. Good night, Father.'

Going up the wide staircase the effort of walking seemed almost too much; he was scarcely aware of what he was doing as he undressed and put on his pyjamas. It was a big room overlooking an acre of lawn, with pines at the back screening the row of bungalows in the next road. It had been his room from the time they'd come to Chertsey; in the big pine chest by the wardrobe were his airgun, his model Vosper boat, his Triang OO train set and control unit and extra rolling-stock and lines and points and a railway station, his Frog Spitfire, the Matchbox and Dinky Toys cars and the boxed games – all in their original boxes, waiting for his son, if ever he had a son. There was a large brass crucifix above the bed and a reproduction of the Madonna of the Rocks on the wall by the door; that had been his choice when he was sixteen. His mother hadn't liked it; she said it wasn't really religious, which was true enough. But beyond the rocks was a grey cold sea to the edge of the world, to Ultima Thule and never mind the world being round; when he'd first looked at that picture he'd started thinking of the black ship, for only a black ship could sail upon that sea, and only the dead would ride in the 1914 Prince Henry Vauxhall, and the 1926 Hispano-Suiza next to the Madonna.

The window was open, letting in the smell of grass and night-scented stock and pine trees; it was colder than was comfortable, but he left it open and went to the bookcase by the door and picked out *The Phoenix and the Carpet*. He took it to the bedside table, switched on the bedside lamp, and went to the door to switch off the main light. The black and white chequered lino was chilly under his feet; his mother had wanted to put in fitted carpet but he had asked her not to change it, not to change either the woodgrain-effect wallpaper; he wanted there to be one room to which nothing was added and nothing taken away, in which he could travel back to innocence or at least comparative innocence. He said his prayers quickly – an Act of Contrition, a Hail Mary, an Our Father: the irreducible minimum when he was tired – and got into bed.

He opened the book, sighed and then closed it and got out of bed and kneeled down again. 'Thank you for all the good thing's You've done for me. Preserve all under this roof from fire and accident and marauders by night. Let me know how best to serve my God and my country.' These were his personal prayers; he had already prayed for the repose of the soul of Father Adrian. He got up, hesitated, and took out a pen and a small notebook from the brief-case beside the bed.

He closed *The Phoenix and the Carpet* and wrote in the note-book:

QUESTIONS
  (1) Who are the employers of Brown and Chambers?
      What did they want me for?
  (2) From where is the leak? There *is* a leak.
  (3) What is the split in FIST about?

He wrote rapidly for five minutes, then his eyes began to close and the pen to slide into hieroglyphics, then totally meaningless squiggles; the pen suddenly slipped from his hand to the floor, and he fell asleep with the light on.

# THIRTY-ONE
## *17 June 1974: 16.00–16.30 Hours*

'I'd like to see Mr Death,' Droylsden said to the large man who had answered the door. 'My name is Droylsden, and I have an appointment.'

The big man looked at him blankly, pulled a long hunting knife from his belt, and started to toss it into the air, catching it by the hilt as it came down.

'Very clever,' Droylsden said. 'Do it again and I'll show you some tricks with a Colt Police Special.' He wondered if Aslan had sent him to the right place. The big man was some eight inches over six foot and his body was in proportion, with broad shoulders, a deep chest, and narrow hips, not shambling and ill-co-ordinated as was so often the case with men of his size. He could handle the knife, and by the way he held himself could handle the huge body; it might be as well to kill him now, because God only knew what was going on behind that big flat face.

A small fat man in a bright red silk dressing-gown came up behind the giant. 'Come on, Sylvester, get out of it,' he said in a Yorkshire accent. 'Get into the kitchen and make us some tea. And put that damned knife away.'

'Sorry about that,' he said as Droylsden followed him into a large room with silver walls and almost ankle-deep thick white fitted carpet with what appeared to be gold thread running through it. 'Sylvester has just learned that trick with the knife and he's very proud of it.' He sank down into a leather and transparent plastic chair and waved Droylsden into the one opposite.

'I wouldn't have thought that he needed a knife,' Droylsden said.

'He's very strong. Broke a man's back across his knees once for a bet. Perfect stranger. He's like a child really: he'll do anything to be noticed. He's an orphan; he's always searching for love. And very shy. He doesn't make friends easily.'

'I should have thought it damned near impossible for him to make friends with anyone except an orang-utan. However, I'm not here to chat about Sylvester, fascinating though he may be.'

'You have a job for me, Mr Droylsden, right?' He opened a huge heart-shaped box of Lindt chocolates and studied the diagram inside, frowning with concentration.

'A job about which there must be no talking.' He caught sight of an unframed painting on an easel. 'God, is that an original Magritte?'

'It is indeed, Mr Droylsden. I'd saw the dealer's balls off with a rusty knife if it weren't. But there's no need to tell me to hold my tongue. That's why I'm so expensive.'

'What would be nice, and what would be worth extra, would be if afterwards you got rid of the chap who did the job.'

Mr Death bit through a strawberry crème. 'Not ethical, Mr Droylsden. Besides, I have a reputation for looking after my boys and girls. If that sort of thing started happening to them, who'd I get to work for me?'

'All right, that's fair enough.' He reached into his briefcase and handed Mr Death a large photo of a man in his late fifties. 'The basic particulars are on the other side. His name should be enough really, but it would be tiresome if you got the wrong chap.'

'I'd give you your money back in that case. Even if the job were eventually done.' Mr Death selected another chocolate.

'Most honourable of you, but we just want the job doing. Have you anyone available?'

A naked blonde of about eighteen appeared at the door and beckoned towards Mr Death. 'Later, later,' he said impatiently, and bit into an orange crème. The girl disappeared, giggling. 'I'm a family man really,' Mr Death said, half apologetically, 'but not in London. I love London, Mr Droylsden: it makes me feel young again. Never got up to any tricks in Bradford. Never made any money in Bradford, come to that . . .'

'I thought you came from the North somehow.'

'Oh, it's a great advantage to me, Mr Droylsden. They trust a man with a Yorkshire accent, God knows why. Except that it sounds so warm and homely . . . Besides, I'm not the only one who comes from the North, am I?'

Droylsden flushed, then laughed. 'Tha's got all tha chairs at home, lad.'

'Very good, Mr Droylsden. I've got three chaps in that particular prison who'll do the job for me. They'll be glad to. Funny chaps, criminals. Very patriotic they are.'

Sylvester came in with a silver tray. 'Tea,' he said. 'I let it brew for five minutes like what you said, Mr Death.'

'Good boy, Sylvester, put it down there.'

Sylvester put the tray down on the glass table nearby, and pulled out a London Classified Directory from under his arm. 'Look,' he said to Droylsden, and tore the directory in two apparently with no effort.

'That's absolutely splendid,' Droylsden said. 'I wish I were just half as strong as you.'

Sylvester blushed and ran out of the room taking the directory with him.

'Goodness, you have made a hit with Sylvester,' Mr Death said.

'As I say, he's like a child. He needs praise, he needs love . . . He doesn't do his tricks for everybody.'

'His affection might become rather embarrassing. Does he ever do any jobs for you?'

'He has done in the past, but he's a bit too conspicuous.' Mr Death poured out a cup of tea. 'I'll be mother. Milk? Sugar? Lemon? Yes, lemon is the best, it brings out the flavour . . . I made the bet which I've just alluded to, actually – when Sylvester broke this chap's back . . . Marvellous, really, all over in a minute . . . It was a very special job, I was asked to do this one very specific thing . . . That was ten years ago, on my fortieth birthday, and I said to Sylvester, "Sylvester, my boy, you've just given me the finest birthday present a man ever had, which is a reputation." ' He put four spoonfuls of sugar into his cup with a silver spoon and stirred the tea slowly. 'Ten thousand, Mr Droylsden. In the usual form.'

'We want it done by Wednesday at the latest.' Droylsden opened his briefcase and took out a bulky brown paper packet. 'Half now, half when the job's done.'

'We might even get it done before. But there are quite a few details to be arranged. And palms to be greased. The country's going to the dogs, Mr Droylsden, corruption everywhere. By the way, is the person in whom we're interested homosexual?'

'He has quite a few vices, but not that.'

'Pity. It could be arranged for him to force his loathsome attentions on some innocent young lad, who would have never heard of such a horrible thing. And in his righteous wrath the innocent young lad – but I needn't spell it out.' He laughed, wheezingly, pushed his cup aside and lit the longest cigar Droylsden had ever seen. 'It would kill two birds with one stone, if you see what I mean.'

'A very tempting proposition, but I don't think that it's on. In any case, the chap's probably been put in solitary by now.' Droylsden rose. 'Thank you for the tea, Mr Death, and I'll be hearing from you.'

'I have two more Magrittes in the next room, and a Picasso. And some other very nice things. No gold wallpaper, the room was designed as a small gallery. A clever young man who not only could do a job for me now and again, but also who I could trust to act as my deputy – why, he could be buying original Magrittes himself in a very short time.'

'That's a great compliment, Mr Death, but I have a contract with my present employer. The penalty clause is rather drastic.'

'That's a shame, Mr Droylsden. Because good men are hard to find.'

Droylsden grinned. 'Nice of you to say so, Mr Death.' He stood up. 'But you will remember what I've said about absolute discretion, won't you? My department employs other good men.'

Mr Death nodded, his face impassive, and chose another chocolate. The naked blonde came into the room again and stood staring at Droylsden, her lips parted. Droylsden glanced at the Magritte, turned abruptly, and walked quickly out of the room.

# THIRTY-TWO
## *17 June 1974: 16.32–16.42 Hours*

'I'm afraid, Xavier, that I have a shock for you,' Aslan said. He went across to the drinks cabinet. 'You'd better have a drink.'

'I don't need a drink. Tell me now.'

Aslan turned away from the drinks cabinet and came to where Xavier was sitting. He put his hand on Xavier's shoulder. 'I fear that the leak is from Reepicheep.'

'Oh, Christ, no!' The tears came to Xavier's eyes. 'Anybody but him . . . It's not the sort of thing I can take.'

'I don't say I'm one hundred per cent certain, and it's been known for the KGB to frame a chap before. One thing is certain: he has a very sizable bank account in Zürich. Forty thousand dollars US . . . That's a beginning.'

'Bank accounts have been forged.'

'The new Chairman of the Council doesn't think so.' He moved away from Xavier. 'Christ, Xavier, if you don't have a drink, how can I have one?'

'A Bison vodka, then.'

'And you are welcome to it, Xavier. Commissar's piss, I call it.' He handed Xavier his drink and sat down at the big desk. 'And, to fill my cup of woe right up, the new Chairman of the Council, the former Controller and Co-ordinator of Security Personnel, is acting out the rôle of King Stork with a vengeance . . . I knew it was coming, Xavier, but I didn't expect the appointment to be confirmed quite as soon . . . Bunty cried when I told her, and, believe me, Bunty doesn't often cry.'

'The former Chairman didn't bother you much.'

'He was all for a quiet life. He had some right bastards on the Council, but as long as he was on my side – or at least not against me – I could get what I wanted. Forwards two steps, backwards one, always advancing . . . Would you like some leave?'

'Why? Do you think I need it?'

'This job in Yorkshire must have taken it out of you.' Aslan's voice was surprisingly gentle. 'Now it's over and you've not cracked, you need time to think. The shit's going to hit the fan as soon as Nigel gathers up the reins into his grimy hands. I assure you that they are grimy, too. You're better out of the way for a while. Better out of Reepicheep's way, too. We can't act yet. You might find it difficult to keep quiet.'

'I will keep quiet if I have to.'

'After what he did to you? I've found out a bit more about Brown and Chambers. They were very nasty people indeed. Nearly as nasty as us, and that's saying something.'

'I'll think about it.' Xavier finished his vodka.

'All right, Xavier, the choice is yours. But see Bunty on your way out and she'll give you the dossier on Reepicheep. It won't make you very happy.'

Xavier got up. The tears had stopped now. At the door he turned, remembering something Father Adrian once had said. 'We were not born to be happy,' he said. 'We were born to do our duty and not complain.' He saw, noted, but could not quite understand Aslan's almost exaggerated reaction of surprise.

# THIRTY-THREE

# *18 June 1974: 15.30–15.45 Hours*

'I'm absolutely awestruck by the speed with which you've grasped it all,' the Manager of Van Norden's Bank said, leaning back a little in his chair and rocking gently. With his white hair and pink round face and half-moon spectacles he seemed almost a parody of all the kindly old professional men – family lawyers, family doctors, but never family accountants or family architects. Or family bankers, come to think of it, though this was a family bank if a bank ever was.

'Twenty-five per cent of your shares are non-voting shares,' she said. 'The rest are owned by the Morgate family, or rather their nominees. That's all I've sorted out, really.'

The Manager shook his finger at her. In contrast to his rather chubby figure, made chubbier by his black coat and waistcoat and old-fashioned gold watch-chain, his hands were long and thin – a pianist's hands on the Michelin man.

'I've been here forty years, Miss Rowmarsh, and I haven't sorted it all out yet. Fortunately, our AGMs are very quiet affairs. Last year, when we had trouble with the heating system, we had it here.' He looked round the room with a certain complacency. 'When I was installed here as Manager thirty years ago, beautiful oak panelling had been covered over with hideous gold and green paper. And the furniture – hideous light-coloured stuff, and a shiny cocktail cabinet – I bought Victorian stuff, like this lovely big mahogany desk and that walnut davenport and that glass-fronted bookcase: they thought me mad at the time but now – why, this furniture's part of the assets of the Bank. Liquid assets: the davenport alone would fetch six hundred . . .'

'You'd say that the policy of Van Norden's was conservative?'

'Gracious me, yes. Mark you, Miss Rowmarsh, all bankers must gamble because of the very nature of their business. It's like the parable of the talents: we can't just *bury* our customers' money.'

'Some of your customers have criticised you for doing business with South Africa and Spain and –' she hesitated – 'other countries.'

He smiled, rather maliciously. 'And other countries, Miss Rowmarsh? You were about to say Portugal and Greece but they're what you call OK countries now. Never mind, we'll do business with Chile to make up for it. You might have added that some customers criticise us for doing business with Iron Curtain countries. Really, who are we to trade with?'

'You have a contented staff apparently. No labour trouble at all.'

'Well, we're a merchant bank, after all. More officers than privates, so as to speak. And we were pioneers in staff welfare. We've always helped our staff with mortgages, their children's education, and so on . . .' He looked out of the window. 'I love this view, Miss Rowmarsh. Cannon Street for me is the real heart of the City. You can see a long way on a fine day like today . . .'

'There is one small point. I'm having some trouble understanding the export figures . . .'

'Say no more, I'll call in the very girl for you. Yes, girl, Miss Rowmarsh – we're not male chauvinist pigs here.' He picked up the 'phone. 'Manager here. Please send in Mrs Dairen with the Morgate file. And make it tea for three, please. With those nice plain chocolate biscuits I had yesterday. Thank you.'

He smiled at her, his smile benign again. 'Actually, I must confess that I'm glad you came today. Things are running so smoothly that there isn't much for me to do.'

'You're tempting fate,' Sally said. 'Better touch wood.'

'No sooner said than done.' He looked up from the desk, at the door. 'Ah, here's Mrs Dairen.'

A tall woman in her thirties came in, carrying a large box-file. Her hair was a pale blonde and her face had an unusual serenity.

'Mrs Dairen, Miss Rowmarsh of the *Argus*,' the Manager said. 'We call Mrs Dairen our Madonna of the Export Accounts, Miss Rowmarsh. She calms down all the irate old gentlemen.'

Mrs Dairen inclined her head towards Sally and pulled up a chair beside her, still holding the box-file, her eyes enquiringly on the Manager.

The Manager looked at his watch. 'Will you be expected back at the *Argus*, Miss Rowmarsh? We can give you a lift back after tea. One of our few perks . . .'

'That's very kind of you, but I'm not going back to the office. This isn't a news article, there's no deadline.'

'Very well, but if you change your mind –'

The Manager nodded to Mrs Dairen; she opened the box-file, pulled out a long hunting-knife and plunged it straight into Sally's heart. Sally screamed, then suddenly, her eyes staring, was still. Mrs Dairen, her serene expression unchanged, forced her back in the chair.

'It's well out of range of the window,' the Manager said. 'I've checked and double-checked.'

Mrs Dairen took Sally's pulse. 'The quickest job yet,' she said in a pleasant contralto voice.

The Manager yawned. 'I could do with my tea,' he said. 'I do hope they remember to bring me some of those nice plain chocolate bickies.'

Mrs Dairen took a packet of Kent and a lighter out of the box-file and lit a cigarette.

'You know I don't like ladies to smoke, Mabel,' the Manager said.

'Fuck you, Buckley,' Mrs Dairen said and blew a lungful of smoke in his face.

# THIRTY-FOUR
# *18 June 1974: 16.00–16.20 Hours*

As Jane went out of Xavier's office, the Chairman of the Security Council stretched out his arm and pinched her bottom. She squealed: 'You're naughty, Brigadier.'

'I know I am, my dear. Senile eroticism. The last flare-up before the fire goes out.'

She smiled at him and continued on her way, her hips waggling in a deliberate Marilyn Monroe parody.

'Bright child that,' said the Chairman of the Security Council. 'Well, not quite, she's nearly thirty, but a child to me . . . Knew her father. One of these days you'll have to know all about the people at HQ, Xavier. Every last one, down to the guards. Though maybe you do . . .'

He went over to the filing cabinet and took out the bottle of Bison vodka and two glasses.

'I have to congratulate you, Brigadier,' Xavier said, accepting the glass of vodka. The Chairman of the Security Council sat down and put his feet on Xavier's desk.

'I've been a long time in the wilderness, Xavier, which makes it all the more acceptable.' He rose suddenly and paced the room, a small stocky figure in the mid-fifties, with a square sunburned face and rumpled brown hair. He had not the presence of Aslan, and his navy-blue suit was unpressed, with papers sticking out of one jacket pocket, but, Xavier reflected, he did have one of Aslan's qualities, which was the air of not giving a damn for what anyone thought of him.

'I was wondering what you wanted from me,' Xavier said.

'I don't really know yet. But there's an organisation chart behind you which needs sorting out. Of course, no organisation on earth was ever run according to the chart, because organisations are collections of human beings and a chart is lines and words. And what complicates everything in our case is the need for security.'

Xavier tossed back his vodka in one gulp and poured himself

213

another. 'There's definitely a need for security,' he said bitterly.

'I heard of your little adventure on the M1. Rather disturbing.'

'What disturbs me as much as the leak, sir, is not knowing what it's all about.'

'One thing which it's about is that Reepicheep has gone missing

'I'm sorry, sir, I don't believe it. At least, if he's gone missing, it's not of his own free will.'

The Chairman lit his pipe. Xavier found the acrid smell strangely reassuring. 'Have you any evidence for that?'

Xavier shrugged. 'I don't know Cyril well – I mean Reepicheep. He lives his own life in his own little circle. But I've worked with him for ten years now and I know he's not a traitor.'

'Traitor.' The Chairman nodded. 'Yes, that's a good word, Xavier. Never mind about going double. Let's say traitor. Is he a puff?'

'Camps it up a bit sometimes, but I've known girls who've gone about with him and the verdict is that he's a premier cocksman. Little chaps generally are –' He stopped, embarrassed.

'That's all right, Xavier. I wouldn't have liked it if you'd said that little chaps are generally puffs. What you're saying is that you have a hunch and be damned to the Swiss bank account. Isn't that it?'

'That's it. But I'm not criticising Aslan. In his position he has to go by the evidence.'

The Chairman poured himself another glass of vodka. 'I'm not criticising him, Xavier. You can't criticise the chap who really nailed Philby – and the Fourth, Fifth, and Sixth Men. I'm not making a formal visit to the Mess to ask if there are any complaints. I'm here because it suits me to come to you rather than have you go to me. And because things are happening.'

'I'd like to know what sort of things.'

'Before you did your last job I should have said that it wasn't your concern. But on Saturday night you proved that you were something more than a hired gun. You obeyed orders that you hated, and yet remained a human being. And, by having him hear your confession, you stated your point of view. Without arguing – how the hell could you, with a gun in your hand? He'd have won then, don't you see?'

'I do see, but I don't see how you know.'

The Chairman sighed. 'These days tape-recorders can work very efficiently from outside a building. Even from a distance. This one was quite near.'

Xavier put down his glass with a bang. 'It's nice to be trusted . . . What shit thought that one up?'

'The sort of shit that you may be one day. When the lack of the information such instruments can obtain might hurt your country.'

'I still haven't had much information from you, sir.'

'An order comes first. Go on leave now and wait until you hear from me. I shall arrange for that nice little girl Jane to give you whatever code numbers you need. She is a nice girl, a genuine blonde, I'm sure, like her mother . . . She is also very clever. I trained her . . . Have you heard of the Committee?'

'Nothing to inspire confidence one way or another.'

'It is there for the express purpose of answering questions.'

'About Operation X, for instance?'

'About anything. About whose daughter Jane really is, if you were ever so damned nosey. But then I could ask if you'd asked the question. If you do go to the Committee, I won't guarantee that you'll always like the answers.' He tore a piece from the document in his jacket pocket and scribbled a number on it. 'Here. Destroy when memorised.' He rose. 'Don't get up.'

'I'll see you again. And thank you.'

The Chairman shook his head. 'You'll see me again – if you live. Don't thank me, Xavier. It never pleases me to put a man aboard the black ship.'

'I wonder how you know about that.'

'I'm confident that you'll work it out.' The Chairman turned abruptly and went out of the room. Xavier looked at the piece of paper for a moment, then, suddenly shivering, set it on fire with his cigarette-lighter.

# THIRTY-FIVE
## *18 June 1974: 20.00–20.15 Hours*

Boris Yuskevitch lay on his bed in Cell 3, Block 4, perfectly contented and relaxed, a short but broad-shouldered and powerful man in his late fifties: a peasant's body, a Slav's body, which didn't seem to match his thin sensitive face with the gold-rimmed glasses. The prison was fifty years old, old enough to have in its atmosphere some trace of humanity, for the prisoners to be able somehow to make for themselves cosy little living areas, corners where there was a tenuous but real privacy, but new enough to be watertight and weathertight with functioning heating and plumbing. And in any case a luxury hotel compared with the Lubyanka in Moscow to which he'd been sent for no good reason in 1947, to be released for no good reason and given promotion to full lieutenant a year later.

There were no quiet cosy moments in the Lubyanka except for the real criminals, the professional criminals, who knew what they were there for and how long they were going to stay and who behaved as if they owned the prison and, one chap in particular, a big chap from Kiev, a petty thief, as if they owned him, until the big chap from Kiev found himself one day suddenly ruptured and with an eye short.

But here it wasn't like that: they were so gentle and kind that it was almost unbelievable, and even the ones referred to in a bated breath as being hard men were just paper tigers. It was difficult to believe that they and the people from CED came from the same race, though not at all difficult to believe that the people from what was now called D15 did.

And here he was safe from CED, and even receiving a certain amount of information that indicated that something was to happen soon, that people at the Centre were at last catching on to the idea that Operation X had had a good run for its money, so to speak; that it was time they pensioned it off with appropriate good wishes and regrets. The messages which he'd received couldn't, naturally, do any more than indicate that there was a ferocious internal battle going on at the Centre at this moment; he had friends who were for Operation X and friends who were against it and enemies who were for it and enemies who were against it and God only knows which side the Director took; and in the meantime he could sit, or rather lie, it out and re-read *Dombey and Son* and have his last cigarette of the day.

He lit his homemade cigarette – he'd been very choosy once, nothing but Balkan Sobranie or Sullivans, but the homemades now tasted better than either – and took out the bookmark from *Dombey and Son*.

He'd been half looking forward to that passage and half dreading it. He knew it was old-fashioned and sentimental, but it always made him cry. He always cried long before Little Paul asked what the wild waves were saying; he couldn't bear the thought of children suffering. He opened the book and almost immediately his eyes moistened, seeing the little figure in bed, so pale and so patient . . .

Ten knocks came from the direction of the wall: O break U, Emergency, Bomb WC, and he was under the bed, the mattress with him, hunched up against the wall, his arms over his head, his hands on his eardrums, and ten seconds after the tongue of flame brighter than the sunlight through the small high window and the bed buckling, wrenched out of its sockets in the concrete floor and the whitewashed wall cracking, red brick underneath, and the explosion, hurting his ears, throbbing inside his head, and the choking smoke and the sweetish smell. And then there came the knowledge that he was alive and his annoyance that his cigarette had gone, his fat, lovely cigarette had disappeared before he could finish it.

# THIRTY-SIX
## *19 June 1974: 3.00–3.07 Hours*

'Such speed,' Yuskevitch said, settling himself more comfortably. 'I really must congratulate you, my dear Major.'

'Brigadier,' said the driver.

'I must congratulate you again. One moment I'm in my prison bed, the next moment I'm blown out of it, the next moment I'm riding in a Rolls, with you, dear Brigadier.'

'It's a very old Rolls, Colonel Yuskevitch.' He passed Yuskevitch a leather-bound flask. 'Scotch is your drink, if I remember.'

'You're a gentleman, Brigadier, and I mean that.' Yuskevitch took a swig from the flask and handed it back. 'Now I'm ready for anything.' He lit a cigarette.

'Ready to answer questions?'

'I did answer all the questions that I could answer. Before my trial.' He was silent, looking along the avenue of oak trees, brown-black and dark green in the moonlight, the foliage of each tree touching the foliage of the tree on the other side, a green tunnel bordered by fields on either side; and beyond it, on either side as far as the eye would reach, conifer plantations, regimented and urban, planned, and boring in daylight but dark and mysterious under the moon. The air through the car window was cool and fresh, the night quiet, and even inside the car it was a good smell – whisky and tobacco and leather upholstery and soap and eau-de-cologne, so different from the prison smell of sweaty feet and carbolic and cabbage and urine.

'You do know, don't you, Colonel Yuskevitch, that we're playing a dangerous game? I'm not promising you anything.'

'With whom am I playing a dangerous game, Brigadier? That's what's puzzling me. I'm sure you're not D15 and you're certainly not CED. D15 wouldn't have moved so quickly, and if you'd been CED, I'd have been a corpse by now.'

'I'm the new Chairman of the Security Council.'

'You're not very well protected. A car in front and a car

behind . . . Is your country's economic situation really as bad as all that?'

'Speed is of the essence. A full-scale convoy can take too long to set up, and attract too much attention –'

There was the sound of gunfire around them and the screaming of tyres and suddenly the Rolls had stopped. Yuskevitch threw himself to the floor for the second time within twenty-four hours. There was silence and the sound of car engines. He heard footsteps. He looked up cautiously; the Brigadier had not moved, and was sitting perfectly still, puffing his pipe. Then the window went down and he leaned to speak to someone outside the car.

'You can't get away with this,' he heard him saying.

'The road's blocked both ways, and we have eight men with Sten guns. Tell Yuskevitch, Brigadier, that the Caucasian mountains reach to the stars.'

Yuskevitch rose stiffly. 'The Black Sea reaches to the Mediterranean.'

The escort cars, both black Austin 1800s with two men in civilian clothes inside, had stopped by the verge. Behind the Austin at the rear of the Rolls was a Rambler shooting-brake. Ahead of the Austin in front was a Ford Falcon estate car and a Land-Rover. Four men in dark clothes and stocking masks were standing by each of the shooting-brakes, their guns at their hips.

'We'll take a man from each of your escort cars, Brigadier. As hostage. Stay here for ten minutes and they'll be quite safe. Ten minutes, no more, no less.' His voice was very quiet, almost bored. The men by the shooting-brakes were tall; this man was Yuskevitch's height, but more slightly built. Yuskevitch couldn't distinguish his features behind the stocking mask; he found this frightening, then firmly suppressed the feeling.

'Come on,' the small man said. 'And don't look so apprehensive. We could have killed you long since if we'd really wanted to.'

Yuskevitch shrugged and got out of the car.

'Goodbye, Brigadier. I hope that you don't get into any trouble on my account.'

'Don't worry, Colonel. I can handle it.'

Yuskevitch and the small man walked away towards the Land-Rover.

'I hope you know what you're doing, sir,' the driver of the Rolls said.

'Everything's under control except human stupidity. We'd better brief the other two.' He got out of the Rolls and drew a deep breath. 'A perfect night.' He looked up at the moon. 'Makes a chap feel young again.'

# THIRTY-SEVEN
## *20 June 1974: 10.00–10.45 Hours*

The entrance hall to Loveless House was old and shabby, with worn brown lino and peeling green paint and stained plaster and a smell of gas. There was a large board to the left of the door listing the departments of Loveless Publications in black letters on a cream background; the lettering was wobbly and amateurish.

A middle-aged guard in a peaked cap, white shirt, black tie, and a navy-blue suit looked up from the *Daily Mirror* as Xavier came in. His hand went up to the lapel of his jacket, went back again, and he sighed. 'Name?'

'Flynn.'

'Flynn what, sir?'

The guard's hand hovered round his lapel again.

'Xavier Aloysius Flynn. Major. I'm to see the Committee at ten.'

'I'll have to see your identification, Major.'

Xavier passed him his CED card. The guard looked at it with an expression which clearly indicated that in his opinion it was a forgery. He handed it back to Xavier, and made a note on a sheet of paper on the desk. 'I'll have to search you, Major.'

Xavier nodded; the guard came over to him and patted his body expertly, looking bored now. He pulled up the reinforced lining of Xavier's right-hand pocket and put it back. 'Now what could that be reinforced for, Major?'

'A teeny-weeny gun to defend my honour with.'

The guard smiled for the first time and went back to the *Daily Mirror*. 'Sixth floor, Major,' he said, jerking his thumb towards the lift at the end of the corridor.

The lift jerked and shuddered its way towards the sixth floor, the smell of gas seeming to grow stronger. Xavier had a powerful sensation of helplessness, of impersonal forces at work, longed for a moment to go out again back into the Haymarket and the sunshine, to have a pot of strong tea at the Tea Centre, to stroll around London with no particular purpose, to be safe and normal in the mainstream, and then found himself entering a door marked, rather to his surprise, INTERNAL SECURITY COMMITTEE; he had not expected anything at Loveless House to be so explicit.

The smell of gas had now disappeared; the room glistened with white and green paint and furniture and there was a silver bowl of red roses on the white plastic and tubular steel desk of the old man who sat there filling in the *Daily Telegraph* crossword puzzle. Next to the bowl of roses, on top of a pile of typescript was a ·455 Webley revolver, as used by the Royal Irish Constabulary, heavy and old-fashioned and not easy to maintain, but a real man-stopper.

The old man stood up. 'Major Flynn?' He held out his hand. 'Delighted to meet you. I'm Kenneth Bohun, Clerk and general factotum.' He moved towards a tray on a small table to the right. 'There's coffee there, just help yourself. And there's coffee and stronger refreshments in the Committee Room, of course.'

'How do you do, Mr Bohun. I'm glad to be here. Rather astounded, in fact.'

The old man chuckled. 'Bert's longing to shoot someone. He is licensed to kill, as they say in the thrillers, and he hasn't killed anyone for quite a while. Neither have I, come to that . . .'

But you have done, thought Xavier; your eyes give you away, just as they give Bert away. You look like a saint with that halo of white hair and gentle expression, but you don't fool me; that Webley isn't an ornament.

'You never know these days,' he said lightly. 'You may get the chance. Bert too.'

'Who knows? I'm not sure, Major, how much the Chairman has told you about the Committee, but we have a little time to spare, so I'll try to put you in the picture. What I'd like you to understand is this: whatever anyone may have said to you, you *can* change your mind now about consulting the Committee. There will be absolutely no recriminations. But bear in mind that there is no guarantee that the Committee will help you. On the contrary, coming here today may be the most foolish thing you've ever done . . .'

'I was told that the Committee was there to answer questions.'

'That is correct. Any question put by *anyone* employed by D15, D16 or CED. Remember that: *anyone*. It does *not* take action; it does *not* make any recommendations to any higher authority. Its personnel are part-time and must be selected and trained early in their careers. It has a hundred members; the actual operative Committee comprises four, one of whom acts as chairman and has the casting vote. So the services of the Committee are always available at twenty-four hours' notice – less if I decide the need is urgent. I can always rustle up four people out of a hundred . . .'

He yawned. 'Sorry, but I've been through this so many times before . . .'

'Who are the members?'

'You will know them when you see them,' Bohun glanced at the electric clock on the wall above the door to the right of the desk. 'The payment for their services was help at an early stage in their careers. And further help when and if necessary. We can often help in ways no-one else can . . . Why are you laughing, Major?'

'I'm sorry. I was just visualising the form which that help might take.' He glanced at the Webley.

'Kindly refrain from doing so. We wouldn't do anything that wasn't entirely legal and proper.' His eyes followed Xavier's. 'A sound reliable gun, though not easy to maintain, and the trigger can make a nasty mess of your finger if you're not very careful. Inside the gun the trigger has an edge like a razor . . .' He sighed and passed Xavier a packet of Silk Cut King Size. 'Please smoke, Major. I know that you're trying to cut down, but proximity to the Committee always has a slightly unnerving effect even upon me. Yes, we helped them all. The star of a play falls ill, the Chairman of the Board has a heart attack . . .'

'I take it that the Committee is made up of the successful in all walks of life?'

'You take it correctly. There is just one more thing. You have not met them here. If by any chance you meet any of them in the great outside, you must be most careful to remember this. During the meeting Christian names are to be used. By them and by you. There is a reason for this. It is imperative that whoever goes before the Committee feels entirely relaxed, free to ask whatever questions they want to ask. You won't feel relaxed, of course.'

Xavier felt an angry flush rising to his cheeks. 'I'm not frightened, Mr Bohun.'

'Of course you're not, Major. That, I may say, is one of your besetting faults and your redeeming graces. You're not frightened of anything; you have in fact a consuming appetite for danger . . . But these people are quite horrible. In comparison with normal decent people, *we* are horrible, Major, but members of the Committee bear the same relation to us as the Ugly-Wuglies to the children who created them . . .'

'Sticks and umbrellas, walking sticks and hockey-sticks, overcoats and hats and school caps . . . I see what you mean. You've done your homework, haven't you?'

'I like you, Major. I've reached the age of sixty – I'm well aware that I look older – because I can make instant decisions about people and almost always be right. So I must again warn you. Having questions answered can break your heart. Or kill you. One way or another.'

There was something missing in the room; it was the sound of traffic. The white Venetian blinds were virtually closed; the room could have been anywhere. 'I'm keeping my appointment,' he said.

Bohun shrugged and picked up the 'phone. 'The Clerk speaking,' he said. 'Ready when you are, Chairman. Yes, very well.' He put down the 'phone, pressed a button under his desk, and a black box, looking like a tape-recorder from where Xavier sat, popped out of his desk to his right. He pressed another button and the door to his right slid open. 'Go straight in,' he said. 'There are no formalities.' He started to fiddle with the controls of the tape-recorder, his whole attention concentrated upon them.

The room which Xavier entered, the door closing behind him as he entered, was newly painted in green and white of the same shade as the room he had just left. Facing him was a long white plastic table with tubular chrome legs; around it were five chrome-and-canvas chairs which, he realised, as he sat at the vacant one at the end of the table by the window, were more comfortable than they appeared. The white Venetian blinds were entirely closed, but the sun outside was so strong that it didn't make any difference.

There was a telephone at the chairman's place at the head of the table, and at each place a sheaf of typescript, a writing-pad, a pencil and a black ballpoint pen with a gold crown and *Ministry of Defence* stamped on it, and a large steel ashtray. There was a small white plastic table by the window with a large coffee percolator, a plain white milk jug and five matching cups and saucers, and a bottle of Chivas Regal, a bottle of Gordon's Gin, a bottle of Bison vodka, a soda syphon, five bottles of Schweppes's Tonic, and one glass. The Committee already had full glasses beside them, and they were each smoking. .

Xavier sat down at the end of the table facing the chairman. To his consternation, he could not for a second remember any of the questions which he intended to ask. Nothing that Bohun had said could cushion the shock of seeing Leonard Sancreed, in a purple silk suit and frilly orange shirt, his hair dyed black, as chairman. On Sancreed's left, his eyes told him, was Octavian Medford, a Left Wing Anglican bishop whose mission of the moment was the reconciliation of Marx with Christ; the round rosy face with the thick black spectacles and its short white hair, so familiar on TV, seemed shrunken and roughened in three dimensions, whilst the face of Cecilia Chambord next to him, so vividly and exactly right in all its dimensions on the stage, seemed now too large, too smoothly made-up, the huge violet eyes staring, the thin-bridged nose almost a beak, the lips not far from being thick.

His eyes told him, his brain refused to accept what it was told, refused again to accept that it was actually Rod Deveron opposite the Bishop and Cecilia Chambord, in a surprisingly conservative navy-blue suit, white shirt and blue spotted bow-tie, smoking one of his long yellow-green American cigars.

The Committee members didn't look up as he came in; they were all laughing quite helplessly. Then Leonard Sancreed looked up from the head of the table.

'Xavier, as you might infer from my position, I'm Chairman. Would you, before we begin the proceedings, like to go to that table and pour yourself a large glass of your favourite tipple? Because you like to sip it, I know, barbarian that you are . . .'

'A kind thought, Leonard,' said the Bishop. 'He will no doubt need a drink before he finishes.' Xavier stared at him, trying to extract some meaning from the words, grew more and more frightened, then said a Hail Mary to himself, taking it slowly, not so much praying as coaxing into his mind the concept of tranquillity, an inner calmness which nothing could shake. The aphasia was replaced by a feeling almost like happiness, the knowledge that help had come, that though the feeling of shock would not vanish, he would be able to remember all the questions that he had come to ask. He filled his glass, brought it to the table, and took a sip, and lit a cigarette.

'There is always this moment of sheer astonishment on the first occasion,' Leonard Sancreed said. 'Followed by blind panic. The dear old Clerk certainly went to town on the Committee ... The Ugly-Wuglies indeed! That's what we were all laughing about when you came in, Xavier. However, let's start. You know who we are already, don't you?'

'I know your public identity. I don't know who you are.'

'Let's get that out of the way,' Leonard Sancreed said briskly. 'We are all in our own peculiar way Left Wing propagandists. We play that part twenty-four hours a day. We'd be no use if we didn't. We don't do any intelligence work. We're not agents. Our public identities are cover. That's all. We are here to answer your questions, or as many as we can. Now let's get on with it.'

The room was silent. Xavier looked at the four faces, now immobile and hard, strangely ageless.

'All right,' he said. 'First question: did Reepicheep leak my code number last Saturday?'

'I'm almost certain that he didn't,' Leonard Sancreed said. 'Does anyone disagree with me? No? Good. Next question, please, Xavier.'

'Then how about the Swiss bank account?'

'He does in fact have one. There's forty thousand dollars to his credit.

'Could it be a forgery?'

'Rod is interested in that sort of thing. He'll tell you.'

Rod Deveron drained his glass, went to the table, and returned with the glass full. 'If it's a forgery, it's a very good one. But there'll have to be more tests. Personally, I'd say that it was genuine.'

'Couldn't he have acquired the money legally?'

'Nothing is more unlikely. He isn't in financial difficulties, but he has no legal means of obtaining so large a sum.'

'Where is he now?'

'Officially, absent from duty without leave,' Leonard Sancreed intervened. 'But Cecilia can throw a little more light on the subject.'

'Orders were given to kill him on the 18th,' Cecilia said. 'Sometime in the afternoon. That's two days ago.' She took a gold compact from her handbag, opened it, and looked at herself, frowning. The sweet, curiously innocent smell of powder drifted across the table. 'To be accurate, orders to find him and kill him. The orders were given to Ninian by Aslan.' She closed the compact and put it back in her handbag.

'My God, I can't believe it. I've known him for ten years –'

'We're here to answer questions, Xavier,' Leonard Sancreed said. 'We're not concerned with how long you've known Reepicheep. Next question please.'

'I haven't finished with this question yet. Shouldn't he have been given a chance to clear himself?'

'How could he clear himself? There would only seem to be one possible source for the money.'

Xavier clenched his fist. He wanted to speak, he wanted to hurl accusations at the four unmoved, slightly bored faces sitting round the plastic table, but anger and grief overcame him; he opened his mouth but no words came.

'Take a deep breath, Xavier,' the Bishop said in a gentle voice. 'Leonard is right. Emotion has no place here.'

'Plastic table, plastic people,' Xavier said in a harsh voice. 'Next question, then. Who hired Chambers and Brown?'

Leonard Sancreed wrinkled his forehead. 'Oh dear, I'll have to pass. Rod, I can see that you're absolutely bursting to speak . . .'

'The KGB,' Rod Deveron said. 'Not their usual style, I agree. But that's the information I was given.'

'But why did they want me?'

Rod Deveron shook his head. 'I wasn't given a reason.'

'Because, Xavier, you are the sort of person you are,' the Bishop said.

'What kind of answer is that?'

'It's the only answer available,' the Bishop said calmly. 'If there were a fuller answer available, I should be delighted to give it to you.' He put his finger-tips together and stared at Xavier benignly. His hands were long, the fingers tapered, with nails glossy from a recent manicure. 'My own surmise – mark you, it's nothing more – is that it's a question not of your ability, not of what secrets you are privy to, but of your essential character.'

Xavier took a drink of vodka; nothing could steady his nerves now, but at least its familiar aromatic taste gave him some sort of footing in the real world. 'What is Operation X?'

'It's a waste of time to ask,' Leonard Sancreed said. 'The Committee, since it has access to all available information, and no axes to grind, and no executive responsibility, can answer most questions. But we're not super-beings.' He smiled at the other three. 'Are we, my dear Ugly-Wuglies? Whatever it is, it's bad for this country. I doubt if it's anything scientific or biological, because biological weapons are unpredictable –'

'All right, you needn't go on. Is Morgate's mixed up in it?'

Leonard Sancreed looked round the table. 'The answer is an unanimous yes.'

'With a qualification,' the Bishop said. 'The wool is being pulled over the eyes of the Morgate family. If you scrutinise the most recent information, there's no doubt about that.'

'I'm not much further forward, am I?' Xavier said bitterly.

'I wouldn't go as far as that,' Leonard Sancreed said, glancing at his watch, a wafer-thin Patek Phillipe with a gold bracelet, 'You know more now than you knew when you came in.'

'I don't know enough. There's Sally Rowmarsh – OK, she's doing a profile of Morgate's. But who's her real employer?'

'That's easy. D15. She was recruited at Sussex University, of all places.'

'What's she up to now?'

'I rather imagine that she's dead. Or wishing that she was dead, which is worse. I only know that she failed to report on Tuesday and since then she hasn't been heard from. She was last seen by two of the staff of Van Norden's bank, hailing a taxi. That would be at about four-thirty.'

'Is it being investigated?'

'Naturally. But with no results so far . . . We really had better get on with it, Xavier, we haven't much time.'

228

Xavier pushed the memory of Sally's body to the back of his mind and said in an unnaturally calm voice: 'Should Yuskevitch be exchanged?'

Leonard Sancreed sighed. 'A purely academic question, Xavier. A bomb exploded in his cell on the 18th, he escaped uninjured. God knows how, he was taken away by D15, on the Chairman's orders, in the early hours of the 19th, and was hijacked, probably by FIST.'

'Who planted the bomb?'

'Freelances commissioned by your Department.'

The Bishop looked up from the pad on which he had drawn a naked man and a naked woman chased by an angel with a flaming sword. 'It was Mr Death.'

'Good old private enterprise ... Any other questions about Yuskevitch, Xavier?'

'I'm not saying that Aslan doesn't know his business, but was it a good idea to try to kill Yuskevitch?'

'I think not myself, and particularly not in such a noisy way. Octavian?'

'I'm terribly sorry, Leonard, but I don't agree with you. The best way of dealing with our Russian brothers and sisters is to kill them. They can't do any more harm then. Believe me, I take no pleasure in it –'

'I'm sure you don't, Octavian. Cecilia?'

'I support Octavian. Frankly, it makes me feel good whenever one of the bastards dies. I hate exchanges and I hate any kind of deal.'

'And God save the Queen! Rod?'

'I'm with you, Leonard. As long as they're alive, we can get something out of them.'

'So I use my casting vote. And I must make something clear to Xavier; I have a shrewd idea that D15 could have extracted much more than they did from Yuskevitch.' He yawned. 'That, Xavier, should wrap it up.'

Xavier drained his glass and, trying as he spoke to hear the words as if spoken by someone else, asked: 'How many other double agents are there in CED?'

'I've looked into this,' Cecilia said. 'There are at least four.'

'Who are they?'

'I don't know. But on the basis of what's been happening recently there can't be any doubt of their existence.'

'How shall I find out who they are?'

'Find Yuskevitch.' She smiled at him: to his annoyance he felt the beginnings of an erection.

'Where is Yuskevitch?'

Leonard Sancreed shrugged. 'We don't know, Xavier.'

'I didn't ask you if you personally knew where he was.'

'There is a distinction to be made, Leonard, and he's made it,' the Bishop said. 'But I'd like to ask you a question, Xavier: is it any of your business?'

'It's not the Committee's function to ask me questions,' Xavier said coldly.

'True. But – and I'm acting in your best interest – you are not primarily an investigator. Very well, then; go to the Deliverer. You'll be given the address on your way out. Your question has been answered. I hope that you will not regret it.'

'Octavian, you're a shit.' Leonard Sancreed's face was white with rage. 'You know what you're doing?'

'My job. And I'm abiding by our constitution. Not allowing sentiment to influence my decisions. And answering the questions which are asked of us.'

'You could have headed him off, damn you! So could Cecilia. The bloody Deliverer's even more trouble than Mr Death. I hate using these bloody freelances ... Well, it's done now ...' He regained control of himself with a visible effort. 'Very well, then. And I apologise to you all – including you, Xavier – for my outburst.'

'Important people are interested in Xavier, after all,' Cecilia said. 'He should be able to cope.' She looked at Xavier, appraising him as if for purchase. 'I can't see what all the fuss is about. If it were a good fuck one wanted, then OK. If it were to have someone killed, then OK. But otherwise –' She shook her head; Xavier watched the performance with no pleasure.

'Thank you, Cecilia,' he said. 'But you may as well answer me a question which has been on my mind for some time. Shall I be made Deputy of CED?'

'I answer that, Xavier,' Leonard Sancreed said. 'There is no doubt about the answer. You will never be made Deputy of CED.

Put it right out of your mind. And now, whether you have any more questions or not, I must declare this meeting closed.'

Xavier rose, nodded at each person in turn, and went towards the door. As he reached the door Octavian rose, putting his hand up. 'Xavier, I wouldn't want you to think me – a plastic person.'

'We all have our job to do, as you pointed out, Octavian.'

'I only want you to know that I shall remember you in my prayers.' He looked at Xavier with a suddenly disconcerting tenderness.

'Thank you, my Lord.' Xavier inclined his head towards him, as if acknowledging his blessing.

# THIRTY-EIGHT
## *20 June 1974: 18.00–18.15 Hours*

The Limes was a substantial house of the early twenties, newly painted white with dark blue woodwork. It was saved from boxiness by the downstairs bay windows and the wood-pillared entrance porch with curious eyebrow-shaped tiles. There were two entrances; the front garden was at least half an acre, and through the gap on the right between the large white garage and the house Xavier could see an expanse of green at least as large again. One of the up-and-over garage doors was open, revealing a silver Mercedes 280CE; Xavier repressed a pang of envy. This was the sort of house he himself would have liked, and the sort of district that he liked: neatly-trimmed hedges of holly and privet, manicured gardens, tree-bordered roads, trees in the garden – here at the Limes a stand of authentic limes – and the quiet respectable commuters living their quiet respectable lives, ten minutes' brisk walk to Woking Station, half an hour to Waterloo on the fast train . . .

He got out of the Mini feeling vaguely discontented. He didn't even feel the same about the Mini any longer since it had been driven by someone else; it was found in a car park in Watford late on Saturday and had been thoroughly examined since. The man who had driven it was simply a low-grade thug whose job was to get it out of the way; but it was in a sense an extension of himself and he didn't like a low-grade thug being in it. He smiled despite himself; what was he but a thug? A high-grade thug who on this fine June evening with the birds singing was ringing the door-bell of the Limes, Salisbury Close, off Oriental Road, equidistant between the two junctions of Onslow Crescent with Oriental Road, and if he had to leave in a hurry, as high-grade thugs often have to, the best way was to the right and then left down Monument Road for more choices . . .

A middle-aged man in a dinner-jacket answered the door. He smiled at Xavier. 'I deliver the goods,' he said in a deep resonant voice.

'I am absolutely confident of your ability to do so,' Xavier replied.

The middle-aged man's hand went away from his jacket pocket. 'Come in, old chap, and have a drink.'

The accent was impeccable, not unlike Hugh Droylsden's, but there was something about the way that *old chap* was enunciated that wasn't English, that was too self-consciously idiomatic.

'You have a nice house,' he said as the Deliverer led him into a small book-lined room.

'That's very kind of you, Major. We've only been here a month Always one has lived in rented houses before but, now we have two little children, we need roots. I have some Bison vodka here.'

'You know my tastes.'

'Mine is a very specialised occupation. Detail is important. That winged high-back chair over there is the most comfortable. Major.' He poured out two glasses from the bottle of vodka on the cupboard beside the door. 'I shall sit opposite you, so. There's a coffee-table on your right on which you'll find Silk Cut King Size cigarettes and an ash-tray. And you are out of range of the window. Nobody is going to shoot me, at least not tonight . . .'

'Your concern for my comfort and my safety is admirable. But couldn't we get down to business, Mr – whatever I call you?'

'Henry will do. It's near enough to my baptismal name. I'm as eager to get down to business, Major, as you are, because I've promised to take my good lady out to dinner.' Dinner came out as *dinnah*, but, Xavier reflected as he looked at the smooth tanned face – smooth except for the savage lines from the nostrils to the corner of the mouth and almost handsome but for the too-flat nose – it would be as well not to let one's amusement show.

'Can you deliver me Yuskevitch, Henry?'

The Deliverer nodded, a strand of fair hair falling into his eyes. He smoothed it back with a curiously girlish gesture. 'It will be tomorrow. Almost certainly.'

'Why not tonight?'

'He isn't entirely his own master. The people he's with have to be very careful. They stay alive only because they take very complicated precautions.'

Xavier lit a cigarette. His chair was very comfortable, the wings giving a sensation of warmth and security, and he couldn't help but be happy, even if only for a second, when surrounded by books which from their appearance were read. 'I'm not interested in FIST at the moment,' he said.

The Deliverer grinned. 'I've told them that. They do not, I regret to say, believe you. They say that they will not join the dance.'

'If I don't deliver Yuskevitch I'll join the dance myself.' Xavier said.

'I believe you. And I want to deliver you Yuskevitch. I have a very serious contract with – well, certain people. If I don't make my quota of deliveries –'

'The penalty clause will come into operation.'

'Exactly, Major. Let me assure you, the sooner I deliver Yuskevitch the better I shall be pleased.' He downed his vodka in a gulp. 'Sometimes, you know, I'd like the whole world to blow up, let them all be in the dance, not just you and me and a few others, Major . . . However, the time is ten tomorrow, which is twenty-two hours. You are to come unarmed and unaccompanied, as he will, and you are to guarantee his safety as far as you are able. He will tell you with whom he wishes to negotiate when he sees you, and not until then.'

'I wonder why he didn't choose someone else.'

'I wonder too, but my job is to deliver.' The Deliverer took a small piece of paper from his pocket. ''Phone this number at six tomorrow, Major. Eighteen hours, that is. I need hardly tell you to destroy it when memorised.' He stood up. 'It's been a pleasure to meet you, Major.' He held out his hand.

Xavier shook it. 'Perhaps we'll meet again.'

'We might, Major. It would be wonderful to think of friendship in our life. But there are only contracts to be fulfilled and that dance, that bloody dance.'

'Then we must take care not to stumble.'

'That's it,' the Deliverer said. 'But we'll have to be damned clever. And damned lucky.'

# THIRTY-NINE
## *21 June 1974: 22.00–22.15 Hours*

Waiting in what had been the lounge bar of the Blue Eagle, Xavier tried to unreel the map of the district in his head, as he always did; but all he could remember was one name, Manchuria Road, and the curious stone ridges, running vertically at regular intervals on the roofs of the terrace houses, not ornamental and having no function that he could perceive. He looked out through the broken window into the moonlight: it was grey rather than silver, the shade in the Bela Lugosi *Dracula* just before the Count revealed himself; but he would have settled for a castle in Transylvania any day rather than this shell of a pub waiting demolition with an unfinished high-rise block next to it. There were lights from the ruler-straight terraces on the edge of the demolition area, but some of the houses were already empty, and soon the monster would grabble up the lights that remained, and the rubble-strewn desolation would grow, and there'd be more high-rise blocks, and they wouldn't be finished either: they weren't for living in, they were the giant's totems, his emblems of conquest. Looking to his left he saw small figures emerge from behind the high-rise block, heard children's voices, caught a glimpse of a feathered headdress. *Bang, you're dead*, and the crack of cap pistols and the distant sound of a train passing through Clapham Junction; and a hand on the shoulder. He threw himself away from the hand by instinct, groping in his jacket pocket for a gun that wasn't there, and saw that it was Yuskevitch, a short man with broad shoulders and a broad, flat, wary, intelligent face and a dark blue car coat and a black ski-cap which did nothing for his appearance.

'Bang, you're dead,' said Yuskevitch grinning. 'It's late for children to be up. How do you do, Major Flynn.'

'How do you do, Colonel Yuskevitch.' He gestured towards the peeling wallpaper, the bare boards. 'I don't think that we need hang about here.'

'It puts me in mind of the siege of Leningrad,' Yuskevitch said. 'Disused buildings are melancholy. It smells too.'

'Mice and damp and rotten wood –'

'We have to wait five minutes. I must make sure that you accept my conditions.'

'I'm unarmed. There's no-one with me. I'll guarantee your safety as far as I'm able. I'll arrange negotiations with whoever you want.'

'You'll put up your hands and come away from the window,' Aslan said, emerging from the passage which once had led from the bar parlour. He was wearing a black suit, black shoes, and a black polo-neck sweater, and carrying what Xavier recognised as a Sterling 9 mm automatic rifle with one of the new night-sights. In Aslan's hand it didn't look heavy.

'I knew it was a gamble, but I thought at least you'd go through the motions of keeping your word,' Yuskevitch said. He spat on the floor at Xavier's feet.

'You're not being quite fair, Boris,' Aslan said, 'Xavier has kept his word. He now sincerely wishes that he hadn't. Without a weapon he cannot kill me, and he knows that since he can't kill me, I shall kill him. And you, of course. That's why I'm here. A senior CED agent is making a deal with a senior KGB agent. What else should I do but kill them?'

'Piers, be reasonable. Operation Midas is closing down. You may delay it, but that's all.' Yuskevitch was edging almost imperceptibly away, his voice calm and unhurried and matter-of-fact.

'Stop that soft-shoe shuffle, Boris, or I'll shoot you through, the balls first and let you suffer a bit. Even if I fixed something up with you, I couldn't fix anything up with Xavier . . . I hope you'll forgive me, Xavier, as a Christian should. I'm not going to say when I shoot you, Xavier, that it will hurt me more than it does you, because I haven't the impudence to tell such a thumping lie, but there will be moments, sitting by the fire with my loved ones, when, thinking of you, my eyes will moisten . . .'

'What made you a traitor?' Xavier asked.

'There isn't time to tell you, Xavier. Traditionally the villain goes on for long enough at this point for help to come or for the hero to get out his throwing-knife. It's enough to say that I refuse to join the lemmings. We won't use silly words like traitor . . . The whole operation's been rather a fuck-up for some time, one lot at the Centre working against another . . . But it hasn't been *wrong*, even then. Thrice drenched in blood, thrice washed in fire, thrice scoured with caustic – Who so clean as we? *You* understand that, Xavier, the need to serve, the need to suffer –'

There was a rush of feet, a chatter of high-pitched voices, and a dozen children, some in cowboy hats and some in Red-Indian head-dresses, rushed screaming and shouting into the room, firing cap guns, milling round Aslan; one child with a false moustache and a full cowboy costume raised his Buntline Special – a beautiful model, even at that moment Xavier couldn't help noticing, a convincing dull blue with a twelve-inch barrel – and aimed it at Aslan, whose eyes were still on Yuskevitch and Xavier, having only momentarily been put off his guard. There was a sharp bang, a red flash, the smell of cordite, and Aslan staggered backwards, putting his hand to his chest, an expression of surprise on his face which was almost comic. His right hand held the rifle still; the child fired again and the rifle dropped with a curiously tinny clang. Aslan looked at the red mess, the whiteness of bone showing through, at the end of his right arm, screamed, and sagged to his knees, supporting himself with his left hand.

Hugh Droylsden and the Chairman came into the room un-hurriedly, Droylsden with a Colt ·38 in his hand.

The child with the Buntline Special peeled off his false mous-tache. 'Xavier, dear boy, you might give me a cigaroo.'

Xavier lit him a cigarette. 'I was told you were dead.'

'You weren't,' the Chairman said, lighting his pipe. 'You were told that orders to kill him had been issued.'

Aslan screamed again, then vomited blood, splashing Xavier's shoes, and fell forward. The Chairman prodded him with his foot. 'Still alive, but only just. A damned good shot, Cyril.' He patted Reepicheep's shoulder. 'That gun has a kick like a mule . . .' He relit his pipe. 'The question is what to do with my old friend Piers. On the whole, it would be best to finish him off. Cyril –'

Aslan lifted his head and said indistinctly: 'Xavier.'

Reepicheep handed Xavier the Buntline Special.

'Xavier,' Aslan said, more clearly now. Xavier knelt beside him. He smiled and looked at the gun. '*Peccavi*,' he said. Xavier

237

took aim at his heart, aiming at the wound in the chest – red with shreds of black wool and white cotton driven into it. Once, twice, three times; Aslan's head fell back.

Xavier knelt down beside Aslan and kissed his forehead, then took out his white handkerchief and covered his face.

He rose. '*Peccavi*,' he said quietly. 'I have sinned. That's a good confession.' He bowed his head. 'Eternal rest grant to him, Lord, and let perpetual light shine upon him. May he rest in peace.' Reepicheep took off his hat and bowed his head.

The Disposer walked in, breaking the silence. He dropped to his knees to look at the corpse, rose, dusted his knees, and looked at Xavier disgustedly.

'The service gets better, doesn't it, Major Flynn? I'll be helping you do the killing next.'

'I don't want to talk about it,' Xavier said. He looked at Reepicheep talking in a low voice to the children, who were not children, who were Reepicheep's friends – it was immediately obvious now that they were midgets, as it had not been obvious two minutes ago.

'We have a great deal to do, Inspector,' the Chairman said coldly to the Disposer.

'I wonder exactly *what* you have to do? Where does *he* fit in, for instance?' He jerked a thumb towards Yuskevitch.

'You were told before you came here that the matter of Colonel Yuskevitch has been cleared at the very highest level.'

The Chairman went over to Yuskevitch. 'We are now going to a place of safety, Colonel, rest assured of that.'

'I'll wait for Major Flynn,' Yuskevitch said.

'You people have rules all of your own, don't you?' the Disposer said to Xavier. 'And now you're killing each other. Tell me what does it feel like to be a murderer?'

'It's a job,' Xavier said in a tired voice. 'A nasty rotten job. You know, Inspector, before modern sanitation they just had cesspits. And the chaps who emptied them at night were called nightsoil men. You can imagine what they smelled like. No-one was so low that they couldn't despise the nightsoil men. But what would they have done without them? We are the nightsoil men.' He looked down at Aslan's body, his face working. Yuskevitch came over to him and took his arm. 'Come on, Xavier, let's go.

And I will put you in the picture about Operation Midas. Operation X, that is . . .' They went out of the room arm-in-arm, Yuskevitch seeming somehow larger, a father-figure, Xavier somehow smaller, bowed by shock.

# FORTY

## *24 June 1974: 11.00–11.30 Hours*

---

'That just about ties it up,' the Chairman said. 'Josef K has really done us proud.' He glanced at the thick sheaf of typescript which Xavier had in his lap. 'Though for the last hour, Xavier, you've been looking at the report upside-down.'

'I'm sorry. But I do grasp the main principle of Operation Midas.'

The Chairman chuckled. 'I know what's needling you. It's strange seeing me here behind Aslan's desk. And Jane in place of Bunty.'

'They were traitors.'

'You can be fond of people just the same.'

Xavier stood up. 'Do you need me any further, sir? I'm not doing much good here.'

'I'm afraid I do need you, Xavier. It isn't like the stories, you know. You're not going to be sent on leave to the Caribbean with the luscious heroine.'

'There aren't any heroines,' Droylsden said.

'And no fiendish plots, just a straightforward funnelling of sterling to the USSR. You have a solid family combine, perfectly legitimate, perfectly efficient. And a family bank. The non-voting shareholders got their dividends fair and square. Sir Geoffrey, Brian and Vanessa sent theirs through to the USSR.'

'They were damned clever,' Droylsden said. 'They even took advantage of inflation. They simply made no provision for it. So the Russians got their motor-bikes – and other things – at least ten per cent cheaper.' He looked fretfully at the litter of papers on his desk. 'Mind you, I'll be glad to hand it all over to Josef K.' He sighed. 'Between us, sometimes I feel you can't win . . . Operation Midas started with Lenin. And Grandfather Everard, all starry-eyed, asking him how he could be saved . . . The question is how can *we* be saved?'

'By doing our duty,' Xavier said flatly.

'Aslan did his duty in a sense. If he was to help with Operation

Midas he had to have a good cover. So he was given Philby and the Fourth and Fifth Man. They'd exhausted their usefulness anyway.'

'What bothers me,' Xavier said, 'is that they really hadn't. The KGB thought that really they'd had a good enough run for their money, surely they'd be rumbled – but if Aslan hadn't blown them, they'd still be around.'

'That's rather unfair, old man,' Droylsden said mildly.

'To hell with being fair. We could only nail down those five traitors – *five* – because they were given us on a plate, and even then three got away. We could only run Operation Purge because we were given the agents on a plate. They were Aslan's cover. And we only got anywhere with FIST with KGB help. Because FIST threatened to muck up Operation Midas –' He stopped. 'That's enough.'

'Oh, no,' the Chairman said. 'Have your say, Xavier. The British Secret Service is incompetent. Isn't that it?'

'Yes, it is. *We* haven't closed down Operation Midas. The KGB has. Because it's too expensive in terms of agents. And because though we wouldn't like it to be made public, neither would they like it to be made public.'

'It has closed down nevertheless,' Droylsden said. 'Morgate's will continue under new management, and the money will flow into this country. Including foreign exchange.'

Xavier laughed. 'That's just what the money won't do any more. The unions will now fuck Morgate's up. Haven't you realised the secret of their success? No labour trouble. The message was got through to a handful of people that if you harmed Morgate's you harmed the good old USSR. Anyone who wouldn't listen or couldn't understand had a fatal accident. And no-one ever thought of looking into it. No-one. Until it was too bloody late.'

'You *are* in a temper, Xavier,' the Chairman said.

'I'm in a temper with everybody. If only I'd gone with Tom Drage that night –'

'You can't live in the past,' Droylsden said.

'Maybe if we did, we mightn't make such a mess of things again.' He stared at Aslan's portrait gallery. 'I hate these bloody photos now.'

'Tear them down if it makes you feel better,' the Director said.

Xavier strode over to the wall and began to pull them down, ripping each across and throwing it on the floor.

'You've still a grudge against us because of Sally Rowmarsh, haven't you?' the Director asked.

'I should have been told that she was from D15.'

'Would that have helped?'

Xavier ripped the photo of Kennedy up.

'I could have *tried* to do something. I might even have done something for that poor little sod Dykenhead. Taken away from his home and tortured to death because he'd stumbled on something odd. And took it to a chap who he thought was from the DTI.'

'In a way you did do something. You killed the two chaps who kidnapped him.'

'I'm damned glad.' He tore down the photo of Churchill. 'I'm even sorry about that poor sod who tried to kill me at my flat. Even if he was KGB. After all, a brother is a brother.'

'Yuskevitch apologised,' Droylsden said. 'Pletnev wasn't given any orders to kill you – he just blew his top when he realised you'd killed his brother.'

'I should have found out who he really was.'

'As you've never been inside the Interrogation Department, it's difficult to see how you could,' the Chairman said. 'You really do need to do quite a lot of hard thinking, don't you?'

'It's all perfectly straightforward,' Xavier said sulkily.

'Is it? Is our present situation straightforward? Morgate's can carry on – virtually no-one there knew about Operation Midas, and of course there was no reason why they should. The bank's a different matter. All the personnel, whether nationals or illegals, took their orders from the KGB, and that's not a story I want to see in the newspapers . . . We'll just have to replace the personnel gradually . . . Then we still have FIST to deal with. We can't rely upon the information we've got from the KGB.'

'And there are some very tricky negotiations with Yuskevitch,' Droylsden said.

Xavier tore down the photo of Hitler. 'Why did he want to deal with *me*? Why not the Chairman?'

'That's something else to be thought about,' the Chairman said.

'It would be interesting to know just what we can charge the Morgates with,' Droylsden said. 'Over the years, at the very least two hundred million quid, a lot of it in hard currency, has been funnelled into the USSR. Which has been a very great help to the USSR. But we're not at war with them, never have been. Really, the money was the Morgates' money. Bunty, of course, could have been nailed for working for the Morgates on Government time, and using her knowledge of CED for improper purposes.'

'It's immaterial now,' the Chairman said. 'She was very quick on the draw with Exit One. I didn't really expect anything else.' He puffed at his pipe contentedly.

Xavier turned away from the photographs. 'I don't know just what you did expect, sir. In your shoes, to be absolutely frank, I'd have taken damned good care to get her alive. Because what I'd expect of Aslan was that he must have been doing something more than service Operation Midas.'

'But you're not in my shoes, Xavier,' the Chairman said.

'I'm not even in the Deputy's shoes, am I? The Committee made that clear to me.'

'Indeed it did. But carry on bellyaching, my dear chap.'

'All the explanations are too pat. Pletnev Junior, who's attached to Morgate's, tailing Tom, realises that I've killed his brother, and takes off after me. Aslan somehow persuades him to say he's from FIST, and then later that night it seems as if someone has taken a pot-shot at me. Their idea was to miss, and give me a real incentive to kill chaps from FIST. Or was it? Because no-one at CED admits to it. There are loose ends all over the place.'

'Ours is a loose organisation,' the Chairman said. 'It has to be tightened up. There are seven hundred and fifty personnel in CED. It'll be quite a job.' He rose. 'I shall now pass on the can. I've enough work of my own.'

'I don't suppose you've decided upon a Director yet, but who's to be Deputy?'

'Hugh, of course.' The Chairman glanced at his watch and went to the door. 'My God, I'm late.' He waved his hand towards the empty chair behind Aslan's desk. 'Why don't you go to your place, Xavier? Much more dignified.'

'My place? I'm not in a mood for jokes, sir.'

'Your place as Director of CED. Confirmed this morning by the Security Council.'

'An official letter is on the way,' Droylsden said.

The Chairman smiled. 'Hugh will carry on tearing up the photos for you. And Yuskevitch and I are coming to see you this afternoon. Jane will give you the details.' He put his hand on the door, then turned back. 'An afterthought, Xavier. Could it be possible that Operation Midas was closed down because it was damaging FIST? Because FIST *ordered* it to be closed down? Just let that keep *you* awake at night too.' He put his hand on the door again.

Xavier walked slowly to Aslan's chair and sat down.

'Why me? After all that's been said –'

Droylsden pulled down a photo. 'What has been said was that you weren't going to be Deputy.' His voice was dry and amused. 'Which was perfectly true. As for the Committee, you didn't ask them the right question.'

'But why me? Why not you?'

'Because I shall make a good Deputy and you wouldn't. But you're Director material. The decision was taken a long time ago.'

'And now I can't bellyache, I'm the chap who's bellyached *at* . . . Leave these photos alone, Hugh. Jane will do it.'

'You can put up some holy pictures and a crucifix.' Droylsden smiled. He went over to the walnut drinks cabinet, poured out two glasses of Bison vodka and brought one over to Xavier. 'You said that you trusted me once.'

'I'll drink to that,' Xavier said. He emptied his glass. 'Christ, I've never felt so lonely.'

His 'phone rang. 'The Morgates? Just a moment.' He covered the 'phone. 'The Morgates are here. Who made the appointment, Hugh?'

'The Chairman. You can put them off if you like. They've had three days of solitary confinement and it'll soften them up a bit more.'

'The sooner we get them in the Interrogation Department the better.'

'You'll have to go there yourself. It isn't pleasant.'

Xavier smiled. 'We are the nightsoil men – who are we to be particular?' He uncovered the 'phone mouthpiece. 'Send them in, Jane.' He put down the 'phone. 'Stay here, Hugh. They'll sit on that sofa facing me. You in this chair beside me on the right.'

244

Jane brought in Sir Geoffrey, Brian and Vanessa Morgate, smiled brightly at him, and said, 'Will you be wanting coffee?'

'I'll let you know if I do.'

Jane smiled again and left the room; his eyes followed the plump little bottom in the tight black dress, then went reluctantly to the Morgates, sitting together on the brown leather sofa as if posing for a family portrait. They were all wearing white towelling hospital gowns and felt slippers. Vanessa, though her face was pale with dark circles under the eyes, continued to be appealing in hers, a little girl lost; her father and her brother were faintly comic, the dressing-gowns well above their knees, keeping their hairy legs tightly together like modest women.

'You'll be broken, Major, broken into little pieces,' Sir Geoffrey said. 'Hijacking us in the middle of the night, taking our clothes, keeping us in a private prison – are you mad?'

'It isn't a private prison,' Xavier said. 'It's an official place of detention.'

'I'm keeping my temper by a great effort, Major, but I can't guarantee to do so any longer. There is a law –'

'Not here. There are drinks and cigarettes in the cabinet behind you, by the way.'

'Leave it to me, Father,' Brian Morgate said. He leaned forward, and as he did so, his dressing-gown came open, exposing his genitals. He flushed scarlet, pulled the dressing-gown together, and held it together. 'Taking our bloody clothes! It's an outrage! All right, the Secret Service is a law unto itself, but you've overreached yourself this time. We're going to be missed, there'll be questions asked – you've *got* to let us out.'

'I'm sorry, Mr Morgate, but that's impossible.'

'Why is it impossible, you bloody lunatic?'

'Because you're dead.' He picked up a newspaper from his desk; Droylsden took it and walked over to the sofa with it. 'On Saturday night on the Hastings road. Your car hit a tree and went up like a bomb. Just as Tom Drage's did.'

Sir Geoffrey went over to the drinks cabinet. 'I think I'll have that drink.'

'I should whilst you have the chance.'

'What are you going to do with us, darling?' Vanessa asked.

'We shall find out all you know.'

245

'I should have thought that you'd already been told everything,' Sir Geoffrey said.

'We've been told as much as Cothill and his deputy want us to know. Marvellous cover that . . . took the KGB twenty years to set it up. Yes, we may even know all that *they* know. But all that *you* know – that's a different matter.'

'I'm sure that you know all that we know. The beauty of Operation X' – there was a genuine note of pride in his voice — 'was its simplicity. It was only necessary for a handful at Morgate's to be informed about it.'

'You can call it Operation Midas now.'

'Over fifty years' work down the drain.' Sir Geoffrey's face contorted as if in actual physical agony. 'May I ask what you've done with Mrs Alvaston?'

'She's co-operating. With enthusiasm.'

'Her attachment to the operation was always emotional rather than ideological.' He held out his glass to Droylsden, who filled it to the brim. He drank half at one gulp, then put his hand over his eyes. 'I suppose that you'll get rid of her when she's exhausted her usefulness,' he said in a half-whisper. He took his hand away from his eyes and glared at Xavier. 'We took you in, didn't we? We made fools of you all these years –'

'That's what you're going to tell us about. All of it.'

'And if we do, what then?'

'I told you, you're dead.'

'You can't do it!' Brian Morgate screamed. He rose and threw himself at Xavier; Droylsden hacked him on the shin and then hit him with the edge of his hand under the nose; he grunted in pain and slumped back on the sofa, his hands to his face, not bothering to hold his dressing-gown together.

'I have to ask you why you did what you did,' Xavier said to Sir Geoffrey.

'I don't see why I should help you,' Sir Geoffrey said. 'I don't think that you would understand.'

'You're wrong there, Daddy,' Vanessa said. 'He understands very well. Cousin Piers always said – says – that a little push at the right time, and he'd have been on our side.'

Xavier looked at her sharply. 'You corrected yourself, didn't you? And we haven't told you.'

She smiled at him 'You'll have to find out, won't you, Xavier?'

'He'll have to find out,' Sir Geoffrey said tonelessly. 'But I don't think that he would ever have come over to us, my dear. He's a very common Irish type, the pious thug. Piers over-estimated him.'

'You didn't really take the trouble to get close to him.'

'Nature didn't equip me to do so, my dear.' The wolfish smile appeared briefly.

'It wasn't just that,' Vanessa said, speaking to Xavier now. 'I want you to believe me. If there'd been time, I might even have been able to make you see what my grandfather saw when he met Lenin in London in 1905. My grandfather was a strange man. Very quiet, withdrawn, a great reader, a great thinker. He'd been on the fringe of Marxism for a while, but there'd never been any public involvement. He wanted to be sure what to do before he committed himself. And Lenin told him: *make money. I don't need any more revolutionaries; in fact I have too many. You can serve me best by becoming a respectable bourgeois, a successful businessman.*'

'It hurt him at the time,' Sir Geoffrey said. 'He wanted to do something spectacular, he wanted to march at the head of the workers. And the Old Man – he always called him the Old Man – *Starets* – said: *Comrade Everard, I ask you to do what is the most difficult, what is the most thankless. And you will have to do it all your life and your children after you . . .*'

'*Your children after you*,' Xavier repeated. 'That says it all. I could almost feel sorry for you.'

'Don't be sorry for us,' Sir Geoffrey said. 'We've always known what we lived for, where we were going. Lenin led my grandfather out of the swamp, and my grandfather made sure that we were never in it.'

'I think you're in it now,' Xavier said. 'The compact group marching alongside' – he frowned – 'the precipitous and difficult path, has made sure of that.'

'We have served a great purpose,' Sir Geoffrey said. 'For over fifty years our lives have had meaning, we have helped to shape history. We have been on the winning side –'

Xavier smiled. 'The winning side has decided that it's exhausted your usefulness now, Sir Geoffrey. Yuskevitch has sold you down the river. Aided and abetted by Cothill and his deputy.'

'We were there to be used,' Sir Geoffrey said. 'We have been used to the utmost. We expected no reward, and that's what you don't understand.'

'Get me a *huge* whisky and a cigarette, love,' Vanessa said to Droylsden. She looked at Xavier intently, crossing her legs with a deliberate carelessness. He looked away from her. 'Ah, Xavier, you still don't look at people . . . Couldn't you consider some sort of – arrangement? We haven't stolen anything, you know. We haven't sold any State secrets –'

'You've harmed my country. My duty is to protect my country. You are traitors. That's all I shall say.'

She took the drink which Droylsden passed her and held her cigarette out to him for a light. 'We still have a lot of money, you know. Some sort of explanation can be fudged up for the car accident –'

Brian Morgate took his hands away from his face. 'It's no use, Vanessa.' He hawked and spat on the red Axminster carpet. 'This bloody Fascist has got us now and he's going to kill us. He's killed Piers already.' His voice rose to a shout. 'He was my friend, he was the only one of the Morgates we could share the secret with, he was a great man, and you killed him. I loved him, I'm not ashamed to say it, he was like a brother to me –' He buried his face in his hands again, not without dignity despite the gaping dressing-gown.

Droylsden watched him, his face impassive. 'We have a busy day ahead, sir,' he said to Xavier. 'We can get nothing more from them here. Shall I send for an escort to take them to the Interrogation Department?'

'No. I want them to find their own way there. Take them into the ante-room and explain to them how to find it. Then issue instructions that they are not to be harmed in any way. And if they want to sit down in the passage and go no further, then let them sit. Because they'll have to go there in the end . . . Do you understand what I want?'

Droylsden nodded. 'Oh yes. It's a refinement that even the KGB has never thought of. If they go under armed guard, they're martyrs, they have some dignity. And they're preparing them-

248

selves for horrible things to happen. Without an escort, they might be going for a bath, a medical examination, a massage. It's five minutes' walk to the Interrogation Department, with five check-points. I imagine that their reaction will be absolute incredulity. Can this really be happening to them?'

'Their reaction will be just the same as Peter Dykenhead's,' Xavier said in a hard voice. 'Dykenhead stumbled across some figures which he couldn't understand – sent in error by Van Norden's – and then finds himself naked in a room with boarded-up windows. With nothing ahead of him but pain and death. They shot his dog . . . Funny, that's what really upset me the most . . . At that, the dog was the lucky one.'

'It was necessary,' Sir Geoffrey said. 'No-one enjoyed it.' He straightened his back and squared his shoulders, suddenly dig-nified, the short dressing-gown no longer ridiculous but cere-monial and proper, worn like a toga. 'We shall walk to our destination briskly, looking straight ahead. We won't be afraid, and perhaps there will be some watching who will remember us with respect.'

'I don't think that they'll remember your son with respect,' Xavier said.

Brian Morgate was whimpering and wringing his hands, his face white with shock. 'You can't do it!' he screamed. 'You can't do it!'

'Be quiet, my dear,' his father said. 'I warned you a long time ago that this could happen.'

Brian clasped his hands together tightly. 'I didn't know it would be like this,' he said in a whisper. 'I'll try, Daddy, I'll try.'

Xavier gasped as if struck, overwhelmed by a flood of pity. 'Get them out of here,' he said to Droylsden.

'Let me send for an escort.'

'Get them out of here. You heard my orders.'

Vanessa and Sir Geoffrey put their arms around Brian Mor-gate's shoulders, but he began to shake uncontrollably.

'You won't like yourself for this, Xavier,' Droylsden said hoarsely.

'I'll like myself still less before I've finished, Hugh.' He looked down and noticed for the first time the thick red-covered MOST SECRET file on his desk; on it was a note *For the immediate attention of the Director CED.*

When the door had closed behind the Morgates and Droylsden he slumped forward, his arms on the desk, his head on his arms, his eyes tightly closed. Very faintly he could still smell Vanessa, her own personal smell. *You don't look at people* . . . The day lay ahead of him and he had no strength left. *I offer this day to You,* he said to himself, *my prayers, my work, my meals, my play, everything to give You glory* . . . *I offer You all the actions of my day as Jesus used to offer You all He did* . . .

He sat up and looked at the TV monitor above the door. The Morgates had stopped just before Checkpoint One, leaning against the wall. Brian was crying, his shoulders heaving. Sir Geoffrey was gesticulating angrily, but Vanessa was standing immobile, her hands folded, her face serene.

He picked up the 'phone. 'Jane, would you come in? Bring your notebook.' He replaced the 'phone and continued to watch the Morgates. When Jane came in and sat down opposite him, he took his eyes away from the monitor with an effort.

'Hugh has gone along to the Interrogation Department,' she said.

'I'll join him presently. There are some matters I want to note first while they're still on my mind. One, Brian Morgate's children. Two boys, nine and eleven. And his wife. And Aslan's wife and two daughters. Nine and eighteen.'

'The Chairman indicated yesterday that he thought it best to tidy up thoroughly. Not immediately, of course.'

'I don't think so. And Vanessa's daughter isn't to be – tidied up either. Once start with that sort of thing and where does it stop? Next, the Chairman –' He paused and looked at the monitor again. Sir Geoffrey was trying to drag Brian Morgate past the checkpoint; he was resisting, still crying. The guard's face was impassive. He looked away at Jane. She looked back at him, calmly. 'You work for me now,' he said. 'Your loyalty is exclusively to me. You will be nearer to me in some ways than Hugh. Do you understand that?'

'It's because I understand that I was chosen. You need not go into this subject again.'

He nodded. 'Very well. We are to mount an investigation into the connection between the Chairman and Igor Maklevitch Director, Scientific and Technical Directorate KGB, Mikhail

Kotolynov, Director, Directorate S, and Boris Yuskevitch, who has much more to tell me. How to liaise with D16 I'm not sure yet. We shall have to start building bridges . . .'

She smiled. 'The Chairman said to me yesterday, knowing I would tell you, that he was re-reading *The Golden Bough*.'

'Rather melodramatic of him.' But he saw the priest of the sacred grove, who had become priest by murdering his predecessor, stalking the grove with drawn sword.

'He has lived like that a long time,' she said, as if commenting on Xavier's thoughts. 'I believe that it agrees with him.'

'It doesn't agree with me. We are going to have a black and white world in future, our side good, their side bad . . .' His voice trailed away. 'That's what it was supposed to be like before . . .'

'In the end,' she said, 'there is a false Aslan, a donkey in a lion's skin. Do you remember? But the real Aslan comes again.'

'The donkey was the dupe of a monkey,' he said. 'Who is the monkey? And that is the next thing to be noted.'

Jane leaned towards Xavier and put her hand over his. He was grateful for its coolness and softness.

'Some of this ground was covered by the Chairman yesterday.'

'We are making our own investigation. Some of the ground has *not* been covered. Cothill and his deputy haven't really spilled all the beans . . . We are no nearer the reason for Dalhart's defection.' He frowned. 'Seems strange to call Aslan that. I wonder why Reepicheep didn't shoot at his gun hand in the first place?'

She took her hand away. 'I'll note that too. Is there anything else?'

He picked up Aslan's gold pen. 'We can have dinner tonight.'

'I'll arrange it.' She moistened her lips; her tongue was very pink and her lips very full. She glanced at the monitor. 'It must be your decision, but I would say that they'd had enough.'

The Morgates had moved on to Checkpoint Two; Brian had slid down to the floor, his back against the wall, a steady trickle growing into a puddle between his legs. His father and his sister were kissing his face, evidently trying to persuade him to get to his feet. He had stopped crying; his face was blank, his eyes staring. Sir Geoffrey was crying now, but Vanessa's eyes were dry. Xavier looked away from the monitor. 'I'll give them five more minutes.'

'It's you I'm worried about, not them.' She rose and came round the desk behind him, putting her hands on his shoulders. 'The end of the day will come and there are ways of forgetting for the night.'

'I'll give you your orders in five more minutes,' he said, relaxing almost imperceptibly under her hands, but not changing his position. He felt her hands leave his shoulders.

When she had gone, he glanced at his watch and wrote on the red-covered file the figures 11.25. *You don't look at people* . . . He found the tears coming despite himself; they seemed to actually smart his eyes. *Oh Christ*, he said aloud, *when will You send the black ship*? He sighed, and opened the file, then closed it and looked at his watch, sniffing childishly, trying to hold back the tears.

## *John Braine*

John Braine was born and educated in Yorkshire, England, the locale for many of his novels. He abandoned his career as a librarian for that of a novelist with the success of his first book, *Room at the Top*, in 1957. He now lives in Surrey, England.